TELL YOU NO LIES

LYNN FRASER

BLOODHOUND
— BOOKS —

Print ISBN: 978-1-5040-8672-1

To all the mothers who are good enough

1

EMMA

I think I know why I did it. It's the baby; everything has been different since she was born. Different. But not how I expected.

The books all said how much giving birth takes out of you. How can you know what it will be like, though? Really? Thomas said I'd be tired, that I shouldn't expect to be able to cope with everything on my own. He suggested his mum come to help. I didn't want that.

'Me and Jenny wouldn't have survived without her,' he said.

Why did he have to keep doing that? I don't need to be reminded. My first child, but not his. I get it. The difference is that I'm not a schoolgirl. I have a degree, a job, a career. I should be able to look after one baby. And this baby was planned. We're both grown-ups. I don't need his mum telling me how to look after my baby.

And I'm not tired.

When I was pregnant, I was tired all the time. In the hospital, after she was born, all I wanted to do was sleep. Not that I could. There were always lights, people moving around, squeaky shoes and clanking wheels, pokings and proddings, and the babies crying, my baby crying the loudest. Hungry, they said. But if she was so hungry, why wouldn't she feed? She refused. She wouldn't latch and she was so angry, angry with me, her face scrunched and her tiny hands in fists, pushing me away.

The nurses were kind. 'She'll get the hang of it,' they said. But she didn't. Or I didn't. Maybe that was what they meant. My baby was hours old and I was already failing as a mother. Everything was harder than I imagined it would be: picking her up properly, changing a nappy, dressing her – I was sure that I was going to break something when I tried to get her limbs into sleeves and legs. Being a mother was hard. Much harder than I expected. I wasn't used to not being good at things, not being in control.

Even while all I wanted to do was sleep, to pull the covers over my head and sleep, I talked to her, sang to her, I rocked her and walked with her, endless walks around the ward. There was a room for mothers to go to feed their babies at night. I couldn't stay there and watch them. Contented babies, kneading fingers, puckered mouths on their mothers' breasts.

I should've known then. I thought it would be better when we came home. That's what they said: *relaxed, back in your home, it'll be better*. It wasn't.

It's all right now, though. I'm much better at the basics and I'm not tired anymore. I understand now and I've adapted. My body has adapted. It's like I'm beyond sleep, Thomas keeps telling me to sit down, go to bed, take a nap. *Sleep while the baby sleeps*. He even repeated that stupid piece of advice. When the baby sleeps is when you can actually get things done.

We talked about how long he'd take as paternity leave before she was born. He wanted to take everything he was allowed straightaway.

'That's such a waste, though. Don't you think?' I said. 'You'll just be sitting around twiddling your thumbs while she sleeps – while I sleep as well.' Because I had expected that I'd need to sleep. 'You'll be bored,' I said. 'Wouldn't it be more fun to have time off when we can do something, go places?'

In the end, he agreed. They're understaffed at work. They're always understaffed. So, he took a week.

I was quite relieved when he went back on Monday. He was just getting in the way, making a mess, moving things, touching the baby all the time.

It's better now. I can have things the way I want them, the way they need to be. I've decided that there's no point sleeping. Why go to sleep if you're just going to get woken up again by the baby crying? Now I think that it's a positive – not needing to sleep, a positive adaptation. It means that I can keep watch. I don't have time to sleep.

And Thomas being here less will help me to keep him safe.

He was working last night. I don't know exactly where, but not in the city. They were out chasing criminals around some sheds in the fens. He doesn't give details and I don't ask. I learnt not to. But it seems harder now. I'd like to know where he is. Why do Cambridge police have to go out to the fens? Don't they have police of their own? He told me that detectives did most of their detecting from behind a desk. He still seems to take every chance he can to be out there, though. What's the draw? Maybe I should worry about that. No. I know Thomas is a good man.

When he came home last night, he crept in like he thought he'd wake me. I was in the nursery. The baby was asleep in the cot. I was watching her, sitting in the dark in the clogged heat, sitting still, trying to withdraw from the fug and everything it held in its molecules. I heard the car draw up, the metal door slamming shut, the sound of his keys when he dropped them on the table in the hall, the tread of his feet on the stairs. I looked over at the cot to see if she stirred.

'Hey, Em? You awake?' He stood in the doorway, the light from the hall casting his shadow across the floor almost to where I was sitting.

I tucked my feet under the chair. 'Shhh, you'll wake her.'

He came in and went to stand over the cot. I saw his hand reaching. I wanted to shout out, tell him to stop. I held the panic inside, spoke softly, all soft-cotton calm. 'She's not been asleep long. Don't wake her. Please.'

His hand pulled back, returned to his side. 'Sorry. Have you had a bad night?'

The baby was stirring now. Had he woken her? He was still standing so close. He should move away.

'Em? You all right?' He was looking at me now.

'Of course. I'm fine.'

He moved to stand by the window, looking down over the park. 'When did you go out?'

'What?' How does he know I've been out? Why is he looking out there?

'You left the door open, not wide, but not properly shut.' He paused.

What should I say? What did he know? Could he know already? I didn't remember not shutting the door. I didn't remember shutting the door. What should I say?

He was speaking again. 'I know it's hard with the baby, but you should probably double-check.'

Check. Double-check. Triple-check. I was always checking. 'Okay,' I said. 'Sorry.'

'Don't apologise, love. It's hard. The pram. The baby. All of it.'

He kept talking, but I couldn't listen. How did I miss the door? How did that happen? I check everything. I check again and again. But I left the door open.

He was still talking. I needed to concentrate on now. I could think about the rest later.

'With the park just next door, you don't know who might pass by and notice. Especially when I'm on nights, you should be careful.' He was still looking out of the window. Why? Could he sense something?

'I am careful.' The door, the door left a fraction open, not quite shut, like that was what we needed to be careful about.

'Maybe it's the catch. I'll check it.' I could see him making a mental note, like he was writing it in one of his little notebooks.

'Okay.' He could check it if it made him feel better. Doors weren't going to save us, though.

It was then that I'd realised that he was looking at me again. 'Where did you go?'

'For a walk.' Why was he questioning me? My skin was clammy under my thin pyjamas. The heat of the day hadn't lifted at all.

A pause, like he expected more, then, 'It seems to have had the desired effect.' He'd smiled.

'What?' What was the desired effect? What was he saying?

He'd nodded over to the baby. 'She's fast off.'

He thought I'd gone out for the baby.

He'd turned from the cot and looked at her again, kept looking at her, studying her. 'Why don't you take the opportunity to go to bed and get some sleep?'

Always going on about sleep. 'She's due a feed soon, so she'll be waking up.'

'I can watch her. I can give her a bottle.'

'No. You'll need to eat something. You won't have eaten, will you? Eat something and go to bed. I can manage.'

'I know you can manage, Em. I'm just saying you don't need to. I'm home now. I can stay with her. Or we can leave her for a few minutes, you know. Babies are more than capable of making you aware when they want something.'

He was thinking. I could see his frown, a slight tightness at his temple. He was quick to release it, but I saw.

'We could have her in with us, move the cot to our room. I could move that chest of–'

'No.' I needed to say more, but say it softer. 'We talked about it. You agreed. It's better like this. Now you're back at work, you need to be able to sleep.' I knew what he was going to say next. He could take more leave. That or something about what he did before. 'It would be too cramped. It's better like this.'

I could see that he still wanted to argue. Like he knew better. Like he was in control. Reminding me again that he was the expert and I was the novice. He'd done it all before. But look how that had turned out. I shouldn't judge him. There are things he doesn't know, can't see, not like I can. I should tell him, make him see what a fool he is. Not yet. I'm not ready to tell him just yet.

This time he'd decided not to say more. He'd come towards me, to kiss me. I'd focused on holding still. I couldn't think about where he'd been. Stay still. I could wash my face when he'd gone.

He kissed my cheek and then said, 'Did you have a shower when you came in?'

How did he know that? 'What do you mean?'

'Your hair's still wet. Did you have a shower?'

I'd tried to stretch my face into a smile, ignore the sense that I was being interrogated. I didn't know if I'd succeeded, so I made a joke, just in case. 'And that's why they made you a detective.'

'Sherlock, that's me.' He'd grinned and then nodded towards the window. 'Do you want me to close the curtains? Perhaps I could open the sash a bit, let in some fresh air. It's still really warm out there, but a breeze–'

'No.' Too harsh. I heard the sharp edges in my voice. Sharp edges cut. Softer. 'No, I don't want to risk the baby getting a chill.'

He'd hesitated, like he might say more, but then didn't. 'Okay, try to get some sleep.'

And then he'd gone away.

I pushed him from the room with my eyes and then checked. It had still been asleep, a small smudge in the expanse of the white cot, chest rising and falling. What did they say? Sleep of the innocent. What did they know?

Should I have told him? No. Not yet. I'm still getting it clear in my head. I need to understand more before I tell him. I'm a scientist. Before the baby, that is what I did – analysis, study, protocols and controls, records. I can do that now. And then I'll tell Thomas. Now is too soon. He wouldn't understand.

But what will I say about last night?

I can't get the picture straight in my head. Or rather there are pictures, but I can't join them together. What came first? Where was I? What did I actually do? There are gaps. It'll be the baby. My brain has been damaged by the baby; it's reached in with acid fingers and dissolved and distorted, mixed everything up, made me forget things. I can't remember, not clearly. And that's what it wants.

Now I know that, though. Now I will concentrate more, be more careful.

I think I understand. I had to do it. That's how I think it was. I need to remember more of what happened. I remember the knife on the ground. I remember the boy down there in the bushes. I remember the blood.

2

JENNY

She hadn't slept all night. Thanks to Jack. Bloody child. Not a child. Still a bloody child.

Jenny was pacing the kitchen eating Coco Pops from the packet. Jack's favourite. If she ate them all that would serve him right. A picture he'd drawn of a car when he was at primary school was still stuck on the fridge door. It was faded and tatty round the edges, but she couldn't bring herself to take it down. You never realise during the years you tire of feigning amazement at their latest artistic endeavour with a crayon and a glue stick how much you'll miss those times when they're a sullen fifteen-year-old who thinks a text saying *staying at mates* gives them permission to not come home at night.

She'd been waiting up for him – not officially, officially she'd been watching some Netflix box set – but when he'd texted she'd gone up to bed determined to – sod him – go to sleep. All the windows had been open and yet there'd been barely a breath of air. She'd thrown off the duvet, punched the pillow back into shape, turned it and turned it again in search of the cool side. There wasn't one. In the end she'd given up and switched on the light – one of the benefits of sleeping alone – and read her book.

She might have dozed a little in the early hours. She'd given up and got up for a cup of tea at five. It was going to be a long day.

What day was it? She pulled back the kitchen door to look at the calendar hung on the back. July was a picture of a posh git in a stupid hat punting under a stone bridge. She only put the calendar up because it was a present from Rose, her mother-in-law, ex-mother-in-law, never legally mother-in-law.

Every month annoyed her. College quads that non-university folk were barred from entering. The class traitors in bowler hats who did the barring. Pictures of King's Parade that showcased the college chapel but must have been taken at dawn to avoid the hordes of Japanese tourists and members of the less than picturesque homeless community who – ironically – were to be the beneficiaries from sales of this calendar that universally erased them. *Where do you live?* Cambridge. *Oh, the university. Oh, so do you go punting?* No, there are people – real people – who actually live in Cambridge, and they do not go punting. They can't afford it, for one thing. They did a survey that found that a huge percentage of kids from the Arbury Estate had never even been to central Cambridge, some three miles away. They certainly weren't swanning up and down the river in stripy blazers.

In her day, they used to drop bricks down onto the student punts as they went under Clare Bridge. Ahh, the good old days. Harder now, with CCTV everywhere. Still, perhaps that was the sort of innocent fun Jack was getting up to, what he was up to last night when he failed to come home and thus annihilated any chance she had of a night's sleep, of any bloody sleep.

The note scrawled on the calendar in the box under the day's date said, 'School 2.30'. Bugger. She'd forgotten that was today. The meeting with Jack's headteacher. A few days ago she'd received the email inviting her – it wasn't an invitation, more a summons – to bring Jack into school for a 'chat' before the new term started.

A chat. These chats were never good. *We'd just like to tell you what a little angel your son is, how well he's doing, how charming and clever he is.* In fact, Jack was clever. They could always wait to tell you that, though. No need for the summons for a *chat. Chats* always meant something wrong – something *you* were doing wrong.

Jack had, to be fair, always been a pretty good kid. Same couldn't be said of a good proportion of the kids he shared a classroom with. Not all schools, all state schools, but Jack's schools. She didn't have the cool million needed to win the postcode lottery by forking out for an Edwardian mansion on Rock Road or something rambling out in Newnham, or a village. Not that she could live in a village – nosy and incestuous as Romsey but with Tories.

The kids in Jack's classes with constant nits, who smelt of not washing, at best, who belted the other kids in the playground because that's what mum did and looked up girls' skirts because that's what dad did, it wasn't their fault. It wasn't even the parents' fault, not really. No support. No education. No money. No hope. No skills – beyond the skills to have more kids and fuck them up, just like they were. Not all of them. Not all the kids. Jack had some nice friends. Just had to hope that he was with them now.

What else did she have to do today? She had a couple of hours' work to do in the Harrisons' garden. They were on holiday and wanted the beds weeding and everything tidied up while they were away. She'd need to check that their irrigation system was working or the whole place would be straw. Heatwaves weren't good for gardens. Her own garden was already more brown than green – professional gardener's equivalent of cobblers' children's shoes. She should go out and give the veg patch a watering before the sun was too high.

Except she was stuck inside waiting for Jack to come home. So she could yell at him, or hug him, little bugger. However mad you got at them, the love still won. Not that she'd be allowed to hug him now. Her instincts were just the same as when he went too high on the swings or crossed a road without looking. She still wanted to grab him, be certain that he was unhurt, and suck him into her body where he'd be safe. Just he was bigger – older – now and she had to treat him differently. Rule one being no touching, no mushy stuff.

A text. And then his phone switched off. No *can I?* No details. No where, which friend, why? When had he started thinking that he was a grown-up and could do this kind of shit? This summer. He'd definitely been worse since the end of school. He'd gone feral. Asleep till lunchtime and then she'd just be thinking that she should go get him up and she'd hear the thump of footsteps on the stairs and the front door slam. He couldn't ever shut the door, always a slam. The bloody thing was going to break one of these days.

She hardly ever saw him. He'd disappear for hours and come in late, often after she'd gone to bed. She should've said something when it started. She'd been relieved that he wasn't on those damn computer games – the constant sound of gunfire and explosions – or somewhere in the dark depths of the internet watching who knew what. She'd policed his computer use when he was younger – rules, time limits, checks on his searches, talks about the dangers of electronic addiction, violent games, pornography.

Their early discussions over shared meals had become more one-way lectures directed at his bowed head, but she'd done all the stuff she was supposed to do. Wasn't he old enough now for her to trust him? Hadn't she done enough?

Where the hell was he? Would he be back for breakfast? He was definitely still eating at home because the fridge and the cupboards were always empty. All those bloody TV programmes on eating for less; let them try their stuff on a household feeding a teenage boy. She found the money, mowed another lawn, pulled more weeds, and kept the cupboards full. No danger that Jack was starving, though scurvy was a possibility.

Her eye caught on the bowl of rotting and wrinkling fruit. The heatwave wasn't helping. She had a bad feeling that a peach was dissolving to putrid liquid under its seemingly perfect surface. Filling that bowl was a ridiculous act of optimism, misplaced optimism. All those hours pureeing fruit and vegetables when he was a baby and now all he ate was processed crap. Her fault, no doubt, for not sitting him down at the table every mealtime to serve up home-cooked meals you ate with a fork and a knife. Obviously her fault, not his dad's.

That familiar spurt of irritation. She shouldn't be doing this on her own. Sure, Tommy was around, but he wasn't *here*. He wasn't the one doing this day to day, every day, wasn't the one trying to navigate the teenage moods, the sulks, the constant tugging on the leash. He wasn't the one cleaning up the crumbs and spills from midnight squirrelling in the kitchen, dragging dirty pants out from under the bed, lying awake worrying about where the hell the little bugger was.

Staying at mates. Was that singular or plural? Some girl whose father was going to turn up on their doorstep claiming that Jack had got his daughter in trouble. Please God let that not run in the family. Jack would make mistakes in his life, but let them at least be different ones to his parents. But wasn't a girlfriend a safer option to some of the alternatives? A bunch of boys crashing out on sofas after an online killing frenzy – that was okay. But what about something darker involving cruising the streets, drink, even drugs. It was possible.

Kids younger than Jack drank. Jenny had a sneaking memory of drinking gin her friend Josie had stolen from her parents' drinks cupboard as they sat on the swings in the park. What had they been? Year 10. Younger than Jack. There wasn't the drugs problem then, not like there was now. Letters from school about the signs to look for. Headlines in the local paper about gangs coming into the city targeting the vulnerable.

And who were the vulnerable? Were the students and the kids of the university academics vulnerable? They bought the stuff – everyone knew that – but they were consumers, didn't get dragged into the darker stuff, no crossing county lines for them, they had people to do that for them, like they had people to make their beds, clean up their mess and trim their lawns.

Was Jack vulnerable? No. She kept him safe; they kept him safe. Two parents, even if they didn't live together. Tommy was police now. He'd know if Jack was into anything bad. Wouldn't he? Though they'd seen less of him since the baby, which he'd promised wouldn't happen. She'd known it would; it was inevitable. Didn't make it right, though. She'd ring him. He could have The Talk with Jack. Schools were back next week and the boy needed to study. You needed qualifications if you didn't want to be vulnerable. He was bright but he was going to have to work if he wanted to get the results he deserved, better results than she and his dad had managed.

If she was going to do this meeting at school, then she was going to have to come back from the Harrisons' in time to have a shower and get changed. What was suitable wear for meetings with headteachers? She felt hot and bothered just thinking about it. Teachers still made her feel itchy, like she was no more than a teenager herself, in trouble again.

Huh, Tommy could do it. She'd send him a message. He'd have some excuse about work, no doubt, or the baby, or *Emma*. He could make time. She had work too. He could do some parenting of his firstborn today. The perfect Emma could look after the no doubt perfect baby.

Even as she internally sneered and raged, she was annoyed with herself. It wasn't like Emma had anything to do with why she and Tommy weren't together, and she'd never done anything to Jenny, not really. Wasn't it un-feminist, or something, to dislike another woman just because she was fucking the man you used to fuck? It was probably in the rule book somewhere. Well, the rule book hadn't met the lovely Emma: PhD from Cambridge, good job, clear-skinned, bouncy-haired, a waist – although there was a chance, a hope, that the waist might have been compromised by childbirth. A slim hope. Hah. No doubt the woman was swanning about in her pre-pregnancy jeans like a bloody Boden-Madonna. And one of those stripy tops. What was it with posh people and stripes?

Jenny went to put the kettle on. Nights without sleep meant days fuelled by caffeine and bad temper. She shouldn't, of course, be drinking caffeine; she had a cupboard full of herbal alternatives. Needs must. She'd do an extra ten minutes' yoga later. It might improve her temper as well. Might.

Maybe she should try Jack's mobile again. See if he'd switched it back on. Where the hell was he?

She wanted to be angry. Really, she was just worried. Your heart walking round outside your body. That's how she'd heard people describe having children. It was true, from the moment they were born, however big they got – Jack was taller than her now – you worried for them, felt their absence when they were away from you like they were part of your own body, which they were really.

Come home, Jack, so I can be mad with you.

3

EMMA

After Thomas went to bed last night, I waited until I knew he'd be asleep – it never took him long – and then I went downstairs to fetch a bottle.

I always had bottles for the next feeds ready in the fridge. As I waited for one to warm, I checked on the washing machine. Finished. I hung out the washing – just a small load. Then put bleach down the sink – its smell clean and cutting – and wiped down the surfaces. Thomas never does. He'd have made himself a drink when he came in, eaten a snack to make up for missing dinner again, standing there without a plate to catch the crumbs, smearing his fingers everywhere.

I went up and collected his work clothes from the wash basket in the bathroom. I looked into the bedroom and saw him lying on his side facing the door. I used to lie behind him, my back against his like it was the wall of a cave. Back before.

I put on another wash. Never know where he's been, what he's touched, been touched by.

I went back up to the nursery, to the window, and continued to watch – the baby in the cot and the clotted shadows below. No one had come into the park while I was gone. I'd know. The glow, down by the side of the house, close, too close, it was still steady, undisturbed, even as the rising light was letting it hide, hide in plain sight.

———————

The sun diluted the darkness to washed ink, warm at the horizon, and the glow faded. And then they came, clanging in through the gate, ripping the silence.

I saw them when they arrived. Through the window, looking down on them, on it. I rested my forehead on the window glass, felt its icy chill cool my brain. The first to come. How long till they found it?

I'd been watching, keeping watch. Since before, since after. They were the first to come into the park since after. Just the two of them. The boy was running ahead. He ran hard into the gate to force it open. The gate's weighted, so it clangs shut. Loud in the morning silence. A second shot of sound as she followed him through. I heard it sharp through the closed window.

They were acting, the boy and the mother, pretending to be a monster, pretending to be frightened. They should've been frightened. But they didn't know. Not yet.

'Boo!'

What does it even mean? Why do people say it? 'Boo!' Explosive consonant and long vowel. A 'b' for blood. Is that it? It should be. It's dangerous. They don't see it.

The boy was young, maybe four or five. Another boy. Was it in him too, already? It was so much harder to see in the sunlight. I'm getting better at it, though, better at seeing. Maybe he was still free of it. Not all were born with it and some had stronger resistance – like Thomas, though he needs my protection to keep him safe from it, especially with his work and Jack and now the baby. He needs me to protect him.

Then the boy was off, running, flying, arms outstretched,

soaring. Eagle or a bomber pilot? Something with prey. Then they played hide and seek. The mother and the boy in the playground. He hid in the bushes – stupid or knowing? – drawn to their still morning-damp darkness and consumed by them. She pretended to look for him.

I realised that I'd stopped breathing, was holding my breath waiting for the moment they found it. I wanted to smash my head against the glass, smash through it, let the sting of split skin soothe. I gasped and my heart heaved in my chest. They were going to find it. Then what?

The mother should've pulled him out of there. But mothers cannot always save their children. (Just like children sometimes kill their mothers.) If they don't know, how can they? And yet still people will say it's their fault. Always the mother's fault.

The mother outside looked worried. She followed the border of the park with her eyes, the fence that disappears behind the undergrowth and then the brick of the house wall that emerges at the other end. She was wondering if there was a break that she couldn't see. Had her boy slipped through a gap in the fence? Had he disappeared? Had he been disappeared? So busy with the game of pretending that she didn't know he was in there; perhaps he wasn't.

She stepped in closer to peer in through the branches. Something touched her face. She flailed to rub it away, panicked, spitting, shaking her head, dragging fingers through her hair. She stepped back and onto something that made her jump again. She rubbed the sole of her shoe on the grass, rubbing something off. She was by the yew trees. Berries. Who thought it a good idea to plant yew trees in a children's playground? The berries are bright and soft-skinned, and poisonous. She'd have trodden some underfoot and felt the soft squish as the sticky flesh popped out from the skin. It happened to me. But that's not why I had to throw the shoes away. I wrapped them in plastic first. Ruined. Gone now. Safe.

The boy darted out from the bushes in a rush of blue and threw himself towards his mother. He was laughing. He was almost in her arms when he tripped and fell. She caught him, lifted him high and kissed him, kept kissing him. He was squirming. A happy ending.

He was back on the ground and she was kneeling, talking to him. She was holding onto his hands and then looking at them. Then looking at her own hands, wiping something on her jeans, running her fingers through his hair, lifting his T-shirt to check him front and back, running her hands over his legs.

I knew what she'd found. Blood. It was now. They'd found it.

He squirmed, trying to get away. She wouldn't let him. She stood and went to look in amongst the bushes. I watched the top of her head disappear, wanted to shout down to tell her to be careful or she'd get it on her shoes.

She came back out into the open quickly. She dragged the boy away, holding him with one hand while, with her other hand, she pulled out a mobile phone. He was protesting, crying, yelling, his face contorted, the top notes piercing the glass skin in between us.

The boy found it, lying in the bushes. He touched it. She was right to be afraid. She was looking around the playground, out into the park, up at the houses. She was looking around, looking for help. I stepped back. I didn't want her to see me watching. I went downstairs. I knew what would happen next. Married to a policeman; I knew. It would take a short while, but the call would come to Thomas.

The mother would need to wash off the blood, get their clothes in the wash. It stains.

4

SANDRA

All night Sandra had lain awake in the tangle of her too-hot bed going over what had happened, going over what was going to happen. It had all been such a mess. She should've kept her mouth shut, stayed out of it, not made it her problem. Alfie, though, when it affected Alfie she couldn't stay out of it. He was what mattered and, especially now, she needed to do what she could, while she could, to make sure that he would be all right.

She'd stared at the ceiling, following the cracks in the plaster, until, eventually, even though it was barely light, she'd thought she may as well get up, put on some washing, go over to Danielle's. Unlike her daughter, her grandson, Alfie, was always up at the crack of dawn. She had her own key, so she wasn't going to disturb anyone.

It was a short walk from Sandra's flat to her daughter's, even though she'd taken the long way round that morning, walking along the road rather than across the park. She kept her mind on the present: curtained windows, bins left out on the path, peeling paint on doors, cars parked half up on the pavement, so you had to turn against the wall to get past.

It was going to be another hot day; she could feel it in the heat of the morning sun as it crept up over the rooftops. She passed the Co-op where she worked, fitting shifts around helping Danielle with Alfie. The shutters were still down. She tilted her head to have a quick look at the area round the side where a couple had set up home a few weeks back, bedding down behind the bins with their cardboard and blankets. Ari, the manager, had moved them on. They hadn't gone far; she'd seen them coming out from behind the barbers further down Mill Road. Maybe he was more tolerant, maybe they were getting some help from the church opposite that had cornered the local market on outreach to the homeless and the local nutters, bless them (the nutters not the church).

Sandra knew the local streets well – the Victorian terraces now colonised by the up-from-London muesli brigade and the broader streets of council-built semi-detacheds added onto them between the wars. She should do; she'd lived in Romsey thirty-five years now, more than half of her life.

Sandra stood in front of her daughter's house. She preferred her own flat. It was just big enough for her, cheap to heat, easy to keep clean. When she'd moved out of the Suez Road house where she'd brought up Danielle and her brother, people told her she was mad to give it up. Council houses in this part of the city were like gold dust. Everyone was being shifted out to the big estates in the Arbury, or further to the new builds in Cambourne. She'd been happy to leave the house, though. She'd been as relieved to get shot of the accumulated rubbish of a failed marriage and two kids as she was to leave behind the rotten floorboards creaking under the carpet and the damp patches in the bathroom. The flat was a new build with straight walls and a white kitchen with room for a washing machine. And no garden to worry about.

Sandra looked over the patch of scrub grass and jagged concrete in front of her. Danielle's front garden was half plastic dumping ground and half building site. Work had begun on the creation of a driveway – the old concrete path was part broken

up and a trench had been dug next to it. There was a circuitous
pathway to the front door marked out by bare patches in the
dying lawn. Scattered either side of this were a child's trike and
sit-in car, and numerous balls and toys. The back garden was in a
similar state.

She'd hoped that she'd brought up her daughter to have
higher standards, a little more pride. She hadn't been around
much when Danielle was older – she'd had to work, make a life
for herself after Brian left – but their home had never looked like
this. She'd dragged the lawn-mower out and cut the grass every
bloody weekend at this time of year. She'd cleaned the windows
and planted up pots of geraniums by the front door. She'd made
the effort.

And when her kids were small, she'd never have still been in
bed while her kids were up and downstairs. You never knew
what they were going to get into, so many hidden dangers –
however many cupboard locks and gates you put up. She'd taken
her eyes off Dean for five minutes once and he'd been trying to
poke bits of his cereal into the electric plug socket. She'd smacked
his hand and he'd cried. You couldn't do that sort of thing
anymore. He hadn't done it again, though.

So here she was. She'd been awake all night, up and dressed
for hours, but at Danielle's the house was still and silent.
Undisturbed. Half of the front windows were still shrouded by
curtains. The nets in the front room looked grey in the sunlight;
she'd take them down and give them a wash. It was good drying
weather, but today wouldn't be the day for it. Another day. Soon.

She tried not to let her gaze be drawn to the glassy eye of
Callum's bedroom window. His curtains were open, as they had
been when she left the night before. What time had it been? After
midnight, the streetlights staining the pavements yellow and
reflecting off the staring windows as she'd looked back.

She could've stayed over. She often did. There was a spare bed
in little Alfie's room since Callum had moved out into his older

brother's old room. She'd needed a break, just a few hours in the quiet calm of her flat to get her strength back. She hadn't slept. She didn't seem to need as much these days, less since... There was time enough for sleep.

She took a breath in and used her key to let herself into the house. 'Yooohoo, it's only me'. It was a whispered shout. She wasn't expecting an answer. She heard the TV in the front room to her left, high-pitched squeals and excited electronic music. She pushed open the door and saw Alfie curled in the shadows on the settee in the flickering light from a cartoon. His eyes were big in the gloom and didn't leave the screen as he fed crisps into his mouth from a packet in his lap.

'Morning, poppet.'

His eyes darted to hers to acknowledge her presence and then back to the screen.

'Are you watching something good?'

'*Spider-Man.*'

'Scooch up and I'll join you for a minute.'

He moved his legs so that she could sit down next to him. She tucked him into her, not minding as his jagged elbows pushed into her side. He was wearing mismatched pyjamas and the trousers reached only halfway to his ankles. She made a note to buy him some new pairs and throw these ones away.

They grew so fast at this age. If only she could place a hand on his head and slow the process down, keep him this young, this innocent, just for a little longer. His hair was sticking every which way like the feathers on a fledgling sparrow. She smoothed it and he let her. Her brother Keith's hair had done that. Alfie had the look of him, not just his hair but around the eyes. They both had those blue eyes that people notice, bright and clear, a light, shiny blue that looks like they're wet, crying or about to cry, even when they're laughing. Lit from inside. And long eyelashes – wasted on a boy, people said. Danielle had had them when she was little. Then she'd grown out of them, grown into them.

Maybe the same would happen to Alfie. Sandra hoped not, hoped he would always be as beautiful as he was right now.

She should open the curtains, get Alfie some proper breakfast, get Danielle up. Just a minute longer. Danielle and Lee would need the sleep. She just wanted a moment more in the peace with Alfie.

She hadn't spent time like this with Shaun and Callum. That was her fault. Maybe things would have turned out differently if she'd been around more, been around for Danielle, and the boys when they were little. They'd made their choices, though, and nothing could be done about that now. Things would be different this time. A new start. Danielle had Lee and he would be a good dad. Alfie would be all right.

Sandra felt the weight of Danielle asleep with Lee above her head. The emptiness of the room next to them – Callum's room – threw the house off balance. It was the box room; a single bed squeezed in under the window and barely room for anything else. Callum didn't care; it'd been Shaun's room and he'd wanted it, wanted his own room, wanted to move in where his big brother had been, desperate to step into his shoes.

Look where that'd got him. As the older one, Callum should've had a claim on the bigger room. He'd left that to Alfie, like he knew. What did they call it these days? Blended families. Made it sound so simple, smooth, when it really wasn't. Lee tried, but he wasn't their dad – and he *was* Alfie's dad. Complicated. Jagged. Shaun and Callum had the first claim on their mum, but Alfie had the stronger claim. Such a mess. Sandra was glad that she hadn't met anyone permanent after Brian, hadn't had a second family. The first was hard enough. Although it did feel like Alfie was hers; another chance to get it right. She was running out of those.

5

EMMA

I couldn't keep watching. I didn't want to be seen at the window.

Thomas is awake now. From the kitchen, I can hear him moving around upstairs. I haven't heard his phone. He doesn't know yet. They'll ring. They'll ring him. He's a detective and he lives right on the scene, the scene of crime, that's what they'll call it.

He's coming down the stairs now. I can hear his tread over the sound of the hot tap. I just need to clean the handles on the cupboards, wipe down the fridge. I need the water to be properly hot. When I turn from the sink, he's standing in the doorway looking round. What's he seeing?

'How long have you been up, Em?' His hair is still uncombed and he's rubbing his eyes.

'She wouldn't settle.' I nod towards the baby lying in her Moses basket. 'I didn't want her to wake you, so I brought her down.'

'I wouldn't have minded. I've got a while before I need to go in. Why don't you go up to bed and see if you can sleep for a bit?'

Again. *Take a nap. Rest. Go to bed. Sleep when the baby sleeps.* I don't need sleep; can't need sleep. I can't rest now.

Let it go. Calm. Not angry. What did they say to me? Turn that frown upside down. Idiots. They just found it easier to look at. Hide the sad. Hide the bad. And the angry. So, sound cheery. 'I'm fine. I've got things to do.'

'What things?' He's laughing. 'The place is spotless, there's washing on the line, that's clearly madam's food for the day.' He's nodding towards the bottles, newly sterilised and filled, ready to go into the fridge. 'What can you have left to do?'

I can't laugh. It's not funny. Is he criticising? Does he really not understand? 'There are always things to do,' I say. 'Feeding, changing, washing, cleaning – it's never-ending.' I should stop now. I can't. The words keep coming. 'I have to stay on top of things. And the baby always wants something and I never know what it is. She cries and I don't know why. I don't know what she wants from me. I try to do what they say in the book. It doesn't work. Nothing works. Nothing will ever work. But I'm trying. I'm trying.'

He's frowning. I've said too much.

'Babies cry, Em. It's what they do – eat, poop, cry. It'll get better, though. Let me–'

Of course. Now that again. The words won't stay inside. 'I'm sorry. I forgot. You're the expert. You've done it before. It's just me being stupid. I suppose you think Jenny did everything better. We can't all be natural mothers. Like her.' She was. Jenny. Natural. Just did it. Made it look easy. She'd only been a child herself when she had Jack, seventeen, but she'd managed, hadn't she? Managed to breastfeed, managed to make it all look easy. And Thomas couldn't see how it had all gone wrong, so Jenny still made her look bad. For now.

I am bad, though – against their standards. Jenny, Thomas, his mother. Bad mother. Good scientist, but bad mother. How could I have thought that I could be a mother? I killed a mother. I can't *be* a mother. How would I know how? It isn't in me. Or maybe it would've been, could've been.

Thomas is still talking, his voice confusing my thoughts.

'I've told you before, Jenny and I were disasters when Jack was born, we had no idea what we were doing. If it hadn't been for my mum, I don't think we'd've ever got the hang of any of it.'

He's thinking back, smiling, imagining them together – him, Jenny and the boy. Now he's back with me, frowning. 'Look, is this about the breastfeeding?'

'No!' It wasn't. I was over that. I'd been sure that I'd be breastfeeding. It hadn't happened. I tried. My milk hadn't come in. They said it happened sometimes. I hadn't been expecting it to happen to me. But I understand now. It isn't my fault. I know it's what they're all thinking, saying behind my back. They're wrong, though. They don't know what I know, what I know now. It isn't my fault. It hated me. It started off pawing and gnawing at me and then it got angry when it came near me. It knew we were different, incompatible. Now I understand why it hated me. And now I'm glad. It's better this way. It's easier to get into a proper routine. And it's safer. Knowing what I know, I couldn't have the baby sucking at me, sucking from me, having our fluids mix through my nipples and bare skin against bare skin. This way I can stay separate and clean and avoid infection. And it'll be easier if I have to…

It isn't my fault.

Thomas interrupts my thoughts. 'Hey, Em, I know you're tired. It doesn't matter. She's fine. Look at her. Look at that lovely fat belly.'

He's leaning over the basket. Leaning over the baby. Again. Why can't he keep his distance? *Don't, don't touch her.* He's bare-chested, just wearing pyjama bottoms. I can see a sheen of sweat on his skin. It's hot again, too hot, airless. I can't open the windows. Even if I do, there's no breeze. We have to keep breathing in the stale air, the sweat and skin dust, the contagion, because out there is worse.

Thomas should shower now, get dressed. He shouldn't be around the baby like that.

Speak calmly, lightly. Move him away. Gently. 'Why don't you go get a shower and I'll make some coffee?'

I got the tone right; he's smiling. I have to keep him safe, protect him. I can't lose Thomas; I won't lose him. There is nothing I won't do to stop that happening. One day he'll know what I've done for him; know that it was for the best.

He's holding out his arm to me. 'Em, come and sit down for a minute.'

I can't.

His phone is ringing. This will be it.

6

JENNY

A key in the door.

'Jack?'

A slam. Again. Obviously Jack. A pounding of enormous feet up the stairs. When did that happen? When did his feet grow so huge? She remembers holding two chubby feet in the palm of one hand, just... yesterday?

Bloody child. Bloody huge-footed child. She should get him back down and make him explain himself, tell her where he's been, tell him not to do it again.

It wasn't that she was one of those overprotective, smothering mothers – she wasn't – but Jack should have discussed where he was going last night, especially if he intended staying out. He wasn't a grown-up, only fifteen, and he was still her responsibility. There she was channelling her mother again. It was like you had kids and got plugged into some kind of *Star Trek* Borg mother entity, where you shared the thoughts and words of generations of the mother-force. As time passed, you assimilated further and further until you could not distinguish yourself from your own mother. You became your mother. What a bloody horrible thought. Jenny had hated her mother for years.

No. She was nothing like her mother. (Her mother would be the first to agree with that. Jenny could see her disapproving face, lips pursed so the wrinkles gathered and pointed like bitter little arrows.) Unlike her mother, Jenny respected her child as his own person. And he showed her the same respect – or that was how she'd planned it. It wasn't that she was trying to stop him growing up or having fun; she really wasn't. He could go out all night. He just needed to talk about it with her first. That wasn't unreasonable. She needed to talk to him now – and check he was all right.

The smell of her coffee drifted up to her nose. Coffee first.

Her mobile rang. Tommy. What did he want? Whatever it was, she could take this opportunity to tell him about the meeting at the school later. He was ringing her, so she couldn't be accused of bothering him at work or interrupting anything. Maybe she could imply that she'd told him about the meeting already. She might have done. She would've done if he'd been around more, if he'd found time for them between the job and the *baby*. She felt a tiny bit bad that she felt such resentment towards a little scrap of newborn humanity. But could she be blamed, really?

Tommy got to start again, have another go at having the perfect family. Family 2.0. Emma wouldn't be coping with a newborn in a one-bedroomed flat when she should've been taking her A-levels and getting pissed. She won't be dressing her baby in stuff from charity shops and having health visitors sticking their noses in day and night like she couldn't look after herself, let alone her own baby.

She answered the call. 'Not forgotten my number then?'

'It's programmed in.'

She would've expected to hear a grin in his voice, but it wasn't there. 'What's up?'

'Is Jack home?'

'In his room.' He didn't need to know that was a recent thing. 'Why?'

'Just checking. Nothing really. I should go.'

'Hang on. Has something happened?'

There was a moment's silence as though his attention was elsewhere, divided. Then, 'There's been an incident– I mean, I've been called out to something involving a kid Jack's age and... I don't know...'

Jenny felt herself softening towards her ex, as she always did. 'And you were worried. It's okay; Jack's here. What's happened?'

'I shouldn't– What the hell. They've found a body, a teenage boy. I just–'

It wasn't Jack. She'd heard him come in. But still her stomach turned and she had to reach for breath. 'Shit. Where? Do you know how it happened?'

'They're saying he was stabbed. It's in the park by ours, Jen. Practically on my doorstep. We don't know what happened yet.'

That's when she should've said that Jack had only just come in, that their son had been out all night. She said nothing.

'It's okay, Jen. It's not Jack. He's with you. I should've known that he would be. You're a good mum. Look, I've got to get on.'

She let him go.

The door to Jack's room was shut. She knocked. She respected his personal space.

No answer.

'Jack.'

Still nothing.

'Jack, I'm coming in.'

He had a bolt on the inside of his door, so he could lock it if he wanted to. It was only fair. She had one on her door too.

When the door opened, she saw Jack lying on his stomach on his bed, earphones in, reading something on his phone. The bed was too small for him really. Really, when did he get that enormous?

'Jack.' She didn't shout, but she had to raise her voice because he clearly hadn't heard her come in.

He turned to look at her. She indicated his ears. *Take them out.* 'Jack, could we talk for a minute?'

'What?'

She waited for him to remove the earphones before speaking again. 'Talk, please.'

'Yeah. What?'

Oh, for the days before the monosyllable became the standard form of communication. 'Jack, I just wanted to say that I'd rather you didn't stay out all night without at least calling me to discuss it.'

'Okay.' He went to put his earphones back in.

'Do you understand what I'm saying, Jack? I'm not being unreasonable.' She really wasn't.

'Yeah. Got it.'

'A text isn't enough. Not really. And you turned your phone off so I couldn't call you. I was worried.'

'Okay.'

He was exasperating. 'Your dad rang this morning.'

That had his attention. He twisted round and sat up. Perhaps she shouldn't have said it like that.

'What did you tell him?'

'I didn't tell him anything. I probably should've, though.' She remembered why she hadn't said anything. 'Where were you last night?'

'I stayed at a mate's. I told you.'

'What mate?'

'Not anyone you know.'

'They can't be that good of a mate then. Try me.'

'Look, I'm not a baby, you know. I texted. There's really no need to involve the police. What did you tell him, anyway?'

'He's not the police. He's your dad. And you're only fifteen. We should know where you are at night.'

'Shit, Mum. Really? What do you think I was doing?' Jack stood up and shoved his phone in his pocket. 'I'm going out.'

This wasn't how Jenny had imagined this talk. 'Where are you going?'

'Out.' He snaked past her, avoiding any possibility of accidental physical contact.

'Out where?' She was talking to his back now as he walked away from her down the hallway.

'Out of here.'

She should tell him to stop, make him stop and explain himself. 'Jack, don't forget the school thing. Be back by one.'

The front door slammed.

That went well. She still didn't know where he'd been all night.

7

EMMA

Thomas got the call, like I knew he would. Right outside his house – they'd have to call him. He was gone in less than fifteen minutes. I heard the shower run for maybe two minutes. Finally washing the muck away. I'll go up with the bleach in a minute.

His hair was still wet when he left. It was cold on my cheek when he kissed me goodbye.

'Sorry, love. I've got to go. I'll call you. Don't worry.'

I'll worry, but not about what he thinks. The body doesn't scare me. The glow has been fading.

I'm back at the window but not too close.

Look at them down there, busy, busy, eyes to the ground, looking down, poking around with sticks, kicking at leaves, shoving their gloved fingers into clumps of grass. They won't find it. Look at them whirring around like white flies in those plastic suits. They could spread the contamination. Paddling in the filth. Breathing it in. Idiots.

All so busy, like they matter, like they have any control. They don't get it. They're stupid, stupidly naïve, like I used to be. They think their plastic suits, their lengths of plastic tape *do* something.

Boundaries. Fences. Gates. Keep out. Keep off the grass. A line in the sand. Police – do not cross. But none of it makes any difference. It's under their feet, right under their noses, all around, inside, all around. No point telling them. They wouldn't hear, wouldn't understand. They think they know. Right and wrong. Good and bad. Guilt and innocence. There are no boundaries. It's all mixed in and mixed up. Like blood.

Blood isn't pure; it's a mix. Mainly plasma and erythrocytes, but then there's the platelets and the white blood cells, the leukocytes, granulocytes, lymphocytes – B cells and T cells – and monocytes. All rushing around the body, carrying the good and the bad from one place to another, a full cycle in less than a minute, seconds from heart to hand, seconds from eye to mind. And there are the infections. Unseen invasions of micro-organisms – viruses, bacteria, protozoa – rushing around the body, pushed and tossed, frothing, growing, spreading, fabulous and evil, dividing and subdividing. All unseen. And inside. I used to think I understood it all. Me in that white coat in the lab thinking I had the control. Not now. Now I see the chaos and all the things I don't know. I thought I had it contained, thought I could see it all with my centrifuge and microscope, thought I knew it all. I knew nothing. But I'm learning. I can beat it.

The baby screamed. I fed it. Changed its foul-smelling nappy. Washed my hands. Washed them again. Hot water. Bleach. I can still smell it on my skin. Now it's sleeping, so I've left it downstairs. I thought about waking it up. The book said to keep to a strict schedule. It didn't work, though. And the books don't understand what I'm dealing with. No one does.

I step closer to the window. But not too close. I want to see. To see and to watch over Thomas.

He's talking to the woman with the child who found it. He's crouched down in front of them. They're sitting on a bench up against the far fence, as far away from it as they can get. That's right, but too late now. The woman looks crumpled. I don't need to be close to know that she's sweating. Even before the sun is high, I can see how hot it is out there. The light glancing off the white plastic, the metal of the climbing frame and slide. Sitting there in the glare, the sweat will be pooling in her armpits and under her breasts.

Will Thomas be breathing in her odour? Move back. Keep away from them, her and the child. The boy is clamped to the mother's side, his arm tucked under hers. He's squirming and kicking at the bench. He wants to break free, to break things, they all do. Does he want to run back, to go back into the bushes? Is he being drawn back? His mother shouldn't have let him go in there. There's always rubbish – mess, dirty things, broken glass, needles. They go in there and they leave their mess. I've watched them.

Thomas is standing up now. Slow to straighten, hands on his thighs. He's been down there for too long. He won't complain; too proud to show he's not as young as he was. I love him, now and forever, ever since I first saw him in The Eagle.

I didn't usually go to the pub after work, but it was someone's birthday. It was packed. I was trying to get back to our table with a drink. He was looking at the blue plaque on the wall. I don't know why I did it. I meant to just say *excuse me* but instead I explained how Crick and Watson didn't discover the structure of DNA on their own, like the plaque implied, how they needed Rosalind Franklin's work with X-rays, how the women never get the credit. He let me rattle on, asked questions and then bought me another drink when I realised that my colleagues had moved on without me.

He wasn't anything like the men I usually dated, when I dated. People at work laughed when I said he was a policeman, firmly town not gown. He made me feel safe. He's always made me feel safe, until now. Now it's my turn to protect him.

So, now step back, darling, step away. Yes, that's right, send the woman and her boy on their way.

8

JENNY

Mid-morning and already hot as hell. Jenny shoved the mower across the Harrisons' beautifully, unnaturally, expensively, green lawn. She was pretty fit, if she did say so herself – rather proud of the defined muscles in her shoulders and legs – and used to heavy gardening, but the morning was already heating up. She wanted to get this done before the sun got any higher in the sky.

At least it was a good job to do when you were annoyed, the anger acted like fuel. Bloody Jack. And bloody Tommy, or Thomas as he called himself – as *she* called him – these days. In fact, bloody men. Moody. Whatever they said about women and hormones, men were moody bastards. Never tell you anything. Hate talking. No thought for other people. Selfish bastards. Jack had been a lovely child. They'd been so close. They'd gone everywhere together. Had to, or she'd never have had a life. The closer Jack got to being a man, the more silent and moody he got. It had to be hormones or genetics, because she hadn't brought him up to be like that. He treated the house like a hotel now. Shit. She was sounding like her mother again. But he did. Walked in, stuff chucked on the floor, grabbed food from the fridge, shut himself away in his room.

Was a time when all he wanted to do was be with her – and she'd been desperate for just five minutes on her own. He used to follow her around; she couldn't even go to the toilet without a little voice at the door: 'Mummy, where are you? What are you doing? Can I come in?' Not that she wanted him to watch her poo – creepy – but an occasional conversation would be nice. They used to talk about everything. She'd even done *that* conversation. Tommy was such a wuss. Tommy. Thomas. Whatever the hell she was supposed to call him. They were both doing her head in.

She needed to tell Tommy that he needed to see more of Jack. She'd read a book about it. How boys needed to grow away from the mother and discover their otherness with a male role model. It was part of them coming of age. Tommy wasn't around enough, especially recently.

He wouldn't have liked it if she'd provided Jack with an alternative father figure. He'd actually had one of her boyfriends police-checked. Gary. Maybe he'd had them all checked. Jack had told his dad that he'd met Gary in the bathroom one morning. She usually got her men friends to leave before Jack got up, or kept her romantic adventures to the nights when Jack was with his dad. This incident had just been a slip-up and Tommy had turned the inquisition on her. Who was he? How long had she known him? What did she know about him? Would he be staying around?

Of course, he'd done everything right when he introduced Jack to Emma. Talked to Jenny first. Asked her permission. Like it had anything to do with her who he was shagging. Built up from short encounters to longer meetings. She'd even met Emma herself before they'd got engaged.

What a horrible evening that'd been. She'd drunk too much wine, even before the pizzas had arrived, and chattered on like an idiot while Emma sat there all cool and stuck-up, smug smile on her face. *I work in a lab at the university. It's too boring to explain.* More like she thought Jenny was too stupid to understand. And, of course, Tommy was all over her – hand on her leg under the table. Did he think she and Jack couldn't see them snogging in the street just as soon as they left? Jack had stuck his fingers in his mouth and made gagging noises. She should've told him off but they'd still been laughing when they got on the bus.

Jack had gone to the wedding. He hadn't wanted to. She was invited but there was no bloody way that she was putting herself through that. It was probably her fault that Jack didn't like Emma. She should feel worse about that than she did. It wasn't like Emma hadn't tried hard with him. Not recently, of course. Family 2.0 apparently didn't have time or space for leftovers from previous failures.

Jenny stopped mowing. She wiped her hands on the back of her shorts and twisted her hair up more securely on top of her head. That was the lawn done.

Her mobile rang as she was unlocking the padlock on her bike. It was Rose, Tommy's mum.

Straight in. 'Have you seen her?'

Jenny knew she meant the new baby. 'No, Rose, why would I have?'

'It's not like I live the other side of the country. Walk across the park, that's all they have to do. I got a picture on my phone when she was born. I couldn't even see her little face properly. Do you think I should go round? I could take a casserole.'

They'd lived on Rose's casseroles when Jack was born, taking it in turns to eat while the other one held him while he screamed. It took them weeks to realise that he was tired and they should be putting him in his cot. Of course it had been Rose who'd told them that. Perfect Emma wouldn't be making those kinds of rookie mistakes. She wasn't going to want Rose turning up on her doorstep unannounced. Jenny didn't care what Emma wanted but she couldn't bear the thought of Rose's feelings being hurt, more than they were already. 'I think you should leave them be, Rose. I'm sure they're just getting used to having a baby in the house, doing the bonding thing. I'm sure they'll bring her to see you soon.'

'I'm not just anyone. That child is my granddaughter.'

'I know. Give them time.'

'It's been two weeks. It'll be her, you know. Emma.'

'Rose...'

'I know you know. She's keeping my son and my grandchild away from me. You never tried to do that.'

The last thing Jenny wanted to do when Jack was a baby was keep Rose away. Her mother hadn't bothered showing her face at all. She'd never to this day met Jack. The last time they'd spoken had been her mother telling her she was a silly slut and should get out of the house before she brought any more shame on her. She'd wanted Jenny to have an abortion. *Get rid. Don't bother coming running to me if you decide to ruin your life.*

'Emma...' Rose's tone added expletives to the name that she would never dream of actually voicing. 'She doesn't think I'm good enough. I bet that child is going to grow up being ashamed of me. Tommy's dad wouldn't have had it, you know.'

Jenny would have so liked to have joined in the bitching session about Emma, but it wouldn't help Rose. 'People are different,' she said. 'You know Emma didn't grow up with a mum. That's got to be hard.' Jenny couldn't help wondering how hard it would have been to grow up without her mother – a bloody relief more like. Rose was more of a mum to her than her mother.

'It's more reason to not shut me out. I'm the only grandparent that poor mite has got.'

What was Jenny supposed to say? She didn't feel at all inclined to carry on defending Emma, or Tommy. They should've taken the baby to see Rose by now. It was cruel not to. At the same time, getting Rose more riled up against Emma wasn't going to help in the long run. Emma wasn't one of them, but she was Tommy's wife and the baby's mum. If Rose wanted to be part of their life, she was going to have to find a way to get along with her daughter-in-law.

'Look, Rose, I'm at work now and I've got to do a thing with Jack, but why don't I come round after that?'

'Would you, love? Not if you're busy.'

'Never too busy for you, Mum. I'll see if I can winkle Jack out of his room and bring him too.' It felt a bit dishonest implying that Jack was spending his time in his room rather than out who-knew-where. Rose was another one, though, who didn't need to know everything about Jack's antics.

'That'd be lovely, sweetheart. I've got some of Jack's favourite biscuits in – at least I think they're his favourites – could be Tommy's. You'll know–'

'It's fine. Any biscuits are Jack's favourites.'

'I'll go and have a tidy round. I'll leave the front door on the catch for you.'

'Rose, don't–' Jenny was standing by her bike outside the Harrisons' house yelling at her mobile phone. 'Rose?'

A woman looked out of her window opposite and Jenny wondered if she should wave. This clearly wasn't behaviour expected of the hired help in St Barnabas Road.

It was too late anyway; Rose had put the phone down. However many times they told her, she insisted on leaving the door open. Times had changed. She shouldn't be doing that anymore.

9

EMMA

The plastic tent is up, squeezed in between the trees and bushes, right up against our wall. The body – the boy – it's still there. Is it still leaking out? Will it seep through, soak into the bricks? I hadn't thought of that.

There was a lot of blood.

That's the only thing clear in my head; not the bit before.

Usually the glow pulses. His is steady now, fading, barely visible, even to me. But while the blood pumped, out, the glow continued to pulse. A heartbeat in the air.

Feel the rhythm of the beat of your heart. With each contraction, blood is pushed around your body. When you cut an artery, like the aorta, every contraction of your heart forces your blood out through the cut, in spurts. Death by exsanguination (*exsanguinatus*: Latin for drained of blood, *sanguis* – I've always thought it was such a beautiful word, despite everything, beautiful – *sanguis*, meaning blood). It happens fast. The average adult body holds eight pints of blood and if you lose half, or maybe two-thirds, you die. And you can lose this amount in seconds when a major artery is cut. You don't have a chance.

He wouldn't have had as much as eight pints. He was only a

child really, thin and wiry, so possibly six pints. It was soaked into the fibres of his clothes. Jeans and a greyish T-shirt. Whenever I saw him, he looked about the same; the result of no imagination and a failure to split your whites and coloureds before washing. (You have to be careful, especially when you can't use a biological detergent – although I think I might start. It might help.) By the end, the boy's T-shirt was black in the dim light, but it would have been bright red. It's probably dried to a darker rust now. You have to act fast to get bloodstains out – soak in cold water before you wash in hot. Get it wrong and you'll never get it out.

The rest of the blood will have soaked into the ground he was lying on, the iron seeping back to the earth's core. Maybe that will cleanse it. Filter it. Maybe the bad protein will degrade and become harmless. If I had my equipment and could take samples, I'd check. I'll have to rely on the glow to tell me. It's hard to see it in sunlight, but I'll check tonight.

It's still early. Hours to wait. I can't keep standing at the window. I should have another shower.

I turn the water up hot. Steam fills the bathroom, clouds the mirror, beads on the wall. I like it. It feels safer under the hot running water. I can think where it can't reach me.

I'm not ready to share my research with anyone yet. I don't know who to trust. I can't tell Thomas. He would want to see the facts. I love that about him; that he values facts. But I don't have them, not yet. I think I have it and then something shifts and it all slides into mess again and I know but I don't know.

Like last night – I know what I did, but I don't know.

If I had someone to work with, maybe, compare findings, but I'm exiled from my world right now. I'm pushed out with the women, with the hormones and the milk and the shit and the draining blood. In the lab, we're all men of science. I don't fit there anymore. I'm out here on my own, with the women who never liked me, who I never knew how to talk to.

How could I talk to them about this? They wouldn't understand. It's better that this one is dead. I can't watch them all. I have to focus close to home, where I can do most good. The evil is in the blood and now I can see the glow, I can see that it's everywhere. Seeing it is a gift and a curse. Other people don't realise. So it's up to me.

People think that it's all about the heart, but it's not. It's the blood. That's where they should look for evil. It's there when you're born, so it's not your fault. But that doesn't make you innocent. People go on about the innocence of children. It's rubbish. A child, a tiny child, can kill a grown adult. And they feed off blood. They are born of blood. They are not innocent.

Out of the shower, I stand in the fog bubble and stare down at my naked body. It's still lumpen and ugly. At least I can't see myself in the mirror. At least I can't see below, where it tore out of me. At least I can't see what it did to me there.

10

SANDRA

Sandra was still sitting on the sofa with her grandson when the ring on the doorbell came; it made her jump. She pulled herself up from the sofa, easing through the ache in her knees and the pain in her side. She moved the curtains aside and saw a man and a woman standing outside the front door looking up at the house. They were seeing what she saw earlier, judging.

The doorbell again and a knock following it. Time to open the door.

Sandra drew back the curtains and raised a hand in acknowledgement to the man and woman now looking in at her. She smiled like she didn't know why they were there. She smiled like she'd tell them what she knew.

A detective and a sergeant. A man and a woman. She couldn't remember what they'd said their names were. Thomas something, maybe. But she couldn't remember the woman's name. They were very serious and trying to be sensitive. Like clergy at a funeral. Sandra felt sorry for them. She wasn't a fan of either profession, but someone had to do it.

She called up to tell Danielle and Lee to come down. Lee clumped down the stairs in an ill-fitting bathrobe looking in

44

need of a scrub and blearily annoyed at being woken up – until he saw what was waiting for him in the hall. He looked at Sandra for guidance.

'You'd better fetch Danielle down, love.' She nodded to encourage him, like she did when Alfie was unsure about doing something new.

Sandra showed their visitors through to the front room. Seeing it through their eyes she wondered if she should've tidied up. The furniture, especially the television, was too big for the room and every available space was strewn with a muddle of discarded clothing, piled up laundry, used cups and plates, crisp wrappers, and toys – action figures, Lego bricks, plastic trucks and diggers. The dining-room table and the floor around it was lost under tools and pieces from a flat-pack that Lee had been constructing – or not constructing – for days now. Sandra tried to keep the mess under control. She was fighting a losing battle.

Still, given their job, these two had probably seen worse, and there was no point worrying what they were going to think of them. Apart from anything else, they'd already know about Shaun.

When Lee reappeared, he'd changed into grey tracksuit bottoms and a T-shirt. Danielle, though, followed him in wearing a T-shirt nightie that barely covered her behind. Sandra couldn't help but wish that her daughter would engage a little more in life and show just a little more self-respect. This wasn't how she'd been brought up. What had happened?

Danielle looked in on the strangers in her front room with a mix of boredom and disorientation. It wasn't just the remains of sleep stopping her eyes focusing, it was the depression, or the drugs the doctor gave her to treat the depression, one or both formed a spongy bubble around Danielle's mind that let very little in and kept her attention somewhat hazy. Sandra knew that she was going to have to do something about this and restore some of her daughter's grip on reality. Just this minute, though, she'd settle for her daughter covering her backside.

'Danielle, love, why don't you sit on the sofa. Lee, move that laundry off the chair, will you? And fetch a hard chair.' Sandra pointed to where his toolbox and various bits of plywood and cardboard currently occupied all of the chairs around the table. 'I'll be back in a minute. Alfie, love, come with Nana.'

Alfie still had his eyes fixed on the cartoon channel and was showing no interest in the new adults crowding into his space. Better it stayed that way. When he ignored her summons, Sandra turned off the television and stilled his protest with a look. 'Now, Alfie. Come with me.'

She fetched a dressing gown for her daughter and settled Alfie on the stairs playing a game on her phone. She refused the detective's offer of his chair and went to lean against the table. The moment couldn't be put off any longer.

The detective spoke to Danielle. 'I'm sorry, Mrs Peters…'

Lee interrupted, 'It's Shaw now.'

Sandra saw the detective cast an irritated look at his colleague before carrying on. 'I'm sorry. Mrs Shaw. Perhaps I could call you Danielle?'

Danielle nodded vaguely. Poor kid. She'd had too much trouble in her life. Lee was looking terrified, but she still had no idea that this was going to be bad. You'd think, given the trouble that had gone before, that she'd have better instincts. Maybe the tablets made it worse. She'd always been something of an innocent, though, a lamb strolling around the slaughterhouse of life. Poor love. Always life's victim. How could she not see that the face on that policeman said loud and clear that this was going to be bad?

'Danielle, this is about your son, Callum…'

'What's the little bugger done now, then? Should I go get him up?'

She didn't even know that he hadn't come home last night.

The detective carried on. 'I'm very sorry…'

Danielle looked away from the detective to Lee and then Sandra. Sandra forced her fingernails into the flesh of her palms and looked to the detective to coax her daughter into focusing on what she was being told.

'This morning a body was found…'

Danielle was shaking her head. Lee went to put his arm round her shoulders but she pushed away, now unable to look anywhere but at the solemn face of the detective.

'…and we have reason to believe that it is your son, Callum.'

'No.' Danielle jerked upright. 'No. No.' She was shaking her head. 'That's not right. No.'

The detective indicated an old school photo of Callum on the windowsill. 'Is that a photograph of Callum, Danielle?'

It was. The boy hadn't changed that much. Same blank eyes and his grandfather's long face. Always skinny, even as a baby. He'd have suited a fringe rather than that dreadful crew cut. He'd never get to grow one now…

The detective looked at Sandra and she nodded. Not the time for crying now.

Danielle was staring at the photograph and still shaking her head. Lee was fiddling with his bloody mobile phone.

The inspector looked genuinely sad. 'I'm very sorry for your loss.' He nodded to Sandra and looked back to Danielle.

'No. Don't be sorry. There's no need for you to be sorry. It's not Callum. It can't be. He'll still be in his bed. He hates mornings. Never gets up before lunchtime. No.'

'Danielle, love, you need to listen to the policeman. Callum's not here.'

Danielle looked at Lee.

Sandra tried again. 'He didn't come home last night, love.'

'No.' Danielle was shaking now. She began to rock back and forth, her body stiff like she was trying to resist the pain, to whine like a creature without words.

Sandra wanted to go to her. But she couldn't. The sofa, the room, the situation was too crowded. She had to stay where she was. There'd be time to comfort her daughter later. For now, she had to stay above the waves. She spoke to the detective. 'Do you know what happened?'

He seemed relieved that someone was asking him something he could answer. 'We don't have any details yet, but it seems that Callum died as a result of a knife wound.'

'I see.'

The room was full of her daughter's sobs. Lee was staring at his wife like he would cry too if he could remember how. Sandra was aware of Alfie sitting on the stairs just outside the door. She needed to do something.

'Lee, I think you should make some tea.'

He looked at her like she'd just suggested he hand over one of his kidneys, and then the realisation clearly hit him that he was being given permission to leave the room. He jumped from the sofa like a man half his age and weight. 'Right. Yes. Tea.'

'Put the kettle on.' Sandra nodded towards the kitchen. As Lee left, she took his place on the sofa and gathered her daughter into her arms. She let her cry into her chest. She shushed and soothed her like she'd done when she was a child. This would take so much more healing than a hurt knee or a broken romance. There would be healing, though. Sandra hid her clenched jaw and dry eyes as she let her daughter cry.

The door to the hall opened and Alfie looked in. 'Nana, the phone...' He saw his mother and stopped, staring at her. He didn't need to see this. Sandra was torn – her daughter in her arms and her grandson across the room.

The sergeant, who had been watching silently in the background, stood up and indicated that she could look after Alfie. Sandra shook her head and disengaged from her daughter. 'Danielle, love, I need to look after Alfie. I won't be long.'

The sergeant nodded towards the space Sandra was leaving on the sofa.

Sandra nodded and held a hand out to Alfie. 'Come on, poppet, Mummy is a bit upset at the moment, but she'll be all right. Why don't we go and get a drink?'

In the kitchen, Lee was staring at the kettle. It wasn't yet on. 'You best go back in. I'll make the tea.'

Lee looked terrified and took a step away from the door.

'It's fine. She'll cry herself out and then the police will want to ask us some questions.'

'What sort of questions?'

'Don't worry. It'll be fine.' She popped Alfie up to sit on the stool she used when she peeled potatoes at the sink. She'd get him some cereal but for now she handed him a banana from the fruit bowl she'd filled the day before.

Lee wasn't moving. 'But…'

Sandra touched his arm as she passed to take the kettle to the tap. 'It'll be fine. Go look after your wife.' He could do that. He was better than the last one. He'd stay, he looked like he'd stay. Danielle needed a man who would stay and little Alfie needed a dad. Boys need dads. Alfie would keep his dad. That was what mattered.

11

EMMA

They're still down there, striding about like they're in charge, wasting their time, blindly nosing around in the evil.

Thomas has gone now. I watched him leave through the gate. He didn't look up. It's better he's gone, away from the body. I wish he hadn't been so close to it. The body. The blood. But now I don't know where he is. It's everywhere, already, and I don't know if where he's gone will be safer or more dangerous. Like the rest of them, he looks like he has the control. He doesn't know what he's dealing with. Those people, the ones he works with, they don't know it, but he's such a nice man, too nice. Look how Jenny gives him the run-around.

And his mum, reeling him in, time after time. If he wasn't so nice, he'd see what they were doing. I thought he was different. I thought he was like me, with me, but now I'm not sure. They are drawing him away and I'm not sure I can save him, keep him safe. He'll have the evil in his DNA; that's why the baby has it. In him it's contained, for now, I think. I wish I could be sure. I wish I knew where he's gone. I saw him leave. He went, but I don't know where. We used to talk about everything, but things seem different now, like there's something between us. It – the baby – it's come between us.

It's crying again. I've left it downstairs, but I can still hear it. I can always hear it. So loud. Fed, cleaned, held, walked. Still crying. It wants to break me. It hates me. It knows I know.

There was a girl at school. We'd moved, me and Dad. He had a new job and he said we needed a change. Really, he needed a change. He didn't want to live where he'd lived with my mother. It wasn't like he could ever forget, having me to look after, but he could live inside walls they hadn't chosen and lived in together. I didn't realise that was what it was about then. I just knew that we weren't living in the same house, I had to leave my bedroom behind, Auntie Jean wasn't next door anymore and I had to go to a new school. I must have been eight. I'd liked school. I was good at school, good at my numbers and reading. Mrs Iliffe used to put my stories and drawings on the wall with drawing pins. I had friends too. At playtime, we'd make daisy chains and play pretend games up on the field.

Then we moved.

The girls at the new school played skipping games I didn't know and they all had best friends already. The teacher said that my old school didn't use the same schemes as they did, so I had to start on the bottom books. I was determined to catch up as quickly as possible, and I did.

The teacher said that I was so good at my maths that I could help the children who were finding it hard. She sent me to sit next to Becky Shipp. I was supposed to show her how to do long division and tell her when she did something wrong. She did it wrong all the time and she smelt funny.

I covered my nose when I leant in to show her how to do it right. She pushed me with her shoulder when we stood up to go out to play and then she found me in the playground and kicked me. She said she'd do worse if I told a teacher. She pinched my arm in the line for lunch and pulled my hair in assembly.

If I had to read out loud in class, I'd see her nudging the person sitting next to her and laughing behind her hand. She went to the same secondary school as I did and, even though we were in different classes, she'd always be in the background, ready to mock and turn people against me. It was because I knew.

The baby knows that I know. If I go near it, it shakes its fists. When I hold it, it kicks me. And it keeps screaming. It's trying to drive me mad, sticking its little claws into my brain and squeezing. It took me a while to see the glow. Now that's all I see. Maybe it got stronger or maybe I was denying the truth to begin with.

I can't love it. I wanted to. I was sure I would be like it said in the books. They all say that you feel this rush of overwhelming love when you have a baby, like nothing you've felt before. No. It didn't happen. I didn't feel it. I felt nothing. Numb. Now I know why.

12

SANDRA

A watched kettle. That's what they say. Not true, of course. Just the watching made the time pass more slowly. She didn't mind that right now. Time could stop now if it wanted. She wasn't daft enough to believe what people said about things not being able to get any worse. Whatever life they'd lived, it wasn't anything like hers.

Sandra braced herself against the Formica work surface and bent over. Her back ached and her chest felt tight. She wasn't getting enough oxygen. She needed to breathe, take a few deep breaths. Standing up, she saw Alfie playing in the garden. Poor kid. One brother in prison and the other one dead. But maybe things would be different, better, for him.

Danielle was hysterical, but Sandra couldn't cry. She would. Later. But not now. Once Danielle stopped crying, they'd ask their questions. They wouldn't get much from her. She was pretty oblivious to what Callum got up to. She wasn't really a bad mother, but things had just got beyond her control. Maybe if she hadn't had to do so much of it on her own. Sandra would never forgive herself for not being around when Callum and Shaun were young. She'd been angry. But it was no excuse. Bloody hell. Now she was going to cry.

The door to the kitchen opened and the detective came in. 'I'm sorry for your loss.'

They really said that. Twice now he'd said it. Suppose it was easier than trying to make up something new every time they had to do this. And it gave them something to say. They couldn't exactly comment on the weather. *Beautiful weather for it. Do you think it'll last? The forecast says it's in for the week. Lovely.*

'My colleague is going to sit with your daughter and her husband for a couple of minutes. I know this is hard, but could I ask you a few questions about Callum?'

He was good at this. It almost seemed like he cared. Lots of policemen she'd come across weren't able to hide the fact that they'd seen it all before and couldn't give a toss. Sandra nodded but carried on getting mugs from the cupboard. Pity none of them matched.

The detective had one of those little notebooks and wrote things down as they talked. You must have to have neat handwriting to be a policeman. Callum had terrible handwriting; might as well have been those Egyptian picture things for all the sense you could make of it. She felt sorry for his teachers. Though his handwriting was probably the least of their worries.

The detective had asked a question.

'Sorry, could you say that again. I'm not with it.'

He made a sympathetic face; he really was very good at this. 'You're Danielle's mum and Mr Shaw is Callum's stepfather?'

'That's right. Danielle and Lee got married about two years ago, but they've been together for about five years. Alfie is his.'

'And Callum's dad?'

'Adam. Peters. Disappeared years ago. Up north, I think.'

'He had no contact with Callum?'

'No. Not since he left. Or his brother. As far as I know.'

'His brother? That's Shaun Peters, is that right?'

'Yes. Shaun's eighteen. He's been in prison, but I'm sure you know that.'

This detective was good. He didn't even raise an eyebrow. He must've been judging. Everyone did. How can you expect people to understand how these things happen, how kids go wrong, how some people can be just wrong from the start? It's not always the parents. It's just life.

The detective continued. 'Is the family in touch with Shaun?'

'No. Everyone was upset. Angry. You know.'

'Were the boys close?'

'Yes and no. They fought, you know. Boys do. Bulls banging heads. But Callum worshipped his brother, looked up to him, you know? I thought, though, that when Shaun went Callum would settle down, but...'

'He didn't?'

She shrugged.

'Was Callum often in trouble?'

'You know. Usual stuff.' The boy was dead. She wasn't going to stand in the kitchen telling tales on him. He was her grandson. She loved him. Despite everything. You just did. Even if you didn't always like them. Sandra could still remember the first time she held Callum. Tiny, he was. Danielle never was very good at looking after herself and eating properly. Probably smoked as well. Sandra had, with both hers, but people hadn't known back then. There were so many things she'd do differently now. Might have stopped it coming to this.

'And do you live here, Mrs...?'

'Chapman. Sandra. No. I've got my own flat. But I come over most days and see to Alfie, and help out. I only live round the corner. But I stayed here last night.'

'Why was that?'

'I was doing the ironing. It got late. I didn't fancy the walk home, so I slept here. There's a spare bed in Alfie's room.'

'Did you see Callum?'

'He was out.'

'No one worried when he didn't come home?'

'He often stays out, with friends, you know?' He was a policeman, he must have seen this before, even if his kids were always in before it got dark, if he always knew where they were. They never knew where Callum was. He'd stopped telling them and they'd stopped asking. It was easier that way. It was actually easier when he was out of the house. He'd disappear for days sometimes, especially since school had closed for the summer.

The kettle boiled and the detective helped Sandra to carry mugs of tea back into the other room. The policewoman was sitting next to Danielle. She'd quietened down and was now just sniffing into a balled-up tissue. She needed to give her nose a good blow. Sandra fought the urge to take the manky tissue off her and give her a fresh one. Hold it to her nose. Make her blow. Life dealt you some dud hands, but you had to hold onto your self-respect.

Lee was leaning against the wall by the door to the hallway. He put his tea on the windowsill and stared at it like he could cool it with his eyes, drink it down and make a quick getaway. Sandra perched herself on the arm of the settee next to Danielle and placed a hand on her knee, pulling the edges of the flimsy dressing gown together as she did.

The detective began his questioning again. He asked if they knew where Callum had been the night before. They didn't. When had they last seen him? This had set Danielle off crying again. Sandra said that she'd seen him leaving the house around teatime, which she had. Danielle had been resting upstairs and Lee had still been at work.

'Do you know who Callum might have been with last night?' The detective had his pen poised but he was disappointed. Danielle shook her head and dabbed at her eyes with the lump of tissue.

'Did he have a girlfriend?'

Danielle perked up, bless her. Something she knew the answer to. 'There was a girl for a while. They split up, I think. Pretty. Black – or mixed, you know? Pretty. Nice girl. So he can't have been all bad, can he?'

'Do you remember her name?' The pen remained hopeful.

'No. Christ. I didn't even know her name. I didn't know his girlfriend's name.'

Before Danielle could launch into renewed sobs, the detective asked another question. 'What about friends? Can you give me names for any of his friends?'

'There was a boy at school. Will something. They were in the same form, I think. He used to come round for him. Not for a while, though.'

'Anyone he had trouble with?'

Danielle shook her head, which could have meant no or I don't know.

At that point they were interrupted by a child's scream from the garden. Alfie. Sandra was first to her feet, but the others weren't far behind.

Alfie had tripped over and was lying sprawled on the path, screaming. The path had been laid years ago on the cheap and needed replacing. It was concrete that had split and subsided. This wasn't the first time Alfie had cracked open his knees on it.

Sandra gritted her teeth. Now wasn't the time to say anything. She'd just get on and clean up his wounds. More blood. Poor lamb had no idea what was going on around him. She rubbed her eyes. There'd be time to cry later. Now she needed to see to Alfie. He was what mattered now.

13

EMMA

I'm not meant to be a mother. I should've known. If you don't have a mother, how can you be a mother? And I'm not good at feelings. My dad said I was hard, unfeeling. When he said it enough times, I believed him. And it was easier not to feel. Where did having feelings get me? Apart from Thomas. But that's different. He's different. He just loved me and so I could love him back.

I thought in the hospital, after it was born, that there was something wrong with me, that I didn't have the right feelings, that something in my chemistry meant that I shouldn't be a mother. And I felt defective, guilty. But now I think it's a good thing, really, because now I can see that there's something wrong with it; I am able to have that distance, perspective. Feelings are not useful in my job. You take the blood sample, you analyse it, you find the disease, you can't cry about it. It's just information. I can use that skill now.

Even if no one else can see it, I know. I know that the fault is not with me. I can take care of the baby, watch it, take responsibility, but not love it. And that's okay. I have to watch to see how it develops, be objective. If I can keep it away from others with the contamination, that might help. Without any nurturing influence the evil might fade, become less powerful. It must be subdued, not allowed to thrive. There's a tipping point after which there is no hope. The evil wins and the only option is to get rid of the contaminated thing. I don't want that. I just want to do the right thing.

But it's so hard to think straight with the screaming and the laughing. I think it's from inside the walls. But I can't think that. I know the baby only cries when Thomas isn't here, though. I know that. It's got clever. He doesn't believe me. I can tell. He does his 'understanding' look. Treats me like I'm a fool. I gave birth; I didn't lose my mind. It sleeps. It's quiet. It's still. And then he leaves and it's just it and me, and it starts. The screaming, the kicking, scrunched up face, skin red – the evil blood rising to the surface. It hates me.

Well, that's fine because I know, and I hate it too. I have to hate it, to be strong. But will I be strong enough, be able to do what has to be done? I didn't know I'd be able to do something like that. But the baby? Will I be able to do that?

14

JENNY

Jack had, in fact, been okay about going to see his gran. It was the trip to the school before that which was the cause of his current sour face.

It wasn't as though Jenny wanted to go to the meeting with the head any more than he did. She wasn't good with authority figures – that's what Tommy said. Teachers always made her feel like a child again. Jenny and Jack were sitting in plastic chairs outside the head's office. She was having flashbacks.

Tommy usually came to parents' evenings and the like. She wasn't completely sure why she wasn't sending him to this meeting. Teachers loved him, of course. Though it hadn't always been like that. Was a time when they used to get into trouble together. Now he was the bloody authority. Ever since he'd joined the police he'd been dodging requests from school for him to join the governors. They used to laugh about it. No one ever asked her. A woman had cornered her in the playground once and tried to convince her to join the PTA. She'd played the single parent card and said she didn't have time.

Tommy – mature, policeman Tommy – was better at this stuff than she was, and so that was better for Jack, wasn't it? Tommy looked more proper, more grown-up. She didn't want the school thinking Jack was some drop-out pikey kid of a stupid, unmarried mother (not that there was anything wrong with not being married or not being academic or, well any of it, but that's what people thought).

She'd brought up Jack properly and he had a dad, a proper one, with a proper job. She couldn't help that she didn't look responsible. Everything about her body was a little bit out of control and seemed to give the wrong impression. She'd always been quite skinny but at about fourteen these enormous boobs had erupted. They seemed to have a mind of their own, always jiggling about in an untidy way and putting ideas in people's heads. That wasn't her fault, though. And she liked the way she dressed; she had her own style. And her hair. Why shouldn't she keep it long? Just because you were over thirty didn't mean you had to have one of those grown-up bobs with every hair always in place. Like Emma.

Emma was part of Tommy's new, neat life. Sometimes she couldn't help resenting that he had another life, that he'd been able to start again. New page. Education. Career. Marriage. Now a new family. Maybe she'd have liked all that. But she'd had Jack with her all the time. He took all of her.

Who was she kidding? It wasn't just having Jack. None of the stuff Tommy had now was her. That was one of the reasons they'd split up. He'd wanted stuff that she didn't. Maybe they could've compromised. For Jack. That's what grown-ups did. Trouble was they weren't grown-ups back then. Not much older than Jack really. And look at the mess they'd gotten themselves into.

Jenny had a mantra running through her head: *I'm the grown-up, I'm the grown-up.* It wasn't helping. It didn't help that she'd gone to the same school. It had changed since she was there – less tatty, new paint job, smart new signage and display boards, must've doubled in size – but it was familiar enough to make her nervous. Was he keeping them waiting on purpose to psych her out? The chairs were just like the ones they used to sit on. She ran her hand along the underside edge of her seat and felt the distinctive texture of solidified chewing gum. Maybe they were the same chairs. Unlikely they'd survive that many years of being chucked about by teenagers. She shifted position and the chair leg screeched against the tiled floor. She flinched and checked to see if there was anyone to notice. What was wrong with her? She was a grown-up.

She nudged Jack and whispered, 'Why are we here?'

He answered without looking up from his shoes. 'You tell me.'

'Look, I'm going to find out soon enough.' She was aware that she'd raised her voice and looked around to check for witnesses. No one. She dropped her voice back to a whisper again. 'Jack, do me a favour will you? Give me a heads-up.'

'Maybe he's seeing everyone.'

'Seems very unlikely. Spill, Jack.'

A sigh before a reluctant response. 'I was in a couple of fights, all right? Nothing really. You know. Stupid stuff. Teachers just overreact.'

Fights? Bloody hell. Why was this the first time she was hearing about this? 'Who started these fights?'

'They did.'

'What were they about?'

'Nothing.'

How could a fight be about nothing? Since when did Jack go around getting into fights? He'd never been the fighting type. She took a breath in and let it out slowly. No need to panic. He was growing up. These things happened. Tommy had been in fights all the time when they were at school. Now was not the time to lose it about this. 'Okay. And is this nothing over now?'

'Yeah.'

'So, I can tell the head that it won't happen again?'

'Yeah.'

'Right.' Jenny bit her tongue. Couldn't they just get this over with? She looked up at the clock on the wall. Was it the same clock she'd stared at all those years ago. Could be. It was a minute since she'd last looked and two minutes past the stated time for the meeting. Her consideration as to how long until they could legitimately leave on the excuse that the appointment had been missed was interrupted by the appearance of a man in a grey suit.

'Ms Richards.' He held out a hand for her to shake. At least he'd checked the records and had her name right. Teachers usually defaulted to calling her Mrs O'Keefe, which just made her feel old, like they were talking about Rose. Rose was Mrs O'Keefe. Though, of course, Emma was as well now. She'd got the ring on the finger.

The head nodded at Jack. 'All right, Jack?'

Jack humphed, but she'd take that over some smart-arse comment.

The head thanked them for coming in as he led them to his office and sat them in a pair of chairs facing him across his desk. He made some small talk about the weather and looking forward to school opening the following week. Seemed unlikely to Jenny but she nodded and smiled. A couple of grunts were extracted from Jack about enjoying the holidays and being ready to study for his exams. Then the head got to the point.

'So, Ms Richards, you will have heard about the trouble Jack had with a couple of his fellow students last year.'

It wasn't a question, thank God, so Jenny adopted a serious face, added a slight frown and nodded. That should do.

'I just wanted us to have this little chat today to put a line under that and be clear that we're starting this year with a clean slate. Jack has always been a good student. There have never been any issues with his behaviour before and he is predicted to do well in his exams. We don't want anything to spoil that, do we?'

Jenny nodded. 'That's right, isn't it Jack? That's what we all want. Yes?' She put an arm around Jack's shoulders. She felt him stiffen and shrug. When did that start happening?

Any further conversation was, thankfully, cut short by the telephone on the desk ringing. The head ignored it, but a moment later there was a knock on the door, which opened to allow a woman to stick her head through.

'I'm so sorry to interrupt, but it's important.' Her eyes widened as she delivered the next part of the message. 'It's the police. They want to talk to you.'

The head nodded. 'Tell them I'll be one minute.'

Jenny and Jack were already getting to their feet having reached an unspoken agreement that this was going to be their escape hatch.

The head apologised as he stood to show them out. 'I think we were more or less done, though. I just wanted to reassure you that we're not expecting any more trouble. Callum Peters has left the school now. I'm sure you'll have a good year, Jack. See you next Wednesday. 8.50. Sharp.'

15

SANDRA

The detective at the house had said he'd come back later. His colleague would stay and he'd let her know as soon as they had any information. He had more questions but they could wait. That was good. He said people would be coming to look at Callum's room, go through his things. She could save them the trouble, but it seemed best to leave them to it. They assumed that she knew nothing and it seemed best to keep it that way.

Before he left, he brought up that someone would need to identify the– He didn't say it. What he'd said was that they'd need a formal identification. Sandra said that she'd do it. So, she came to the morgue on her own and waited in a corridor to look at her grandson's dead body so someone could tick a box.

It wasn't like Danielle would be able to do it. She was in pieces. But even if she could've come, Sandra wouldn't have let her. This was down to her. No mother should have to identify her child's body and Danielle wasn't strong enough. Despite everything, there was still an innocence about her. She still believed that things would work out. Sandra wasn't sure if that meant that she had done her job right or wrong. She'd done her best and then she hadn't done her best and now she was trying to make up for that.

Sandra had seen dead bodies before. She hadn't made it to the hospital in time when her mum died, but she'd gone into the ward and behind the curtains they'd pulled around her bed. Her mum had never been a big woman, but she'd already shrunk, like she'd deflated when the breath left her body. Had they been close? She never really thought about it. They didn't analyse things like they do nowadays. It was her mum and then she died. She was old; that's what happened to old people. Callum wasn't old, though. A child, a whole life not lived. He'd never be a man, have kids of his own.

Everyone had been very kind. It was all done very sensitively. She couldn't fault them on that. She knew it was their job, that they had training on how to do it, how to handle people like her in situations like this. Still, she was grateful.

It was Callum; obviously it was Callum. She wasn't allowed to touch him. Most of him was covered up. It was like he was tucked in, asleep, but not. He'd looked so like himself and so not like himself.

His hair was too tidy; it never lay flat like that. It was already difficult to remember how he'd been the last time she'd seen him. Not as peaceful as this. She preferred remembering as he'd been when he was little. Not that he'd ever been what you'd call a happy kid, not like Alfie. With Callum it was like he'd had tiny razor blades in his blood, nicking him, stinging, making him spiteful in response to the discomfort of just living.

He'd looked calm lying there in that room, stiller, tidier, than he had ever looked alive. He'd looked younger, more like a child. That was just death playing tricks, though. Callum hadn't been a child for years and definitely not since his brother went.

Should she have felt more? Should she have been more upset? She felt numb. Maybe some part of her had been preparing for this day – no, she could never have imagined this. Prison, though, like his brother, she'd been expecting that. She'd never been as close to the older boys, Shaun and Callum, but maybe she'd also been putting distance between herself and them, a distance that wasn't there between her and little Alfie. He was her hope for the future; he was the one.

Shaun going away should've given Callum a chance to take a different path. Rather than escaping his brother's shadow, though, he'd stepped into it, taken it on like a new skin. He was drawn to trouble, to the ones who dealt in trouble, like a bee to nectar, like a fly to shit more like. He couldn't seem to help himself. Maybe if his dad had been around. Danielle just couldn't cope, bless her.

Sandra had tried, she'd tried talking to him. Lee had tried talking to him, when he wasn't yelling at him. But could you blame him? He'd tried his best, tried to treat him like his own when he and Danielle got together – maybe less so since Alfie came along. Even after that Lee had bought him presents – trainers, games consoles, phones – the little sod had sold them. He said he'd lost them or they'd been nicked, but he'd sold them. There'd been meetings at school and social workers. Nothing got through to him. And this is how it had ended. Under a sheet in a morgue with police looking on.

In the back of the car going back to the house, Sandra looked out the window and let the familiar streets of the city drift past her eyes, vaguely noticing the changes: the cranes filling the sky behind the hospital, the modern flats jutting out from the smooth runs of mid-nineteenth-century housing, the new roundabouts and road markings.

She wondered how the city would look in ten, twenty years' time. It'd changed so much since she'd come up from London when she married Brian. It was all about the university then.

Brian's dad had been a porter at one of the colleges and his mum had been a bedder, one of the housekeeping staff. Brian hadn't wanted to stay in Cambridge, but it was what he knew. He wasn't happy, and maybe that was why he'd turned mean, or maybe he'd always been mean and she just didn't see it at first. When he'd died – not even forty – and she'd had the kids and work, she just hadn't had the energy to move anywhere – back to London, somewhere new to start again.

As she got out of the car back at Danielle's, Lee was at the bins. He nodded as she walked towards him. After all, what was there to say?

The bins were kept away from the house at the front of the garden. Sandra nodded up towards the house. 'Police still here, I suppose.'

'Yeah. Bloody kettle's going to wear out if she makes much more tea.'

Sandra smiled. 'Something they can do, I suppose.' She turned her back to the windows and lowered her voice. 'It's probably best if we stick to the story that I stayed over last night.'

Lee glanced back at the house and didn't say anything.

'Danielle went up to bed about nine, we watched TV and then I slept over.'

Lee hesitated and then let the lid of the bin bang down. 'Sandra, I didn't...'

Sandra put a hand on his arm. 'You don't need to tell me. I don't want to know. Let's just keep it simple.'

He nodded as he turned away. She followed him back up the garden to the house.

16

EMMA

People thought I was weird at school. I liked school, liked science – even though I was a girl – did my homework, didn't go to parties, didn't have a mum. It was different, better, when I came to Cambridge. There were more people like me, and there was the science. It was why I stayed – degree, PhD, work in the labs. I'd found my place, or thought I had; they're trying to take it from me.

A city of science and scientists. Built on order and logic, you'd think it would be safe, wouldn't you? When I first came, it was still a small city, only a city at all because of the university, just a neat flare on the edge of the fens. Now it's oozing out, over the surrounding villages, filling in the gaps with new estates and science parks. The boards on the edge of the new developments say, 'Cambridge is evolving'. Natural and inevitable and all for the best – that's what they want you to think. Who could disagree with the benefits of evolution in the place where Darwin did his learning? The shine from medieval study rooms and chapels is so pretty and the bright lights of the laboratories so clean, what bad could happen here? I thought I'd be safe here and then I thought I'd be safe with Thomas, and now nothing is safe.

The contagion. You'd be amazed at how much there is out there and the places it finds to thrive. Take this park, with its blue fencing and safety gates, the red swings and yellow slide, the mulch underfoot to soften hard landings. It's where toddlers take their first steps. I see them. When the windows are open, I hear them. (Not now, now I know that the windows have to stay shut.) On the swings, they squeal, excited at the feel of air rushing into their faces as they swing really high, but really not that high. This is where dads bring the kids while mum has a lie-in and mums come to gossip with their friends – nods and waves and smiling kids, all nice and safe. But look closer and you'll see the chipping paint, the hard earth emerging underfoot, the kid blocking the slide on purpose, the sneaky shove off the climbing frame, the bitter single fathers and the bored, inattentive mothers, the bad mothers, anchored to the screens of their mobile phones to stay sane (it'll take more than that).

Then, when the little ones go home, for grey fish fingers and bedtime gaming, the teenagers come. They think they're invisible: slouching in the shadows; shoulders hunched; furtive, twitching fingers; hoodies pulled over their heads like cowls. They should carry scythes. I've been watching them, coming and going, their bikes sprawled on pathways while they sneak about in the bushes doing their dirty business. At night they flicker in and out of the yellow streetlights like moths, secret destroyers. But I see them. I watch. What else can I do, trapped in here day after day, night after night. I watch their pulsing glow.

They bring cans, and bottles that they discard and smash, leaving jagged teeth on the soft ground. The girls and the boys sit on the swings and on top of the climbing frame to smoke and snog and scream, and pretend to laugh. Laughing like hyenas smelling blood, snouts in blood.

Then there's the other stuff that goes on in the shadows at the edges. I've seen the needles and the flaccid condoms left under the trees. I've seen the graffiti; spray paint and scratched words in wood and stone, dirty words, dirty thoughts – anger, jealousy, fucking and hating. And I see them, doing their dirty deals. Innocence is a lie, a whitewash. Danger and infection. The spores are everywhere. I can see them. I can see the creeping, seeping mould. The pulse of evil in the dirty darkness.

I've seen Jack – Thomas's Jack – out there, in the park, with the hyenas. I've seen him sitting with them, close enough to touch, touching, nudges and shoves, sharing food, passing cans from mouth to mouth. He's infected. And if he's infected…

And the boy. He came every night, sometimes alone and sometimes not. There is never pure darkness in a city and the streetlights in the park mucky it further, so I can see the playground quite clearly. Coming and going, on his phone, always on his phone, lurking, favouring the dim shadows. The council let the bushes and trees grow wild around the edges of the park. They don't know or care about the dangers that can hide and grow there. But I saw his glow, strong and steady. I watched from the window. Better to look out. I watched every night from the chair by the window. I can see out and still watch the baby. With the lights off, I could watch their twin glows in the darkness.

I know. I see. I think that's why I had to do it.

I should tell Thomas. I can't tell Thomas. Maybe he would understand? But if he didn't… It's too much, too much to think about, too much to do, too much responsibility. Too much.

17

JENNY

When Rose let them in, Jack headed straight for the kitchen. 'Can I have a biscuit, Gran?'

'Of course, sweetheart. You know where they are.' She kissed Jenny on the cheek and patted her arm. 'Tea?'

Jenny nodded and shut the door behind her. She followed Rose through into the kitchen, passing Jack in the narrow corridor as he was heading to the front room trying to shove two biscuits in his mouth at the same time as doing something with his phone. They hadn't talked much on the way back from school. He didn't want to tell her anything and she wasn't wholly sure that she wanted to know. Of course she wanted to know, but maybe later.

Rose was filling the kettle. Jenny leant against the fridge and peered past Rose to look out at her small garden, more of a yard really – mostly grass with a neat flower bed down one side and a crazy-paved path down the other, leading to the bin store and the back gate at the end. The grass was more yellow than green, but it was all still as neat as ever. Presumably Tommy still found time to come and mow the grass for his mum. That was something. 'It's looking a bit parched out there. We could do with some rain.'

Rose followed Jenny's eyes to look out at the garden. 'I've been chucking the washing-up water on the rose, my rose, the one Tom planted for me when we moved in. Kissed me right there in the garden he did. Said I was his lovely Rose.'

Jenny smiled. She'd lost count of the times she'd heard this story.

Rose was playing with her wedding ring, twisting it in its permanent valley on her finger. 'This'll go to Tommy when I die. I hope he'll hand it down to little Isa. If her mother will let him.'

'Of course she will. Don't worry about that. Or about dying, for that matter.' She hesitated and then added, 'I'm pretty sure they're calling her Isabella, though.'

'I had a cousin Isobel; we called her Isa. You're probably right, though. Isabella. Bit foreign. But pretty.' Rose placed a hand on Jenny's arm and leaned in. 'Her face when I call him Tommy. Right sour, like she expected treacle and got lemon. It's all *Thomas* now, don't you know. He's gone posh on us.'

Jenny didn't disagree but made sure her face didn't reveal that.

Rose patted her arm. 'Good on the lad. Making something of himself. Shame he'd had to leave so much of himself behind when he did. Don't know what his dad would've had to say.'

Jenny remembered some of the things Tom had had to say about her and Tommy. He'd been silently furious when she'd got pregnant. *Bloody fools* was all he'd been heard to say on the subject. Then he hadn't approved of them not getting married and then not approved again when they'd split up. Then his only shared opinion was, *a boy needs his dad*. He wasn't so wrong about that.

Rose was back playing with her rings. 'I'm not getting any younger. My engagement ring, that's yours.'

Jenny opened her mouth to protest.

'No. It's not worth much. It's yours, though. You've been like a daughter to me.'

The unspoken reference to Emma was left to hang in the air. Jenny touched Rose's arm, feeling the softness of her crepey skin, and pointed back out into the garden. 'You've done well with that fuchsia. It's looking lovely. We might have to cut it back a bit when it's finished flowering.'

Rose leaned against her slightly as they stood side by side looking out of the window. 'Of course it's only a small garden but Tom was so proud when we bought this house. Of course, we wouldn't be able to afford it now. And where are the youngsters supposed to live? Not even any council houses for them. Not round here. I blame Maggie. Have you seen the price they're asking for these now? I nearly spat my tea out when Tommy told me what it's worth now. I hate to think how much he paid for that house he's in. Of course, Emma is earning good money. You know she's going back to work, don't you?'

'Most women do now.'

'Yes, but she wants to go straight back, put that poor little baby in a nursery. And who'll look after Tommy?'

'I think he's big enough to look after himself.'

'He does a very hard job, though. Long hours. Stressful. The least he deserves when he gets home is to find his dinner ready. My Tom–'

Jenny gritted her teeth. Her Tom had always come home to a hot meal. At least she wasn't the subject of these comparisons with the good old days but she neither wanted to join in this particular attack on Emma or be placed in the position of defender. 'At least this weather is good for the washing. I swear I got a load dry in half an hour the other day.' She looked out of the window again and saw the back fence next to the gate vibrate and bow. Through the open window she heard the wood scream in protest. The fence sagged forward under the weight of a figure – a close-shaven head and a black T-shirt – sprawled not so much against it as on it, like it was a big wooden hammock. He was a teenager, maybe Jack's age,

74

certainly past that soft stage – if this lad had ever had a soft stage.

Rose had seen and was banging her fist on the open window. 'Oi, you! Get off my fence.'

There was the sound of running feet down the alley. A bang and a rattle of the bolt as something crashed into next door's gate. There was a yelling and swearing from the lad on the fence, scrabbling to get up, the wood snapping and collapsing under him.

Rose was at the back door, yanking it open, a pair of kitchen scissors in her hand.

'Rose. No. Don't go out there.'

Jack appeared behind them. 'What's going–' He looked out the window and then, somehow, he was past Jenny and Rose and running down the path.

Jenny yelled after him. 'Jack! No!'

Already he was at the fence. Jenny heard him speak to the lad now standing on the broken fence. 'Fuck off.'

Jenny looked at Rose, though why the hell she was worried about Jack swearing in front of his gran at a moment like this she wasn't sure. She wanted to go after Jack but at the same time she needed to keep Rose inside.

The lad facing Jack was staring him down, mean-faced and flushed with fury. He stamped on the fence so it cracked and further collapsed under him. 'What the fuck you looking at?' His face was ugly and contorted. He looked like he was deciding what to do next. His body flexed.

Jenny saw the partial figures of another couple of boys in the alley behind.

Jack was talking to them. She couldn't hear what he was saying. He gestured at them and the boy on the fence stepped back into the alley. Now it was Jack standing on the fence. The boys were backing away and Jack was following them into and down the alley. Now Jenny couldn't stay still. 'Stay here, Rose.'

As she started out the back door, Jack came back up the garden, calm as you like, hands in his pockets. 'It's all right, they've gone.'

'You shouldn't have confronted them like that, Jack.'

'They broke Gran's fence.'

'Yes, but it's only a fence. I was worried about you.'

'I'm all right, aren't I? You can't let them get away with stuff.'

Rose was watching out the window as they came back into the kitchen. Jenny saw that she was still holding the scissors in her shaking hand. 'Let me take those off you.'

Rose didn't speak.

'Shall I finish making the tea and we'll go through to the other room?' Jenny moved to close and lock the back door.

Rose reached to squeeze Jack's arm. 'Thank you, sweetheart, but you shouldn't have done that. You should've let me or your mum look after it.'

Jack smiled. 'You can't deal with wankers like that–'

Rose interrupted. 'Language, Jack.'

Jack grinned and nodded. 'You need to be careful, Gran. They're not nice kids mucking about.'

Jenny frowned. He wasn't wrong, but how did he know? She moved out of the way to let Rose get the milk from the fridge. How much did Jack know about these kids? Perhaps here with Rose would be a good time to ask. 'Do you know any of these "not nice" kids, Jack?'

He cast her a scowl while Rose answered for him. 'Jack wouldn't know any nasty lads like that. He's got more sense, haven't you, love?'

Jack let himself be pulled into a hug by Rose. 'That's right, Gran.' He stuck his tongue out at Jenny over his gran's shoulder. 'I might know *of* them. The fat lad. Shaven head. Tinge of a ginge. Total plank. Lives up the Arbury. Don't know what he's doing round here.'

'Up to no good, I'd say.' Rose finished making the tea and handed Jack the biscuit tin. He tried to open it to take one and she waved him away, indicating that he should take the whole tin. He didn't need to be told that twice.

Jenny was studying her son, trying to discern how much he knew about the underbelly of Cambridge life. Jack narrowed his eyes at her as he left the kitchen with the biscuit tin.

While they drank their tea, Rose asked about the incident at the rec. 'Her next door. Foreign. Nice woman, though. Quiet. We were out front earlier and she said they found a body. Police everywhere, she said. Was Tommy there?'

Jenny weighed up whether she should tell Rose what Tommy had told her on the phone earlier. Was it meant to be confidential? Would it just worry Rose more? She decided that Rose would find out soon enough anyway – clearly the Romsey jungle drums were already at work. 'I think someone was hurt there last night. I think there was a knife involved.'

'A knife? I keep seeing on the news about the knife crime in cities, in London, up north. But in Cambridge? Was it them druggies?'

'I don't know any details, Rose. Try not to worry.'

'Of course I worry. About Jack. And about Tommy. I saw on the news just the other week about that young girl policewoman–'

Jenny corrected it in her head. *Female police officer.*

'–She stopped some man for something and he stabbed her. She died. Just like that.'

'I'm sure Tommy is very careful and he can look after himself, Rose.'

'Yes, I know, but what about Jack?'

'You said yourself, he's a good lad. He stays out of trouble.' Who was she convincing? Rose or herself? Because, of course, Jack hadn't stayed out of trouble. He'd just walked straight into trouble. She'd watched him. What had he said to those lads to make them back off? What exactly had happened out there?

And, of course, he still hadn't told her where he was the night before.

18

EMMA

The hallway is the coolest place in the house. No windows apart from the half-moon of glass above the front door that lets light trickle down onto the floorboards, turning them pied golden grey. I lie in the grey. The floor is comfortingly hard, and smooth against my cheek. The walls muffle the sound of high-pitched crying. I'm floating in shadow and wood. Just a minute. I just need a minute.

I called Thomas. He didn't answer. Busy. Working.

He hasn't called me back. It's been so long; I don't know how long.

The days are endless here on my own, just me and the baby, for hours and hours. A feed every two hours. That's six in twelve hours, at fifteen minutes each, that's one and a half hours. Nappy changes, assume six, five minutes each, that's another half an hour, leaving ten hours to fill. And if Thomas works late, like he did yesterday, that's even more.

I just service the baby. It's all I exist for now. I am its slave. Bottles and equipment need sterilising, I need to clean down the changing table, get washing going, hang it outside in the fresh air, the baby needs to be fed, changed and dressed, and then it spits and shits and vomits and I have to do it all again.

Endless.

I can't concentrate on anything; my mind is too buzzy. I can't read or watch television, not that there's anything on. I just wait and listen to it scream at me.

I could clean the floor again. The cracks and ridges of these boards must hold millions of particles of dust and dirt, skin and–

I called Thomas and he didn't answer. Why isn't he answering? Where is he? He said I should call him if there was a problem, but when I call him he doesn't answer. He said I could call and that he would be there. Why did he lie to me? Why doesn't he answer? Maybe he's already changing. The baby and that boy; he could be contaminated. Why isn't he answering the phone?

I want him to hear the screaming. Then he might understand. I want to speak to him. If I can get him to answer his phone, he will hear the crying and he will know that I'm not lying, not making it up. But he's not answering.

Maybe if I could go to those things that mothers go to, those groups and coffee mornings. Thomas says I should – NCT, baby massage, all that stuff. He's given me leaflets and found websites. But he doesn't want to go. Why would I want to? How can I? I wouldn't know what to say.

I've never known what to say to other women. It was just me and Dad and we talked about proper things, when we talked, and then I did science and there were fewer and fewer women and I was okay with that, I liked it. And, anyway, what if I did? What if I went out there? How could I face them when all my baby does is scream? They would look at me and they would know and I would know that they were judging. That would be worse than this.

The only thing I have in common with those women is that we have given birth. I don't want to talk about that, exchange stories of breaking waters and contractions and dilation and stitches. Giving birth was horrible, far worse than I ever imagined. I want to forget it. It's disgusting. And private. I've never sat in a café discussing my vagina before, so why would I want to now?

And I don't want people pawing the baby, cross-infecting, spreading disease. That's what I'm fighting against, so why go somewhere that will facilitate it? For now, I have to do this here, on my own. I'd like Thomas's support, but I'll do it without him if I have to. He still hasn't rung.

To begin with, I thought that I was just a failure and that I would have to learn to live with that and with people feeling sorry for me and talking about me and how bad I was at being a mother. Now I can do what I'm good at; there's something that I can do. I can see what they can't. I can act when they can't. I can do things I never thought I could, would never have believed I could do if I hadn't seen it. I'll save Thomas. He's what matters.

The phone. Thomas. Not the right time, though. It's gone to sleep. Quiet now. Like it knew, knew to stop crying, stop now. I need to answer though, know that he's all right.

'Emma? It's me? What's happened?'

'Where have you been?' I have to know, but I try to make it sound casual.

'In a meeting. What's up?'

'You didn't answer your phone. I called. I called again.' I sit up in the hallway with my back against the wall.

'It was on silent. Has something happened?'

'No. But I couldn't reach you.'

'Is Isabella all right?'

'Yes.' That's all he cared about. Was the baby all right? What could I tell him?

'And you're okay? Do you need me to come home?'

He doesn't mean it. I can tell. He won't come home. 'I wanted to know where you were. That's all. I was worried about you.'

'About me? You don't need to worry about me, Emma. I'm fine. I've just been tied up, busy.'

'With the case? The thing that happened in the park? What they found here?'

'Yes. Is that what's worrying you? What they found in the park? There's no need to worry. I promise. I'll tell you about it later.'

What can he tell me that I don't know? He thinks he's the one that knows things, sees things. He's waiting for me to say something, to tell him that it's okay to go, to go back to paddling in the evil, to leave me alone with the baby again. I don't want to. I want to tell him, to explain, but I can't. 'I just wanted to talk to you.' It's all I can say.

'Look, as long as you and Isabella are okay, I really need to go. We can talk when I get home.'

'When? When will you be home?'

'As early as I can. But I really must go now. I'm sorry.'

I don't know what to say. I stay silent. Don't give him the answer he wants, can't. I pick at the gaps between the skirting board and the floor. Black muck. I'll need to find something to scrape it out, whatever is hiding there.

'Okay, darling,' he says. 'I'll see you later.'

The phone goes dead in my hand. *Later.* When is later? When is too late? The whining is starting in the other room, the whining and then the scream. It's off again. It knows.

19

JENNY

When they got back from Rose's, Jack slouched off to his room, slamming the door shut behind him. Partly to annoy him, Jenny decided to put some washing on and knocked on his door to make him hand out the dirty clothes that she knew were strewn across his floor. He scooped them up and handed them to her at the door, letting it close again in her face.

She talked to the door. 'Thanks, Mum, for doing my washing and taking such good care of me, like a bloody servant.'

She was still muttering to herself as she stuffed the clothes into the washing machine. She checked the pockets of jeans and shorts as she went, pulling out sweet wrappers, a pen, a couple of tissues – God, they made a mess of a wash, you were picking the bits off for days. As she tipped up the last pair of trousers and gave them a shake, something heavy clattered to the floor. She rocked back and sat with her back against the oven, unable to touch the object lying on the kitchen lino in front of her.

She sent him a text first:

Can you come round after work? Need to talk.

He rang back a few minutes later. Jenny hesitated before picking up. She didn't want to do this on the phone; she just wanted him to come round.

He was clearly in work mode and anyone who didn't know him would think he was a rude arse. (She knew him – he was a rude arse.) 'What do you want, Jenny? This really isn't a good time.'

When was a good time these days? 'My apologies for interrupting your new life with the needs of your old life.'

'Not now, Jenny. I have neither the time nor the headspace. What is it that can't wait?'

She really hadn't meant to get into it on the phone but, well, he was an arse. 'It's about your son. Or had you forgotten you had a son? Tall boy, looks like you, fifteen going on twenty-one. You need to sort him out.'

'Why do I need to sort my son out and why do I need to do it right now?'

'Well, first of all, he didn't come home last night and–'

'Woah. What do you mean he didn't come home last night? You said he was there when I called this morning.'

'Well, he was, he was back by then.'

'So where had he been?'

This wasn't the discussion she'd wanted to have. Why had she mentioned last night? 'He said he stayed at a friend's.'

'Okay. So what is it about that that requires my immediate attention? My teenage son had a sleepover.'

'It wasn't a sleepover, as such. He sent me a text to say he was going to stay with a friend. But that's not good enough. He didn't ask. He didn't tell me what friend.'

'So, don't tell me; tell him.'

'He needs to tell me where he's going in advance. How do I know if he's telling the truth? He turned his phone off – like you do, I know that's what you do – so how do I *know* that's where he was, or *exactly* where he was or who he was with?'

'Jen, I've been telling you that the boy needs more rules for years. You're the one who's all about freedom of bloody expression and letting him discover his own boundaries.'

'Don't chuck stuff back at me. You left me on my own to do it, remember. He didn't come home. I was worried.'

'It's the summer holidays. He'll settle down when they go back to school next week.'

'You need to talk to him.'

'Okay. When I see him on Sunday, I'll have a word.'

'No. Today. I had to go see the school today. He's been getting into fights.'

'Why am I just hearing about this now? I'm at work, in the middle of something.'

'Because today was the first time I knew about it. And now I'm telling you. His father.'

'Well, we can talk about it at the weekend, before he goes back to school.' He seemed to hesitate and then added, 'Who was he getting into fights with? Did the head give you any names?'

'I can't remember.' Jenny cast her mind back to the head's office and what he'd told her. 'Hang on, yeah, some boy called Callum. I'd never heard of him before. Callum Peters.'

The phone went quiet and Jenny wondered if they'd been cut off. 'Tommy?' She was readying herself to continue the argument about whether the conversation could wait until the weekend.

'I'll be round after work. I can't give you a time, but I'll be there. See you later.'

20

SANDRA

They'd come to search Callum's room. They'd wanted to know about the bolt.

'Shaun put it on himself,' Sandra had told them. 'Said he wanted privacy. Didn't like people going in his room. Neither of them did.'

'And how did it get broken?' they asked.

Sandra had shaken her head. 'Can't remember. Lots of things got broken around those boys.'

The doctor had prescribed some stronger tablets for Danielle and she was sitting, hollow-eyed, in front of the TV with Lee and Alfie. The policewoman was making more tea.

Sandra was in Alfie's room, folding and putting away clothes. Shorts and T-shirts in primary colours that smelt of fabric softener and the iron. Danielle told her not to bother ironing Alfie's clothes, that no one did these days. She liked to do it; she liked his things to be nice. Most of his clothes were things that she'd bought for him. She liked him to have nice things, always avoided the mean slogans and green and grey camouflage patterns that started so young. She wanted him to be a child, a proper child, for as long as possible.

As soon as Callum had moved into the other bedroom, Lee had painted this room in a pale blue and Sandra had carefully applied a border of planets and moons. The moons were yellow like cheese. It wouldn't be long before he knew that the moon wasn't really made of cheese.

Callum's room – what had been Shaun's room – couldn't be any different. It smelt different. Testosterone, cigarette smoke and something else, something bad.

Nearly half of one wall was painted black; whoever had started the job had simply given up and the colour petered out with a few half-hearted, streaky brushstrokes. The grey carpet was barely visible beneath the layer of dirty clothes and rubbish – crumbs, crisp packets, cans, chocolate wrappers – strewn across the floor.

No one was supposed to go in there. The bed hadn't been changed for weeks. Special permission had to be obtained for Sandra to go in and do it while he watched over her from the doorway.

Periodically, he transferred a pile of clothes onto the bathroom floor in the expectation that they would be washed for him. There'd been a tangle of his jeans in the laundry basket when Sandra last put together a load. There'd be no point washing them now. They wouldn't be keeping them for Alfie. What would they do with them? What would they do with all his stuff?

Sandra passed the closed door as she went downstairs. She could hear them moving around in there. Two of them. There wouldn't be room for any more. Barely room for them. How long would it take them? Would they tell them what they found? She hadn't told them where to look.

It hadn't taken her long. Callum had been out. She'd reached under the mattress, feeling along from the foot of the bed to the pillow end. That's where she'd felt the plastic bag. She'd pulled it out and known what would be inside before she'd looked. She recognised it from crime shows on TV. She'd put it back and kept looking. She'd found more in a sports bag at the back of the wardrobe, along with greasy rolls of cash. She'd put that back as well. Would they find her fingerprints on it? Even if they did, would she have to say she'd found it? Would it matter if they knew? Would they expect her to have called the police on him? Perhaps it would have been better if she had. Prison was better than what had happened, wasn't it? She'd left the drugs and the money. She'd shut the door. She hadn't been able to stop herself picking up a mug that had been used as an ashtray. That was how he'd known she'd been in there.

The same detective came back to ask them some more questions. He said his name again. It was Thomas. Thomas O'Keefe. They sat in the front room again. The policewoman took Alfie upstairs to play in his room.

Sandra was expecting him to ask them about what they must have found in Callum's room. Instead, he started by asking about school.

'Were you aware that Callum had been in trouble at school?'

Lee snorted.

The detective didn't react but continued. 'Specifically that there had been fights?'

Sandra looked to Danielle. She looked so young and so old at the same time. Her skin was dull and there were deep ridges running from her nose to her chin, across her brow, wrinkles around her mouth. Nicotine and unhappiness were very bad for the complexion.

It was clear that Danielle wasn't going to answer the detective's question, that she barely knew what was happening now, let alone what had happened in the past hours, days or weeks. So Sandra nodded. 'Yes. There were always fights.' The boys had fought with each other at home and with other kids away from home, in the park, at school. In trouble everywhere – in school and out. Always bruises and bashed knuckles and other parents on the doorstep complaining. They were angry, maybe even born angry but certainly angry later, and everyone had to suffer. So, yes, they knew there were fights.

The detective made a note in his book. 'Do you know any details of the fights that happened at school recently?'

Sandra looked at Danielle again and, this time, reached across to pat her knee to get her attention. She was always being called up to the school. About Shaun and Callum. Up and down like a bloody yo-yo. You'd think they'd get the idea and give up. It was just something she did because it was expected. Same for them, presumably, call the parents, as expected. So off Danielle had gone. It'd happened before and it would happen again. She went and sat in the headteacher's office, he said serious things, she nodded and then she came home. 'Danielle, love, do you know anything about any fights Callum got into up at the school last year?'

Danielle looked out from a long way away and shook her head. Sandra answered the detective for her. 'I'm sorry. We can't help you. The boys were always in trouble. I'm not aware of any details.'

The detective continued, 'Okay. I'm not sure how to ask this question?'

'Best just ask it. Is it about drugs?' They'd know. No point being coy about it.

'Yes. It is. Were you aware of Callum being involved with drugs?'

Danielle looked blank, so Sandra answered. 'Yes. I was.' That probably put her in the wrong. She'd read the leaflets the school and police had provided when Shaun started getting into trouble.

Callum had shown all the signs: the eyes, odd behaviour, sneaking about. The stuff he'd sold – that was what that was about – nicking money from her purse, the disappearances... All that even before what she'd found in his room. Knowing, and knowing what to do about it were different things, though.

Should she have reported it? They wouldn't have done anything if she did. That's how it'd been with Shaun. They had to wait until someone did something serious, until someone got hurt, before they did anything.

'Was anyone else aware?'

'You mean Danielle?' Was she even listening? 'Yes and no. She didn't want to know. And she has Alfie and Lee. And Lee, he only has eyes for Alfie.'

'But you knew?'

'Yes. I'd seen it before.'

'With Shaun?' The detective hesitated and then added, 'What happened?'

There had to be police records on Shaun, but maybe he wanted her version of events. She could oblige. 'Shaun started nicking his mum's fags when he was about nine and I'd guess he started smoking other stuff – taking other stuff – when he went to secondary school. He didn't get on well at school, so he went less and less. He hung out with bad types and, I suppose, one thing led to another. Not a very original story, I'm afraid.'

'And when he was arrested?'

'A pub landlord challenged him and Shaun punched him – poor man ended up in hospital with a head injury. Then, rather than just leaving, he smashed up some furniture and threatened a few customers with a broken bottle. Always had a violent temper. The pub was on Mill Road, a stone's throw from the police station, so when he stepped out the door your lot were waiting for him with open cuffs. And he had drugs on him, of course.'

The detective nodded. Her version obviously fitted with the one he already knew.

'And Callum?' he said.

'It only got really bad after Shaun went, like he stepped into his brother's empty shoes but had to prove they fitted. Of course, the network of bad friendships was already in place for him to pick up. Nothing anyone could do to stop him. And...' Sandra wasn't sure if she should say any more. Should she tell him about Shaun? About Alfie? What good could it do. 'I don't know what else I can tell you?'

'Thank you, Sandra. I'm sorry no one was able to help the boys before it all went so wrong.'

Sandra shrugged. It happened. You couldn't rely on help coming from outside. That wasn't how it worked. She'd been brought up on an estate in South London. They policed the place themselves. No point waiting for some friendly neighbourhood copper to sort out trouble. They had better things – people – to worry about.

21

JENNY

Jenny was sitting on the front step attempting to read a book. It wasn't a very good book; she'd picked it up in the charity shop on Mill Road and suspected at the time that the cover was a little too pink.

It was after six. She should probably go in and find something for tea. She needed a shower and it was probably cooler inside the house, but Jack was in there and she hadn't worked out how to talk to him yet. She was waiting for Tommy.

Jenny lifted a hand to check her hair. She'd coiled it on top of her head and stuck a combed grip in it when she got up that morning. Now most of it had escaped and was in various stages of drooping and hanging down. She released the grip, attached it to the bottom of her vest, and ran her fingers through the dark hair that now hung to her shoulders. She divided it into three thick hanks and was plaiting it over one shoulder when Tommy's car pulled up. She could tell his mood from the way he drove; it wasn't good.

She stayed seated and finished off her plait as she called out, 'Nice of you to join us...' She'd meant it to be cheery, a friendly dig, but perhaps it had come out with a bit more edge than she intended, or Tommy was really mad.

He certainly looked far from friendly. 'Just don't. Not now. Not today.'

'I knew I shouldn't have told you. Just forget it. I'll deal with it myself.'

'No, Jen. You should have told me what was going on before.'

'I didn't know what was going on, that anything was going on.' And when had she seen him recently to tell him anything?

'Well, that's the problem, isn't it.' He had his bloody sanctimonious voice on.

'So, what would you have done? Not ignored him for the past six months? And, by the way, while we're on the subject, perhaps you could call your mother. She's upset at never seeing her new grandchild. Remember your mother, old lady, gave birth to you, lives a couple of streets that way?'

A door slammed upstairs.

A stab of guilt. 'Tommy, he can hear us. Let's not do this now.'

'Agreed.' Tommy suddenly became calm and looked – she wouldn't have thought it possible – even more serious. 'You're right. We shouldn't be shouting about this out here. Let's go inside.'

Inside, he slumped heavily onto the sofa. It sagged and seemed to attempt to swallow him, its various multicoloured drapes collapsing onto him from all sides. He attempted to lift himself out of the cushiony morass but gave up and slumped back. He looked exhausted. 'Jen, I don't want to argue.'

'Well then, don't.' Even Jenny knew she sounded childish. Why did he make her behave like this? It was so infuriating. She hadn't even told him what she wanted to tell him yet.

'Do you really not know where Jack was last night?'

'Not exactly. He said with friends.'

'Did he lie to you about where he was going?'

Where did that come from? 'Jack wouldn't lie to me.'

Tommy was keeping his voice low. 'What about last night?'

'He didn't lie; he just didn't tell me where he was.' Jenny sat on the edge of the armchair.

'No, I mean, do you know where he was?'

'I told you. With friends.'

'What friends?'

'I didn't ask.' She should have made Jack tell her where he was. But he was so hard to talk to these days. It was so hard to get anything out of him and, when she pushed it, the atmosphere between them became toxic. She wanted them to be friends, didn't want things to end up like they had been between her and her mother. She didn't want to say any of this, though.

'Okay, we'll leave that for now. School. What exactly has been happening at school?'

This must be what he was like at work, questioning people. 'Said there'd been trouble. Fighting. With a couple of students. But head said that the main one had left now.'

'Callum Peters?'

'Yeah. So that's probably the end of it, isn't it? It's not what–'

He interrupted her. 'Jenny, I shouldn't tell you, but they'll be releasing the name soon. The dead boy was Callum Peters. Callum Peters is the boy who was found dead this morning, the one I told you about.'

'Oh.'

'Yeah, oh.'

What the hell? But, no. That was ridiculous. What was he even trying to say? 'That's got nothing to do with Jack, though, has it? He doesn't go to the rec. He says only losers hang out there?'

'A boy who is at school with our son, who our son has been fighting with, was stabbed last night and we don't even know where our son spent the night.'

'He was stabbed?' Jenny tugged at her plait feeling the pain in the roots of her hair. This was her fault. She should have been stricter with Jack, like Tommy had said all along, kept him safer.

She'd thought she knew better. Her mother being strict had done nothing to save her and Tommy's dad had just screwed him up. Her relationship with Jack was going to be different, based on mutual respect and love. Nothing could happen to him if she loved him enough. He would be free but he would stay out of trouble because he knew he was loved. And he was such a lovely boy, she knew he was. But… Callum Peters. Stabbed.

Thomas was talking again and Jenny concentrated on listening. 'Have you heard the names Will Collinson? Or Adele McDonald? Are they friends of Jack?'

'Don't ring any bells. I don't think so. Why?'

'Nothing. They're friends of Callum Peters.'

'I've not heard of them. But I can't know the names of everyone Jack knows.' Did he think she should? Should she?

'No, I know. I'm not saying you should. I'm just asking.'

Jenny looked at Thomas still sunk in the sofa, framed by her collection of rugs and cushions. He didn't look as though he was accusing her of anything. Not now. He just looked tired. She wished she could pull one of the rugs over him and let him sleep, just where he was. And the world could just wait until they were all ready to deal with whatever came next. She could curl up next to him and they could both sleep while Jack was safe in his room upstairs, like they used to.

22

EMMA

If you put your head under the bathwater, the sounds above are smothered and, within a moment, the loudest noise is the blood pumping in your ears, the rhythm of your heart beating. Breathe slow and the beat slows. You half lie, half float. Water cups your face and your hair spreads and floats like waterweed. And the beat is loud and everything else is drowned.

It's still screaming. Even though I can't hear it, I can feel the vibrations in the air on my skin lying just out the water, on my island face. I'll sink lower and let the water settle over it.

He needs to come home and be a witness, see it for the animal it is. The screaming, clawing animal. Babies have sharp fingernails. I never knew that. The nails look so tiny and new. You imagine them to be soft, but they're not; sharp, they can draw blood.

Red blood cells live for about 120 days. Assuming my hypothesis is right, and I got this ability to see from the mixing of bloods, either with the baby or through the transfusion, I should have it for a while longer. Maybe I'll always have it now. My knowledge is growing and I am strong. With the ability to see, comes a natural defence in my blood, but watching and fighting and watching and keeping it away and not doing anything else is *so* hard.

Now, the water, cooling around my body, is washing me clean, rinsing away the taint of it, sweat and spit, drool and snot and wee and shit, all pouring out of it and all carrying the evil. I added just a splash of bleach to the bath. Its tang under my nose is comforting. I have to be clean to stop the evil proteins having something to cling onto, to climb from that body to mine, to spread and multiply. I'm learning all the time, learning its tricks, but I can't fight it alone, not always, not much more. The evil in every one of them has to be purged.

I push myself up out of the water and hear the crying again. And the phone. Again.

It's not him. He doesn't ring. I have to call him and he doesn't want to talk to me, I can tell. Them, out there, they're luring him away from me. We should've moved away, like I wanted. To a village, at least. Put some miles between us.

It'll be his mother on the phone again. She rang before. She thinks he'll be home by now. He isn't. I thought he'd be home by now. But he isn't. Not late, he said. As early as I can, he said. But this is not early and the thing is screaming and he has to see it screaming and to understand. We were supposed to do this thing together; he promised. But that isn't him on the phone; that's his mother. Rose. By any other name would smell as sweet? Not sweet. Not little old lady sweet. She hates me. She likes the other one and her son. But he chose me. And together we have to deal with this thing we have created; together we have to make it right. I want to do it together, but if I can't, if he won't, I will do it alone. But not because he is with them. No.

After the baby, I noticed something not right in other people. When I saw it in the boy in the park, that's when I started to work it all out. After that I saw it everywhere, but I had to focus. It's right to start close.

The front door.

'Em? Where are you?'

He's home. I have to answer him. I must be normal, so that he knows it's not me.

'I'm in the bath, darling.'

He's outside the bathroom door. It's locked.

'But the baby is screaming. Can't you hear her?'

Of course I can.

And now it's stopped. So now he'll think that it's me, that I'm the poisonous one.

Out of the bath, wrapped in bath-robe and towel, I go to find him.

Thomas is in the nursery, holding the baby, stroking its back. 'It's okay, baby, it's okay little one, Daddy's home. It's okay.'

He turns when I come to the doorway. Smiles.

'How do you women make towels stay on your head like that?' And then he looks serious.

'Was she crying long, Em? Poor little mite. I know it's okay for babies to cry but she seemed really distressed. She was all red in the face and sweaty, like she'd been crying for a while. Poor little scrap.'

'She was okay. I needed a bath. I thought you'd be home earlier. She's always crying.'

'I can't believe that!' He patted the baby's nappy-fat bottom. 'Is she hungry?'

'She's been fed. She's been changed. She just cries.'

'She really is so tiny and so perfect.' He whispers into her ear, 'Is Mummy a bit tired? Were you just a bit lonely in this big cot all on your own?'

In my head, I'm screaming. How would you know anything? You weren't here. You haven't been here all day. It doesn't matter what I do or don't do, it screams at me.

I say nothing.

He continues to speak in his soft, baby-friendly voice: 'Well, she's all right now, aren't you, little one?'

'I just wanted to finish in the bath.'

'You should've gone in the bath when I got home. I'd've watched her while you had a good long soak.'

I don't want a long soak. I just needed to get clean. A few minutes to get clean. Before I watch again. He can't watch it like I do. It's down to me. I have to do it. He's picking it up, holding it. I wish he wouldn't. But I can't say anything about that.

Instead, I say, 'You'd better get changed. You smell.' I should smile. I smile. 'Have a shower or something. I'll stick that shirt in the wash. I can take your suit to the dry cleaners tomorrow. This weather everything gets so sweaty and smelly. Just leave it on the chair in the bedroom.'

He's not saying anything. He's still holding it. Too close. Too long.

'You can put her down; she'll be fine.' Smile. 'Go get a shower, darling. I'll make you something to eat.'

Thomas does have a shower, but he puts the baby in the Moses basket in the bathroom and sings nursery rhymes. I can hear him.

'Three blind mice, see how they run, they all ran after the farmer's wife, who cut off their tails...' He gets out of the shower. I can hear his feet across the bathroom, going closer. 'Don't you worry, little one. No one's cutting any tails off around here.'

He's showered now. That's better. Washed away the poisons from out there. I'll get away when we've finished eating and clean the bathroom. Bleach. I'm not sure if it works but I have to try. I put just a dash in the bath water. Not much. Just a splash. I'm not stupid. I understand the chemistry.

He's brought the Moses basket down with him. He's bathed the baby too. Changed her. 'How come all her clothes are white? I'm all for rejection of the gendering thing, but shouldn't she have something pretty? Didn't my mum give us some nice bits and pieces when we told her you were having a girl?' He smiles. 'Do you remember how excited she was? I don't think I've seen any of them?'

'They'll be around somewhere.' I'm not using any of that frilly stuff. Too hard to keep clean. I need everything to go in a hot wash. We don't need anything from his mother. 'Let me take her. Go sit down, relax, while I finish dinner. It's late. You're late.' Don't make a fuss. Don't say anything. 'You must be hungry.'

'I, um, yeah, that'd be great.'

Can I ask him? Can I ask him about his day? Must keep it natural, neutral. No suspicions. No arguments. Not between him and me. How to start? 'How did it go today?' Ask about the case, the boy? No. Too much. Ask why he was late? No. Just wait. Be patient. Wait.

Finally, he says, 'The body they found out there–' He nods towards the side of the house nearest the park. Close. Too close. Keep your face neutral. Listen. Let him tell you.

'–it was a lad, fifteen, called Callum Peters.'

A name. He had a name. Callum. Fifteen. Younger than I thought. Younger and older. He'd gone from looking older to younger.

'He was stabbed. Well, that's what initial forensics are saying, but we haven't found a weapon and we're waiting to know more.'

Know more. No weapon. Is he watching me? Why is he looking at me when he says that?

'There's no need to worry. Whatever the weapon was, it's not out there anymore.'

I nod and smile.

'And we're pretty sure that it'll be drugs-related. There were drugs found in the boy's home. He's been in trouble, been in care, he's on the system for criminal damage, shoplifting… The move on to drugs is pretty typical. His brother was involved in dealing. We're looking into family and friends but we're pretty sure that it'll be linked to drugs.'

He's stopped talking. It was like he'd forgotten who he was talking to for a minute.

'I'm sorry. I shouldn't be telling you all of this. It's just... No. You don't need to be worried. You've got to focus on you and Isabella. Tell me about Isabella. Tell me about your day.'

'No, what is it? What's worrying you? What shouldn't you tell me? Nothing you've just said won't be online by tomorrow. What is it?'

'It's Jack.'

Stay still. Don't react. Don't move away. Don't do anything. That boy. What about him? Look interested, caring, not too interested. Stay very still.

'I had a call from Jenny–'

That woman. Always ringing, calling him, calling him back. She couldn't have him. No reaction. Breathe in and out.

'It turns out that Jack had some trouble at school with Callum Peters. I'm sure it's nothing. It'll be nothing. But it'll be difficult, it could be difficult, if it comes up in the investigation, that's all.'

Sound casual, just curious. 'Jack and the boy were friends?' They were from the same pack, connected, cross-infected. A fisted hand behind my back to sink nails into flesh. Don't react.

'No. Not friends. More the opposite. And Jenny doesn't think that Jack is friends with any of the other kids who've come up in connection with Callum. Jack's a good lad.'

He's not good. Not. Good. No, they're all connected, all cross-infected. I've seen them all out in the park, hanging off the climbing frame like monkeys in the jungle, picking at themselves, squawking, fighting, showing off. It's in their blood. It's in that boy's blood. Thomas should stay away from him. Has he seen him? Has he been near him? He said Jenny called, but... I have to ask. But calmly.

'Is that where you were? After work? Why you were late?'

'Don't look like that, Em.'

I failed. I gave myself away.

The crease in his forehead says that he's annoyed. 'I wasn't that late. Jenny rang. I had to talk to her. She was worried. I was worried. And Jack *is* my son.'

'Yes. But–'

'Please, not this again, Em. Jack's part of my family too, our family. We've been so preoccupied with the baby that maybe we've neglected–'

I can't listen to this. I can't. I need to tell him. But I can't. I turn away to the sink and turn on the tap.

'Oh, come on Em, sit down.'

'I have to get on. Clear up. Make food. Sort out the next feed.'

'Let me help.'

'No, you're tired.'

'So are you. Let me help.'

'No. I'd rather do it myself. I know what I'm doing. I'd rather you didn't get in the way.'

I have my back to him. I think I can hear him start to stand. But then he sits again. 'If you're sure.'

There's silence between us for a few minutes and then he says, 'Mum rang today and I haven't had a chance to get back to her. I'd better give her a call.'

On the phone to her his voice changes, like he's going back to them. He doesn't talk like that when he's with me, that fenland-estuary voice. He doesn't sound like that with me.

His voice rises. 'Did you call the police, Mum?'

Why did she need to call the police? What did anything that had happened have to do with her?

'Mum, that's not the same thing. Calling me is not calling the police.'

She was always looking for an excuse to ring him. We shouldn't have bought this house. It's too close. I knew. I shouldn't have let him persuade me. It wouldn't have happened if we'd been somewhere else.

'I might not be available, Mum. I might be doing something

else or not be able to take your call. Call 999 and they will send a patrol car straight out. I don't want to scare you, but there's bad stuff goes on out there.'

Out there? Outside. Strangers. That wasn't where the bad was, not the bad they needed to worry about.

'Jack?'

Why are they talking about that boy? Him again. Always him. He's the bad.

'I'll talk to him. That was reckless.'

He's listening to her again, chattering away. Doesn't she know it's late? I haven't seen him, haven't had him here all day, and now she's dragging him away. He's mine. He might've been hers once but now he's mine. I need him with me. They're talking about what happened in the park. Will he tell her something he hasn't told me? Do they have secrets?

'Mum, you know I can't. But, no, it wasn't paedophiles. We are following up a number of lines of enquiry.'

The formal language. Policeman Thomas. What were those lines of enquiry? What did they know? What could they tell from what was left out there?

'I'll come and look at the fence as soon as I get a chance. I've got to go now.'

He's lowered his voice. They're whispering together. Whispering secrets. I can hear my name. Talking about me. How dare he talk to her about me? What is he saying? What poison is she dripping in his ear? I can't hear. Something about *tired*. I'm not tired. I don't need to sleep. They'll not catch me out like that. He's saying goodbye. I'll need to look like I'm doing something, not listening. I don't want them to know I know.

'Mum, make sure you shut the downstairs windows and lock the back door tonight, okay?'

She doesn't need to do that. She's one of them, one of the infected ones. What does Rose know about what happened out there? Did she send that boy? Send him to spy on me? What does

Thomas know? Thomas and those policemen out there? Flies. Flies. Like flies. Swarming. Feet paddled in it. Blood fizzing with it.

He should be finishing the call, finishing with her, but he says, 'I'll pop over, just quickly. Okay?'

All of them circling. Buzzing.

23

SANDRA

Sandra handed Lee a cup of tea as he walked through the door from work.

'Don't know about tea. I could do with something stronger.'

'I know, love, but I think it's best if we all stay sober right now.' Sandra patted his arm as she walked back towards the kitchen.

He followed her. 'I didn't mean it. I know. And thanks. For the tea. And for looking after Dani and Alfie. Has she gone?'

'Police liaison woman?'

Lee nodded.

'Yeah.'

'Thank Christ for that.'

'They were here, the police, going through Callum's room. And the rest of the house. I told them that he's barely – *was* barely – in the rest of the house. They were asking questions about what we knew. About Shaun. About his friends. Wasn't much we could tell them that they didn't already know.'

'They came to my work. Porter who showed them into the kitchen looked like his eyes might burst out of his face. They had to ask him to leave or I swear he'd have stayed to listen in.'

'They didn't take you anywhere else, though?'

'No, said it was informal, but something about talking away from the family. Nothing I could say in front of Dani.' Lee nodded up at the ceiling. 'How is she?'

'Doctor came and gave her something to calm her down.' Sandra couldn't help thinking that tranquillising was not what her daughter needed. She'd been out of it for months, years really. The girl needed to get a grip. She didn't know what was wrong with her. Didn't take after her. Brian, maybe. He hadn't been big on responsibility.

Danielle had always been a bit out of it; 'off with the fairies,' her dad had called it. She never seemed to quite focus on everything, always staring into space or wandering off. It's what she'd been like at school. 'Doesn't concentrate,' they'd said. Maybe if she'd done a bit better for herself at school she wouldn't have fallen in with the Peters lad, wouldn't have got herself pregnant at seventeen. 'What else am I going to do, Mum?' she'd said.

Get a job. A career even. Something going somewhere. Meet a proper working bloke who can keep a roof over your head. Get married. Then think about having kids. Not that Sandra had said any of those things. What was the point? She'd had her own life to worry about then.

She'd been seeing Steve from the Press warehouse, going to aerobics, earning enough to buy nice things and go out of a weekend. It'd been her chance to live a bit, have some fun. She hadn't wanted to be saddled with looking after grandkids so soon. Of course, now there was nothing she wanted more. Little Alfie was the apple of her eye. All too late now, though, wasn't it? No. Not too late. Not too late for Alfie. She could still see to that.

Lee was eating a piece of ham out of a packet from the fridge.

'Come on, give that here and I'll make you a sandwich.'

'I'm a chef, Sandra, I think I can make a sandwich.'

'Yeah, well, you're not, are you? You're eating meat from out of the fridge while you've still got your shoes on. Go and take them off and I'll make you up a plate of something.'

Lee went off to remove his shoes and came back to lean in the doorway as Sandra buttered bread and sliced a tomato for him. She found a packet of crisps and poured them onto the plate.

'Getting a bit posh now, aren't we? You'll be serving it up on the bread board next.'

'It was all baskets in my day. Chips in a basket. Chicken in a basket. Scampi in a basket.'

'Can't see either catching on with that lot at top table.'

'Can you imagine? So, Professor blah-blah, what wine shall we serve with the scampi à la basket? Will it be a sharing board for the lamb cutlets or individual boards?'

They laughed and it was like everything was normal for a couple of minutes.

Sandra sat with Lee in the lounge as he ate his supper. 'What did you tell them about you and Callum, you and Shaun?'

'Not much. Just said they were part of the package. Dani's kids. Kind of marry one, get two free.'

'Not a great package. The boys I mean. Shaun was already off the rails and Callum not far behind when you met Danielle.'

'Yeah, well, it is what it is. I wanted Dani and they came too.' Lee was quiet for a minute, eating.

Sandra waited.

'They asked about his friends. Callum's. I told them I didn't know any of his friends. Weren't none that came round the house that I saw. He's just been hanging round the house like a bad smell since school finished. I told them I told him to get a job.'

'Did they ask you if you argued about it?'

'Yeah.'

'What did you say?'

'I said *a bit*. Didn't seem worth denying.'

'Just about the job, though. That's what you told them you argued about?'

Lee nodded.

'Did they ask about Shaun?'

'Police always ask about Shaun. I told them good riddance, that he was banged up and I'd asked him not to come back.'

'Is that what you said?'

Lee dropped the piece of bread he'd been eating onto his plate. 'I said I didn't fucking ask him, I fucking told him to stay the fuck away. I said I told him if he disrespected his mother or took one step back inside our home again, I'd fucking kill him. All right?'

'Okay.' So Lee had lost his temper. The police would know that he had a temper.

'Yeah, I know. I should've kept my bloody stupid mouth shut.'

'You need to try to keep your temper in front of them, Lee, love. Did they ask you where you were?'

'Yeah. Like on the telly. Enquiries.'

'What did you say?'

'I told them the truth. I was at work and then at home. Got in about nine. Dani went to bed about ten. Then I went up a bit later.'

'You told them I was here? That I stayed?'

'I did. Like you said. Watched television. You stayed the night on the sofa.'

'Good.'

Lee put his plate down on the floor next to his feet and looked at Sandra. 'I didn't see him, you know.'

'You went out looking for him, though.'

'Yeah, but I didn't find him. I've got nothing to hide. Do you hear me, Sandra? You don't need to protect me.'

'You know how these things go, Lee. Evil stepdad.'

Lee went to protest, as he had every right to do. He'd never been evil. Some might say he'd had the patience of a saint with those boys. They were her flesh and blood but...

'I know you're not evil, Lee. The police don't, though. And

they're questioning you about where you were. If we start telling them about the fight and how you went out after Callum – well, they're going to start jumping to conclusions. I've seen it on the telly. How the police go for someone because they want a quick and easy result.'

'You watch too many of them crime programmes, Sandra.'

'They're based on real life, though. They always go for the family. Danielle can't lose you, Lee. Alfie can't lose his dad. I'll not let it happen. I'll not see them left on their own.'

'Hey, come on, Sandra, they won't be. They've got us.'

'I plan to be around for as long as I can, but I won't always be here.'

'Course you will. You're not old. Got miles left on the clock yet. Spring chicken.'

'Yeah, well, in your line of work, you know what happens to spring chickens. Let's just keep some things to ourselves, shall we? The police are looking at Callum's so-called friends, that drugs crowd that Shaun introduced him to. Let them focus on them, rather than closer to home, eh?'

'You know best, Mum. Now, got any chocolate stashed in those cupboards?'

Sandra hauled herself up from her chair to go dig out something from the secret treats stash she kept for Alfie. She bit her lip to keep the wince of pain to herself. Secrets. They were all keeping secrets. Except maybe Danielle. Moved in with those bloody fairies.

24

EMMA

I pretended to be asleep when he got back from his mother's. He doesn't know that I don't need to sleep anymore.

I watch the baby and I watch out there, through the window, comings and goings. People. Adults. Children. All dirty, contaminated. The glow of the evil is inside them. It leaked from that boy, into the ground, into the air, thinning and diminishing away from its host, soft like dying embers, dying. I'd go mad if I didn't look beyond these walls that jitter with its constant, constant crying, holding in the stench of puke and shit, and blood. Always blood. The metallic stab of blood.

The smell. It turns my stomach. I can't eat. Everything tastes of metal, the tang of it on my tongue is foul. I can't wash it away. It's everywhere.

Even Thomas. When he's been with them all day, I can smell it on him. But it's not in him, not yet. His mother, Jack and that woman, they all want to infect him, take him away from me. And the baby. All of them, drawing him away, drawing him in, pulling him close so that it can infect him, bring out the bad in him, claim him. But he's mine. Him and me. We were family. We were happy. I don't want the baby. I want Thomas. Like before. It was okay before. It was safe.

I got up when I knew Thomas was asleep. I edged out from under the thin cover – all I could bear in the heat – careful not to disturb him. I didn't need light. I'd been staring into the darkness, so my eyes had adjusted. He was snoring. He snores when he's in a deep sleep. At least I knew he was safe, away from them for a while.

I'm back in my chair in the nursery. I can't sleep. I have to keep watch.

I'm looking for signs and patterns. Trying to understand more. Sometimes I think that I can defeat it. I know that the baby cries less when it's outside. Why is that? Maybe the contagion is dissipated by contact with fresh air and thrives in enclosed spaces. But the evil in that boy was strong outside, so maybe it wants to be outside so it can spread. I wish I knew. I wish there was someone I could talk to or a reliable reference source. I've looked on the internet for research papers on the subject, but there's nothing that seems to be exactly in this area. It means I'll be the first if I write it up.

The secret will be in the mix. In the combination. People think blood types are such absolutes, but they're not. Your blood type can be A, but there's an O hiding in your DNA. I'm type A. So's Thomas. I made sure I knew, in case anything ever happened. The baby is type O. Somewhere an O was masked by an A, but now, in it, in the baby, it's in plain sight.

The wrong mix can create evil and it can make you too weak to fight the evil. I'm protected but Thomas isn't. And the baby is evil. And the other child, Jack. I checked his blood type. And I was right. Thomas keeps emergency information for everyone in the front of an old address book – phone numbers, passport numbers, blood types. His mother. Jack. That woman. They all come before me.

Jack. His other child. He has it. I should have known before, but until now I haven't been able to see it. He always hated me. He was always sullen and rude. I tried to be understanding. Now I really understand. I thought it was me; there was something wrong with me. But it's not that. It's the evil in his blood. I'll have to do something. I know I can, now.

What if Thomas doesn't understand? I should warn him. But I can't. Not yet. I don't want to involve him until I'm sure. Especially the bit about the baby. And Jack. Thomas doesn't really understand science, not the detail. He might not understand the implications and what needs to be done.

It's morning now. I watched the dawn again, light poking its fingers into dark spaces, exposing dust in the air. The baby cried only a little in the night – restless to be fed but then quiet again. Not like during the day. It's asleep again now. Apparently asleep. Waiting. Thomas is getting ready for work – dressing, eating, drinking coffee, checking his phone. He'll be gone soon and it'll start again. Maybe if he stays it will be fooled and start when he's still here. Then he'd see.

'Thomas?'

He looks at me over the phone in his hand.

'Could you maybe go in a bit later today?'

'I wish I could but with the, you know, the case. There's so much to do. We've to look at CCTV and there's more people to talk to.' Now he's putting bread in the toaster. 'Do you want some?'

I shake my head.

'You know, if you need a break, Mum would take the baby for a couple of hours.'

'No.' That woman isn't getting her hands on it. No.

He frowns. 'I know she's old, but she's quite capable, you

know, Em. And she's great with kids, babies. Look how brilliantly I turned out.'

He was being funny. I should laugh. I can't. 'I'm okay on my own. I'd rather be on my own. I'm not ready to see other people yet.'

'My mum is hardly other people.'

He looked over at me, must have seen something I hadn't caught.

'Okay. But you'd be doing me a favour if you'd give her a ring in a couple of days. Invite her round to see the baby at least. She really wants to see her, whether or not you'll take advantage of her babysitting skills. Some kids wrecked her back fence yesterday and I think she's a bit rattled. I should probably pop in on her again, but I have to get to work.'

I just won't answer. I'll let him think I'm going along with this. I'm not, though. I'm not. No. She's trying to get him away from me, get him round there. Kids and fences. It'll be a ploy. Pulling him in. Why can't he see it?

He's eating toast and licking his fingers. I bite my lip.

'I'll try to be home early. I know I said that yesterday, but I'll try. But I might have to go back round to see Jack.'

Back round? What was he saying? He said last night that Jenny had called. Did he say he'd been round there? He didn't. I'd remember.

He's combing his hair in the hall mirror now – already edging towards the door – so I have to talk to his back. 'When did you see Jack?'

'I went round to talk to Jenny after work yesterday. I told you.'

He doesn't look at me. He's hiding things. He didn't tell me, hadn't told me that he'd been in that house, been with them. Been with that boy. And then he'd come home, come into this house. How could he? How could he not tell me? I didn't know he was going to be with that boy, that he'd been with him. I should've known. I was worrying about the dead one, not him. I worried about the wrong one. They're all around. And he doesn't know. He's too good, can't see the danger all around. And her on the phone, always on the phone. Her and his mother. Tommy they call him. Name for a dog not a grown man. All circling. Breathing on him. Touching him. Stay calm. Keep my voice calm.

'You didn't say you went there.'

'Sorry, didn't I? But, yes, I did. It wasn't important. Just popped in to talk about Jack.'

Defensive. He knows he didn't tell me. He kept it from me.

Now he's checking his watch. He wants to get away, wants to get away from telling me. 'You said, you implied, that you just talked on the phone. You didn't say you went there.'

'Didn't I? It's not important, is it? I do have to see them, you know. Jack and Jenny. We've been through this.'

We had. But that was before, before I knew what I know now, know the danger they pose, to Thomas. I can see them, in my head, standing together, heads bent together, almost touching, touching. Had he put his arm round the boy? He does that. I've seen it. Did he feel the pull of the blood, of one of his own? Was Thomas already like them, already infected? I'd see it if he was. Wouldn't I? When the contagion in the blood is strong, I can see it really clearly now. I saw it. In the baby. In that boy in the park. They can't have Thomas. I won't let them. I'll do it again, if I have to. I've still got the knife. It was in my hand. I didn't know what to do with it. I kept it.

Thomas is talking. He's picking up his keys, putting on his jacket. 'I've got to go now, Em. We can talk later. I don't want you to worry.'

He kisses me, kisses his fingers and touches the baby's head. He should wash his hands now. Fingers in his mouth. Fingers touching everything. Fingers on the baby. I can't tell him to wash his hands, now, just as he's going.

He turns as he's opening the front door. 'If you do go out today, make sure that you shut the door properly, yeah? There's nothing to worry about. I can't imagine any criminal types being around while we're still in the park, but, you know, just check it's closed properly.' He stopped and looked back. 'You didn't see anything, did you? When you were in the park?'

Smile. Not too much. Just enough to be reassuring, innocent. 'No. Sorry.'

He's nodding. 'No, that's good. Better. Okay, see you later.'

The click of the door. It'll start again in a minute. I just have this moment in the quiet to think. What to do?

25

JENNY

Jenny hadn't slept a wink. She hadn't been able to settle after Tommy went. She hadn't told him. Not all of it. Not the most important bit. She should've told him.

While she went round and round thinking about what she should've done, should've said, should do now, should think, about anything but what she couldn't think, she'd ended up cleaning the bathroom, hoovering (except in Jack's room, of course), watering the plants, emptying the bin and sorting the recycling, tidying the drawer in the kitchen that hadn't be closing properly for months and sorting out her invoicing.

She'd finally gone to bed and then got up again and changed the sheets. It hadn't helped. She'd been too hot to sleep then. She'd got up and made herself one of those camomile teas. Tasted like wee, and made her wee. Once she was done with the weeing, she must have dropped off for a bit, but then she was awake again at four, since when she'd laid awake trying to work out the best time to ring Tommy, deciding not to ring him, deciding to text him and then deciding again that she needed to call him, talk to him face to face. Again. Talk to him and tell him this time.

She'd called him when she knew he'd be on his way to work.

It wasn't ideal, but better than calling him at home. He'd been annoyed, answering her on hands-free. 'What is it, Jenny? I'm on my way to work. Can you make it quick?'

That had annoyed her, like always. Some things were reliably constant then. 'Good morning to you as well.'

'Jenny, I'm not in the mood. What do you want?'

'I don't want anything. Just thought I should let you know that I found a knife in your son's pocket. Bye then. Have a nice day.'

Obviously, she hadn't put the phone down. She listened to the silence on the line as he took in what she'd just flung at him.

'All right. I'm on my way. I'll just call work. Is he there?'

'Yeah. Not up yet.'

He hadn't said goodbye and he'd skipped the pleasantries when she let him in less than ten minutes later. 'Show it to me.'

She'd been carrying it around in her dressing-gown pocket and now she placed the penknife into Tommy's hand. At least he hadn't pulled out his plastic gloves – dad Tommy not policeman Tommy.

'Where did you find it?'

'Pocket of his jeans. I wasn't looking. I was just checking the pockets before I put them in the wash.' She didn't tell him when she'd found it.

'Did you ask him about it?'

'No.'

'And you didn't know he had it, had a knife?'

'No!'

'I'm not accusing you of anything. I'm just asking. Okay?'

She nodded.

'The jeans. Do you know when he last wore them?'

'No. He's got a couple of pairs that look the same.' He was wondering what she'd been trying not to think about. Had he been wearing the jeans the night he was out all night? The night... Nope. She wasn't going to think it.

They were talking in the hall and were unaware that Jack had come out of his room and was listening to them from the top of the stairs until he spoke.

'That's mine. What are you doing with it? What's *he* doing here again?'

Jenny stood between Jack and his dad. 'Jack, I wasn't checking on you. It just fell out of your pocket. But a knife, Jack. What were you thinking?'

'Everyone has them. It's no big deal, all right?' He came stamping down the stairs and held out his hand. 'Just give it here.' He reached round Jenny to demand that his dad give him back the knife. 'Give it. It's mine.'

Thomas stepped back. 'I think we need a chat, Jack.'

'Little chat down the station? Want to rough me up a bit, do you?'

Jenny was surprised by the cynicism and anger in Jack's voice. 'Jack, it's your dad.'

'Is it? Thought you'd called the pigs on me.'

'Jack!'

'It's okay, Jen.' Thomas indicated that they should move out of the hall into the front room and led the way. 'Why don't we sit down?'

Jenny pushed a reluctant Jack ahead of her into the room, but she couldn't make him sit. He stood scowling in the doorway. She perched on the arm of the sofa. 'Jack, love, I didn't know you had a knife. You know I don't like them. I thought we'd talked about this.'

'It's just a penknife, Mum.'

Thomas stepped forward and bent his head to look into his son's face. He spoke softly. 'Jack, I'm not accusing you of anything.'

Jack looked at him under his fringe that needed cutting, his eyes the mirror of his dad's.

Thomas carried on. 'It's just...'

Wrong thing to say. Jack was alert again and his head was suddenly upright, his eyes glaring. 'Just what?'

'We're your parents; we worry about this stuff. Knives are serious. All knives. People get hurt. It can be just an accident, but people get hurt.'

Jack was silent, staring at his dad, daring him to say the wrong thing. Jenny wished she could intervene. Trouble was she didn't know herself what was the right thing or the wrong thing to say. It was like watching someone defuse an unexploded bomb.

'Look, Jack, a lad your age was found dead yesterday morning. Your mum says you knew him.'

Jack stepped back. 'You're talking about Callum Peters, aren't you? No need to look so surprised. You've heard of the internet, right? Everyone knows. Callum Peters was a knob and he's better off dead.'

'Jack!' Jenny was shocked to hear Jack talk like that.

Thomas was trying to keep his tone light but there was a distinct edge of policeman to it that Jack was not going to miss.

'Your mum said you knew Callum, that you'd had some trouble with him. Did you see him when you were out the other night?'

Boom. Jack was off. As he stormed from the room, he yelled back, 'Now we have it. So what? I'm under suspicion, am I? Under arrest? Thanks Dad. Or should that be Detective Dad?'

Jenny heard the front door open and then slam. She saw Jack, still in his pyjamas, marching down the front path, breaking into a run.

Thomas made a move to follow him.

'Don't. You won't catch him. And it's not a good look, chasing your teenage son down the street. He'll come back. I'll talk to him.'

'What went wrong? I didn't mean to upset him. But–'

'Yeah, I know. It was never going to be easy, Tommy. I say the wrong thing all the time these days. Why do you think I called you and didn't talk to him myself?'

Tommy leant against the wall. 'I'm glad you called.' He looked at Jenny and must have seen the eyebrow she couldn't help but raise. 'Really I am.' He sighed. 'I should've talked to him last night.'

'You had to get home. And we didn't–' She nodded towards the knife, not quite able to speak the lie that she hadn't known, hadn't told him before. 'Just try to remember that he needs a father not a policeman.'

'Yeah, okay.' Thomas nodded and continued to stare out of the window. 'Jack looked rough this morning. Are you sure he's not on anything?'

'What did I just say? Yes, I'm sure! You look rough – are you on anything?' They were back on opposite sides again.

'Okay.' Thomas's tone was back to business. 'What do you know about the fighting at school?'

'I've told you everything I know.'

'And you hadn't heard anything about the problem with Callum Peters before? His name hadn't come up?'

'*Come up*? What, you mean during our long chats over dinner about the detailed ins and outs of what he did that day? I know you don't live with a teenage boy, but you were one once.'

'Okay, okay. I get it. Monosyllabic. Tells you nothing. I've taken my eye off the ball. I admit it. I'll be around more.'

'Will you? What's Emma going to say about that?'

'She'll understand. She's had a rough time, but it'll get easier now, and she's always understood that Jack is my son and I need to be his father.'

Jenny was working very hard to look like she believed him. Now was not the time for another round of the argument they'd been having ever since they split up and ever since he got together with Emma. She'd let him have his fantasy today. She decided that less was probably more in terms of the conversation right now. 'Okay,' she said.

Thomas looked like he expected more. When she didn't continue, he said, 'Okay. Will you try asking him about the other night when he comes in? He's clearly not going to talk to me.'

Jenny nodded.

He turned the knife over in his hand. 'And I'll hang onto this. We'll talk later? You'll call me if anything happens? If you're worried about anything?'

Jenny nodded again. Was he confiscating his son's knife or taking it into evidence? It wasn't clear. She didn't want to ask.

'Okay.' Thomas checked his watch. 'Look, I'm going to have to go.'

As Thomas let himself out of the front door, he looked back. 'I know I'm probably asking the impossible, but can you try and keep him at home or try to keep track of where he is? Just for a couple of days?'

'I'll try. I'm sorry if I implied you weren't a good dad, Tommy, you are, okay?'

Tommy shrugged. 'Knives, Jenny.'

'One knife. And he won't have ever used it.'

'How do we know, though? How can we know?'

26

SANDRA

'No! Just no!' Sandra swung round to confront the gaggle of women a few paces behind her on the pavement, close enough for her and Danielle to hear every word they said – as intended.

She'd seen them as they came out of the Co-op. Tricia Baxter, what looked like one of her girls and a couple of scruffy extras Sandra couldn't place but could see were from the same tribe. They were always there at the school gates, smoking on the benches in the kids' playgrounds, propping up the bar in the pub, dragging back half of Primark on the number two bus come benefits day, watching like baggy vultures ready to pick over the remains of other people's troubles.

Without looking back, Sandra said, 'Danielle, love, take Alfie home. I'll be back in a minute.'

Faced with Sandra obstructing their way ahead, the women slowed to a halt, uncertain but projecting cockiness. Tricia Baxter sucked deeply on her cigarette and stepped forward to lock eyes with Sandra. Head tilted to one side, fag smouldering between yellow fingers held level with her right ear, she said, 'Problem?'

Sandra had gone with Danielle and Alfie to pick up a few bits and pieces from the Co-op on Mill Road. It was the first time Danielle had been outside since they heard the news about Callum. She couldn't stay indoors forever, not with young Alfie, and Sandra knew the longer she left it, the harder it would be. So, like Danielle was a child again, Sandra had got her out of bed, helped her blow her nose and wash her face, and encouraged her to get dressed. Standing behind her grown daughter, brushing out her hair, Sandra had wondered where the years had gone. How had they come to this place?

Not least because of the pills the doctor had given her, Danielle had retreated to somewhere very far off. She did what her mother told her to. She held Alfie's hand; she walked to the shop; she picked bread off the shelf; she let her mother pay; and she let her mother guide her back towards her house. She didn't hear the women behind them talking. Her mother did.

Sandra looked through Tricia Baxter at the motley crew with her. Tricia's daughter had thin blonde hair pulled back in a ponytail, face drawn on with a heavy hand – eyebrows like monstrous caterpillars skulking above spider's legs lashes and thick, black eyeliner. The girl had been an ugly baby, an ugly teenager and had grown into a very ugly woman. The other two women were clearly of her generation, probably not that old but looking like they'd been through the wash a few too many times. They were nothing, existing to reflect and project the older woman's nasty words.

Sandra had known Tricia since she'd first moved to Cambridge. She'd say she was a cow, but that would be doing cows a disservice. One of the problems of never moving very far was that you never escaped people like Tricia Baxter, to whom you were bound by years of walking the same pavements and scraping the same shit off your shoes. They hadn't liked each other thirty years ago; they didn't like each other now.

Sandra made it clear that she was addressing herself to Tricia, rather than her followers. 'All right, that's enough.'

Tricia flicked out a tip of tongue and picked a fleck of tobacco off it. 'What?'

'Stop spreading malicious gossip and talking out of your backside about stuff that has nothing to do with you. That's what.'

'Affects all of us round here, dunnit? Bad apples, those boys, always have been, every one of 'em.'

'Just. Shut. Up.' Sandra felt tired. Why had she decided to confront this bloody woman? When little Alfie was there it had seemed so important to make her stop talking. Now she just couldn't be bothered. But she'd started it.

'Everyone knows they were trouble. Selling drugs to kiddies.' The gaggle nodded their heads in agreement.

'It's none of your business, Trish, but that never has stopped you sticking your nose in.'

'Course it's our business. Affects our kids, dunnit?' More nodding from the gaggle and then Tricia added, 'At least somebody sorted one of 'em.'

Sandra knew of old that Tricia Baxter had an evil mouth on her, but still she was surprised at how low she would go. 'Just leave other people alone, Tricia, and concentrate on looking after your own.'

'Always have, haven't I?' Tricia patted her daughter's arm. 'And she looks after hers 'n'all. Not like your girl, Dani. Let those boys run wild. And she must've known.'

'Danielle did her best.' Sandra knew that sounded weak.

'My arse she did. Too busy lining up a new daddy. And there must be something dodgy about him, if you ask me, taking on that lot. Wouldn't be surprised if he didn't have something to do with it.'

'Nobody did ask you. And Lee tries his best; he looks after Danielle and Alfie. He's a good man.'

Tricia sneered. 'Like you'd know one of those if it slapped you round the gob.' One of the gaggle tittered and Tricia grinned.

'Crap parents. Crap kids. One in prison. One stabbed. Someone should call social services and get that little one out of there. He'll be just the same otherwise – if he hasn't started already.'

Sandra stepped forward and slapped Tricia round the face. Tricia's mouth fell open and, as the slap reverberated down her arm, a long tail of ash fell off the end of her cigarette. She looked like a toddler who'd dropped her ice cream. There was a pause before she lunged forward to shove Sandra and, at the same time, released a deep-throated yell. 'You fucking bitch. I'll 'ave you!'

Sandra stepped away and avoided Tricia's first strike. What had she been thinking? She hadn't been thinking. She couldn't have a physical fight in the street. But that woman shouldn't talk about Alfie like that. He was a good boy. He'd be all right.

Tricia had stopped. Her raised hand dropped down by her side. She and the others were looking at something behind Sandra's back. She heard a shout. A man's voice.

'Oi! I don't think so!'

Sandra turned and saw the detective, the one who'd been asking them questions at the house, walking rapidly towards them. He must have seen what she'd done. What would he be thinking? She felt very small and very stupid.

He reached the women and placed himself between Sandra and Tricia. 'What's going on here, ladies?' He held up his warrant card. 'Anyone want to tell me?'

Tricia pointed at Sandra around the detective's body. 'She hit me. That's assault, that is.' She looked so pleased with herself for finding the right word. The other women nodded along.

The detective looked at Sandra. 'I'm sure she didn't mean to,' he said.

'I'm afraid I did,' Sandra said.

The detective's voice softened when he spoke to Tricia again. 'Mrs Baxter, isn't it?'

Tricia grinned. 'Yeah, that's right.'

Sandra wondered why the stupid woman was so pleased that a police detective knew her name.

'I'm sure you must appreciate what a difficult time this is for Sandra.' The detective stepped alongside Sandra to face her accusers with her. 'But if she did assault you, I will understand if you want to press charges and we will go to the station and take a full statement.'

Tricia was clearly enjoying the spotlight and replied almost coquettishly. 'No. Of course not. Such a dreadful thing to happen.' It was sickening to watch. Sandra was rather tempted to slap the old cow again. Not a cow. She must remember that. Warm, friendly creatures cows. Useful to society.

The detective turned back to Sandra. 'Can I walk you home?'

Sandra nodded and they left Tricia and the others staring after them, at least waiting until they were out of earshot to start up again.

The detective took off his suit jacket as he walked beside Sandra and hung it over his shoulder. Sandra took a sideways glance. He was quite good-looking. Shame Danielle couldn't have found herself a man like that. He'd have kept the boys on the straight and narrow. She felt disloyal – not that Lee hadn't tried.

They walked in silence until they reached Danielle's house, then the detective said, 'Could I ask you a couple of questions? Save me disturbing your daughter.'

Sandra would rather he didn't see the house in the state it had been earlier, and still was, no doubt. She just didn't have the energy needed to keep the tide of chaos at bay. She saved what energy she had for Alfie. 'Is out here all right?' she said.

'Of course.' He nodded towards a bundle of gardening tools by the front door. 'Who's the gardener?'

Sandra could see the detective's eyes scanning the barren tip that was Danielle's front garden. Not a single thing growing that wasn't a weed. Even the scant grass was mostly moss, clover and dandelions. 'It's me,' she said.

'You have a garden?'

'No. I live in a flat. I'm a community gardener.'

'What's that then?'

He was trying to make her feel comfortable. What was it he wanted to ask her? She'd have to wait and see. 'A few of us look after the open spaces, cut things back when the council don't, plant up small flower beds, that sort of thing. Always carry a pair of scissors or secateurs in my bag for snipping back a bit of creeping ivy or annoying bramble.' Sandra put her hand in her pocket; empty right now.

'Right.'

It was pretty obvious that gardening and the clearing of weeds from public parks was not a subject that interested him. She might as well make it easier for him. 'What would you like to know?'

The detective looked grateful. 'Did you know any of Callum's friends from school?'

'No, not really. Saw one or two lads around more than others, I think.'

'Danielle mentioned a boy called Will before. Do you think she'd be able to remember any others?'

'Don't think so. Callum and the rest of the family lived somewhat parallel lives. He took food out of the fridge, accepted clean clothes, came and went pretty much as he liked.' Sandra took her mind back to times she'd seen Callum. He'd usually been alone. She did remember one boy, hanging around at the gate before school. And there'd been that girl for a while. He was a secretive kid, though.

'Other than Will, any names you heard from school? Anyone he had trouble with?'

'I'm sorry, I don't think I can help you.' Sandra hoped he wouldn't want to talk to Danielle right now. She barely remembered her own name, the state she was in, and there was no telling what she might say.

Thankfully the detective seemed happy to change the subject. 'What can you tell me about Danielle's husband, Lee?'

'He's a good enough man. Good enough husband. Good dad to little Alfie. Dotes on the boy. He's got a job. Pays the bills on time.'

'And before he met Danielle?'

'Can't help you there. I wasn't around so much.' She hadn't been. And she felt bad about that. Coulda. Shoulda. No point thinking about that now.

Another question. 'How did Lee get on with the older boys, Shaun and Callum?'

Perhaps that was what the policeman really wanted to know. 'They had their moments. Boys growing up. A man in the house who's not their dad. It was difficult at times.'

'Did those difficulties ever become physical?'

No point lying. 'Once or twice with Shaun. Over the drugs. How he spoke to his mum. But then Shaun went to prison.' Sandra studied the detective's face. How much did he know?

'Does Lee have a temper?'

'Show me a man who doesn't? Anyone really.' Sandra had a flashback to her own behaviour earlier. She shouldn't have done that. Bloody hell. She was losing her mind. She'd slapped Tricia Baxter. She was never going to hear the end of that.

Another question: 'What about Callum?'

Lee and Callum. 'They sparred. But Callum fought with everyone. Kids at school…'

'But did Callum fight with Lee?'

'Sometimes. There was shouting. Lee loves Danielle and wants to look after her, and Alfie.'

'What about the night Callum died?'

'Nothing special. Why?'

'Nothing. Did Lee go out at all?'

Sandra frowned. 'No. He stayed in. We all stayed in. Danielle went to bed. Lee and I watched television for a bit.' Should she say something more? What had been on? She couldn't remember. She didn't have to, though, because the detective's phone rang. He ignored it and it stopped ringing, but then started up again.

He looked flustered, embarrassed. Real man inside the competent policeman, then. 'I'm very sorry. Do you mind...?' He asked her permission to answer his phone.

'Of course. It could be urgent.'

He took a few steps back out of the front garden onto the pavement and answered his phone. Sandra couldn't catch most of what he was saying because he had his back turned to her. Didn't seem like a professional call, though. He was telling someone to calm down. He finished the call and walked back towards her.

'I'm sorry about that, Sandra. And I'm sorry but I'm going to have to go.'

Sandra felt for him. He looked flustered, shaken off his steady perch. 'Thank you. For earlier. I don't know what came over me.'

'Don't worry. Difficult times.'

He looked as though he had difficult times of his own.

He walked quickly away in the direction of Mill Road and when he thought he was out of sight, he broke into a loping run. Sandra wasn't the only one with troubles.

27

EMMA

Thomas has to spend time – proper time – with the baby so that he can see what it has inside, what it is.

This morning he was so desperate to get away. I couldn't let him leave me all day, couldn't let him be away all day. I rang him, made him answer my call. I told him that I had a doctor's appointment, that I couldn't take the baby, that he'd forgotten he'd said he'd look after the baby.

'I have to go to the doctor's. I did tell you. Have you forgotten?'

'No. Did you? Are you all right, Em?' He sounded worried. I don't want him to be worried about me.

'I'm fine. I just need to get the site of the stitches checked.' He hates talking about the stitches and the cuts and the tears and all those other intimate indignities of giving birth.

'Right. Okay. Does it have to be now? I'm–'

'I have an appointment. I told you. Your mind has been elsewhere. You probably forgot.'

'Yes, you're right. Sorry.'

He was stuck then. He was trying to think of a way out, but

his mind would be muddled by thoughts of raw flesh and mess and pain. 'I need to go, Thomas. For my appointment.'

'You can't take Isabella with you?'

'No!' I was angry. He said I should calm down. I don't like him to see the anger, the rage inside me, the fear. I need to keep control. He said he would come, though.

I've got the baby ready. She's in her seat. There's a bag with nappies and milk. All he has to do is take her. I don't want to discuss it. He'll talk me out of it, make me stay. I won't. He will look after it and it won't be able to keep up the act; it will reveal itself and then he will know.

I'm at the nursery window while I wait. I'm keeping an eye on the park. The police tape is still out there. They've taken their tent down and now the tape is just around the area in the bushes where he lay. Will they have left the blood down there? Will it be sinking down and being sucked up by the weeds and bushes and trees, breathed out through the leaves?

Some people come too close. They can't see it in the air, still traces left in the air for them to breathe in, to get inside them. Fewer children than usual. Parents spooked, not wanting to have to explain, not wanting to have to think about what could happen to them, their children. They should think about it and then they'd be better prepared.

I've seen Thomas's mother out there, walking round the paths in the semi-dark. She looks up at the house. I see her slow and look up. I know when she will turn her head and I step back so she can't see me. I know what she wants to do. It's a trap. She hopes our eyes will meet, she'll wave and then she'll have an excuse to knock on the door. I made Thomas tell her that I wasn't comfortable with unplanned visits, unexpected visits. I made him tell her before I agreed to buy the house. Too close. I knew it was too close.

And already those other women are back. Community

gardeners they call themselves. I've seen the posters attached to the railings. They come with their flowered gloves that won't protect them, and supermarket bags of tools for snipping and cutting and pulling up. When they take down the tape, they'll start up again, cut and the plants will bleed infection. They want to make things better. That's what I want. To keep people safe from the barbs and prickles and the sharp-edged brokenness inside other people, pumping round in their blood, turning them putrid, tainted with a rotten infection that can contaminate others. Can contaminate everyone.

The council should maintain the park, cut back the growth and clear the rubbish. It's why we pay our taxes. Instead, these volunteers come nibbling away at the chaos.

I've never had time for volunteering. I was studying and then I was working. The baby thing was always part of the plan, the natural progression some might say, but I wanted to wait until I was established before taking a break. I agreed that I'd take six months' leave. I thought three, maybe, and he said I'd need a year, but I can't be away that long. I might lose it all.

I've trained for years to get to where I am, I don't want to get behind, and the lab is under pressure – recruitment across the hospital is frozen because of the lack of money, but it doesn't mean there's any less work. Some people can't take the pressure and they become sloppy, standards suffer, things will be missed and mistakes made. I need to get back. I want to get back; that's not wrong. I'm good at what I do there. But at least now I'm not actually wasting my time.

I expected to have nothing to think about, being away from work and at home with the baby. I knew there'd be things to do, but what would there be for my mind? I thought that whole part of my brain would be left fallow, or that it would go fuzzy and useless. What is it they call it? Baby brain. Hormones messing with your mental processes.

It's all rubbish, though, I've never been more alert and I can see things so clearly, things I've never noticed before. It's amazing. I'm keeping notes, especially now I'm sure no one has written it up yet. I'll share my findings when I get back to the lab. I can't believe no one has seen it before. Of course, if it is to do with the blood, it's exactly my field. It seems most likely that it's in the rhesus protein and maybe how that combines with blood type. I don't have it completely clear yet. I'm rhesus negative and the baby is rhesus positive.

He's here. I hear the front door and go downstairs. He's carrying his jacket and I can see the wet patches on his shirt. Sweaty. It would be better if he wasn't; if he was clean. The dirt and sweat are like a bridge that lets the evil cross over. That can't be helped right now. He's going to try to get away. I can tell from his face – all reasonable with an underlayer of pleading.

'Emma, look, love, I'm right in the middle of something really important.'

See? He's trying to get away. I won't let him. 'No, Thomas, this is important. I'm still bleeding. I need to go to my check-up and how can the doctor examine me with a baby screaming?'

'Em, this is why I said I should take more leave. But you said to go back and now it's–'

'Are you going to make me lug the pushchair up the steps at the surgery, sit in the waiting room full of sick people with her?'

He's beaten. 'Okay, but just an hour, yes?'

'I'll be back as soon as I can. You have everything you need in that bag.' No excuses.

He's still watching as I walk off, like he can't believe I've gone. He'll see now why I have to go. He'll see. The baby was quiet when I handed it over. Made it easier. For once its sneaky manipulation worked in my favour.

Of course, I'll put on a good face for the doctor. *Yes, all healing nicely. No problems.* Like I did when that health visitor came round. She had her notebook and the sympathetic tilt to her head, the bored look in her eyes. She kept checking her watch. She had a questionnaire to see if I was depressed. Transparent.

Easy to tell her what she wanted to hear so that she'd put a little tick in the box next to my name.

I don't need people interfering. I want an end to the indignity of being poked at, fingers up inside me, fingers in my brain. Public property. A playground for their cutting, snipping, poking, digging. How do I know if they have it and are trying to trick me? How do I know if they're on its side? Smile and tell them what they want to hear, that's the best way.

And let Thomas see what it's like. So he'll believe me when I explain.

28

JENNY

'You want to watch what you're doing with those things.' Jenny pointed to the knitting needles Rose was holding when she opened the door. They were bundled up in what looked like the sleeve of a baby's cardigan in palest pink. Rose had knitted numerous versions of that same garment for Jack in his early months and years, new versions in ever bigger sizes and brighter colours arriving as the seasons passed. He must've been about eight when she had to tell Rose to stop because he wouldn't wear them anymore. She'd nodded. 'Tommy was the same. Such a shame when they grow up so fast.'

Now the same patterns were out. Different shade of wool, that was all. Jenny had wondered if she'd have another, a girl. Not now. She was done.

Rose stabbed the needles into the ball of wool. 'Nice surprise. You coming in?'

'I wanted to see if you were okay after yesterday.'

'I'm fine. Take more than some little vandals to upset me.'

Jenny remembered Rose's hand shaking, white as she held those scissors so tight. 'Did you call the police about it? Like we talked about.'

'I called Tommy.'

'Not the same thing.'

'That's what he said. What's the point having a son in the police if you can't call them, rather than hanging on for some constable or secretary to tell you to fill in some form on the interweb?'

Jenny had given up correcting Rose's version of the internet. It drove Jack crazy. That and the way she pronounced pizza. He'd correct her, every time, and, every time, she'd respond with a flutter of her hands to bat him away. They were lovely together. Jenny secretly hoped that the new baby wouldn't get that special relationship with Rose that Jack had. She didn't like herself for the hope, but it was there.

'Shall I put the kettle on?' Rose added.

'I didn't want to disturb you.'

'You're never a disturbance. I'm just watching some rubbish on the telly. I shouldn't. Waste of time. Watching other people spend stupid amounts of money on houses and moaning about the size of the third bedroom. Should know when they're well off. Don't know why they want to keep moving anyway. Me and Tom were quite happy in one place. Come on through, then.'

Jenny hadn't intended to stay but dutifully followed Rose inside.

They were drinking tea and watching some impossibly orange women looking at villas in Spain when the doorbell went.

Rose looked out the window. 'It's Tommy. And he's got the baby with him.' She sounded so thrilled.

Jenny considered an escape over the broken fence out the back. She didn't want to see Tommy again. She certainly didn't want to see him with his new daughter in tow.

Tommy walked in holding the baby against one shoulder and holding his jacket and a flowered changing bag in his free hand. He was red in the face and sweating. Still he managed to sound officious when he said, 'Mum, I told you to always put the security chain on when you don't know who's at the door.' Then he noticed Jenny and looked embarrassed.

'I just popped in to check on your mum. After yesterday.'

He nodded. 'Thanks.'

'I don't need your thanks for checking on Rose.'

He was about to protest when Rose hurried in, her eyes seeking out her granddaughter. 'What a lovely surprise. Is everything all right? Shouldn't you be at work?' Even as she was expressing concern, she was grinning and holding out her arms to take the baby.

'She smells, Mum. Needs a nappy change.'

'I'll do it.' Rose twitched her fingers, eager to take the baby. 'Naughty Mummy not change your nappy, Isabella? Come to Nana.'

'No. You're all right, Mum. I can manage.'

Jenny and Rose watched as Tommy got down on his hands and knees and expertly changed his daughter's nappy. It wasn't like Jenny hadn't seen Tommy change a nappy before, but this seemed too intimate. She shouldn't be here, shouldn't be witnessing this. He was another woman's husband caring for his child with another woman.

Rose was watching. 'Where's madam, then?'

Tommy stood up and lifted the baby into the air. 'Up you come, Bella Isabella. All clean.' He handed the baby over to his mum and answered her question. 'You mean Emma? She needed to go to the doctor. I forgot.'

'I see,' said Rose, who obviously didn't see. 'And work?'

'Yes, well, that's the problem. I wondered if you could watch Isabella for me for an hour.'

'Of course I will. Is Emma happy with that?'

'Why wouldn't she be? You're Isabella's grandmother.' A slight sucking in of her lips was Rose's only response to that. Jenny was proud of her.

Isabella was wide awake and restless in her grandmother's

arms. Rose gave the baby her finger and smiled as the baby clutched it in her tiny fingers. She barely looked at Tommy – had, obviously, completely forgotten Jenny was there – as she said, 'Okay. Off you go then.'

Jenny watched how Tommy struggled to pull his eyes from his new baby. 'There's milk and nappies in the bag. She's due a feed in about an hour, but I should be back by then.'

'We'll be fine, won't we, Isabella? Isabella and Granny will be just fine.'

Jenny knew when she was surplus to requirements. 'I should be getting off. I'll leave you to it, Rose. I'll call later.'

As Jenny followed Tommy down the narrow hallway, neither of them inclined to speak, the doorbell rang. 'I'll get it, Mum.' Tommy opened the door.

It was Jack standing on the doorstep. He glanced between them, suspicion written all over his face. 'What are you two doing here?' He had a scowl for his dad. Jenny felt quite honoured to be excluded from that particular look.

'I'm just leaving,' Tommy said.

'Figures,' said Jack.

Jenny considered telling Jack off for how he was speaking to his dad, but decided Tommy could fight his own battles. 'I'm off to work. I'll see you later. Not too much later, though, yeah?' She was relieved that Tommy stayed quiet.

Jack rolled his eyes but gave a slight nod that she decided to take to mean *Yes mother, I will indeed see you later but it's been so lovely to run into you so unexpectedly and I would never dream of being late*. She should probably stop reading so much Jane Austen.

Jack was looking away down the street and, following his gaze, Jenny saw a pretty girl walking down the pavement towards them. She pushed a wheelie bin out of the way to make room to carry on. Having negotiated that, she saw Jack. She obviously recognised him.

Jenny looked at Jack to check his reaction. He looked

embarrassed. Maybe there was something between them? Jenny had been wondering when Jack might get a girlfriend, might bring a girl home – or a boy, of course. She wasn't prejudiced, she didn't mind which.

Although looking at Jack's face now, she had a feeling that whenever it happened it would be a girl. This girl was lovely-looking. Quite dark. Lovely curls. You couldn't see much of her figure under the giant sweatshirt she was wearing. It was good that girls didn't always feel the need to dress for boys. What would she have done if she'd had a girl who wanted to wander the streets half naked? Having a boy was bad enough. Worse thing would have been having to feel some sympathetic kinship with her own mother. She was glad she had a boy. Despite that little pink cardigan.

Jack stepped out of the way to let the girl by.

'All right?' she said.

Jack nodded. 'Yeah.'

As the girl passed in front of the open door, she looked at Tommy. She seemed to frown and she looked back as she carried on.

They all watched her walking away and then Tommy said, 'Do you know that girl?'

'Adele? She's in my year. Why?'

'She knew Callum Peters, the boy who died. Do you know her boyfriend?'

Shame, thought Jenny. The girl already had a boyfriend.

Jack was fidgeting on the spot. 'Will? He's a tosser.' He sneered and glanced away at the girl's retreating back.

Tommy raised his eyebrows. 'Will Collinson was, apparently, friends with Callum Peters at some point. By all accounts, he seems like a good lad, nice parents, good results at school. Seems an unlikely friendship.'

Jack made a snorting noise.

Tommy was giving Jack his I'm-looking-into-your-head look.

'Do you know something about Will Collinson I should know? Was the connection that girl? Adele? Is that what you were fighting with Callum about?'

Jack stared back at his dad, purposely blank.

How do you like that then, Tommy? I get that look every time I ask our son anything. Teflon.

Tommy was persistent, though. 'Jack, are you involved in anything I should know about?'

Now Jack was shouting. Tommy should've seen that coming. His lack of practice dealing with Jack was showing. Why did he have to wind him up by accusing him all the time?

Jack's face was flushed and his hands were curled into fists. 'Yeah, I'm shagging Adele McDonald, I'm a drug addict, and a pusher, and I murdered Callum Peters.'

'Jack, that's not funny.' Jenny reached out to touch Jack's arm. He shrugged her off. Now she was unsure what to do.

Jack was glaring at his dad. 'It's what you think, though, isn't it?'

'No. It isn't. But, look son...'

Rose appeared in the hallway behind and looked between Tommy and Jack over the baby's head. 'Tommy? Jack? Is everything all right?'

Jack spoke to Rose. 'I'll see you later, Gran.' And then he was off. Jenny watched him lope down the street.

Jenny watched Tommy watching after Jack, saw him raise his hand to his mouth and chew at the corner of a nail. He'd never quite got out of that habit. He'd told her that his dad used to smack him across his knuckles when he saw him doing it, even tried rubbing engine oil under his nails to put him off.

Rose looked worried. 'Is everything all right, Tommy?'

'Second time today that's happened. I'm not doing very well at this dad lark.'

'You're doing your best – he's a teenager,' Rose said. 'He's not really involved with the dead boy, though, is he?'

'I'm sure there's nothing to worry about, Mum. Don't worry. I'll be back in an hour. You'll be all right with this little one.' Tommy placed a hand on his daughter's head as he passed Rose in the corridor.

'Of course I will. Now off you go.'

They both seemed to have forgotten Jenny was there. Tommy passed her and shrugged. 'I know. Don't say it.'

'I didn't say anything.'

'You didn't have to. Look, I've got to go. I'll sort it later, okay?'

'Okay.'

Jenny wanted to be angry with Tommy, but she felt sorry for him. What a complicated mess it all was. Maybe old Tom had been right. They were bloody idiots. They should've got married and, despite apparent evidence to the contrary just now, a boy did need his dad.

29

EMMA

I spent most of my time at the doctor's in the waiting room, perched on the edge of one of those horrible plastic chairs trying not to touch anything. Other people. All watching. Checking me over. I forced my shoulders to relax, looked bland, calm.

The doctor, a man, looked at the computer screen more than me. Better that way. Once I was on the table, lying behind the curtain on that sheet of blue paper they pull out from a roll, then I had to let him look. But he was looking at pulpy flesh and scars. That was all. I went to another place, a bubble of quiet and clean, without plastic gloves and intrusion. *How am I? Fine. All under control. Just a quick check-up. Everything fine. Of course. Everything fine. Little laugh. Yes, tired, a bit, of course. But fine. Establishing a routine. Doing great.*

I walked home. Odd to feel the sun on my face. Everything seemed a little too bright – and dirty. I squinted and tried to keep looking ahead, just ahead, not at the houses and cars, the broken pavements encrusted with muck and dirt, the people. I haven't been outside much. I haven't been out since the other night, in the park.

I'm relieved as I turn in towards our front door. I call out as I come in. It's quiet. Too quiet. Where are they? *Where are they?*

Thomas is not here. And the baby is not here. The house is empty. They were supposed to stay here. He was supposed to stay here with the baby so that he would see and understand. We would be together. Together we would decide what to do. But they're not here. Not here. It's made him go somewhere. Where?

There's no magic. This evil is not supernatural. It is just a disease. It can't make people disappear. The baby, though, or one of the others... Thomas could have been influenced. Where would they go? I should never have left them. Never have left Thomas alone with the baby. It's clever. The helplessness, the weakness, all a disguise. They are born with a talent for manipulation. That's what the big eyes are about and the finger grabbing. Designed to draw you to them and hold you. I've read about it. The books think it's all about survival of the species. It can be so much more.

I am calm; I must be calm. Where would Thomas go? He didn't want to be here, at home. Where would he be instead? Work. It'll be work. Thomas is a good man; he works hard. He'd go back to work. Would he take the baby there?

He's not answering his phone. He never answers his phone. I will not stop ringing. Again. Again. Unanswered, ignored. But what if something has happened? What if Thomas is hurt? Has it hurt him? Could it hurt him? I was a fool. Stupid. Stupid. Stupid. How could I leave it? I have to watch, control, always. Stupid. Answer the phone, Thomas.

He answers.

'Where are you? Are you all right? Why aren't you here? You were supposed to be staying with the baby. Is the baby with you? Where are you?'

'Whoa, slow down, Em. Everything's fine. Calm down.'

I can't calm down. No. No. He's right. Calm down. I should laugh. Ha ha ha, look at me being so silly. I can't do that. I can't make a laugh come. 'Okay, so have you gone for a walk or something?'

'Look, Em, don't overreact, but I had to go back to work.'

'With the baby?'

'No.'

No? Not with the baby? He's not with the baby?

'I had to go back to work, so I dropped Isabella over at my mum's. She's–'

'No! Why would you do that? You were supposed to watch her. How could you take the baby there? It'll make everything worse! Don't you see?'

'What are you talking about? She's my mum, for God's sake. She used to have Jack all the time when he was a baby.'

'I don't want her near the baby. I told you. This morning. I told you. You knew. You were supposed to be with her. She can't be there–'

'Look, I'm not going to argue with you about this now. I'm on my way to pick her up. I'll see you soon.'

He's put the phone down. Thomas put the phone down and he's going there and the baby's there, there with her, and they'll all be together. Blood will call to blood. Wolves circling. I have to be there. I have to protect Thomas.

Across the park. If I run, it's not far.

Outside. Through the gate. Into the park. I can't run. I'm hobbled, ripped, broken. It broke me for just this. To stop me. To slow me down. But I'll get there. It's not far. I'm stronger than it thinks. I'm healing. I've healed. I'll heal again.

A woman on the path. Too slow. Move aside. I pass on the grass and feel the ground hard and dry underfoot, smell the dust from too-dry earth.

They're all together, all of them. Gathered together. Probably laughing. Everybody is laughing. Laughing at me because I can't stop them. I thought I could. I thought I was strong enough. But it's strong too. It's affected my mind. Evil mind-waves, vibrations from the blood, escaping through the sound-waves, the screams, to affect my mind and stop me thinking clearly. Hah, so clever. I thought I was getting away to think and making Thomas see, but it was clever, cleverer than me, it used that weakness, took advantage of the opportunity and they all came together.

They made Thomas betray me. He betrayed me. Went to them, took it to them. He just cares about the boy, the boys, the evil boys. He's their thing, their puppet. They make him lie for them. My good, honest Thomas, lying, not doing what he said he would. I should tell him, explain. But he wouldn't believe me. Would he believe me? No, not now, not yet, especially not now. Perhaps it's getting stronger. That'll be it. The contagion in the baby, getting stronger, pulling him away from me.

Run. Must run.

30

SANDRA

There were more police back to talk to Danielle. Sandra had opened the door to them. It was Sandra who did most things in the house. Lee came and went to work. When he was at home he sat and stared at Danielle with a tragic look on his face. No use to man nor beast.

Sandra had got used to expecting little or nothing from men, though. She was mothering them all: putting food on the table, clearing it away, making cups of tea, tucking Alfie and Danielle into bed, answering the phone and answering the door. She should be exhausted, had a sense that some part of her was, but she couldn't sleep, so she kept going – hoovering, cleaning the bath, sweeping the front, more tea.

This time it'd been the nice family liaison girl – Janice, that was her name – and a different detective to the one before. She didn't like this one as much; seemed a bit full of himself, posh voice, probably one of those fast-track out of the university types. Wrong side of the tracks here, literally – Romsey was built on the other side of the railway tracks to the university, streets of tiny Victorian two-up two-downs, nothing like the big houses on the other side and the colleges in the middle.

Sandra had introduced herself as Mrs Chapman. The new policeman seemed to think she was some kind of home help and she saw no reason to disabuse him of this fact. She'd left them to it. Good luck to him getting any sense out of Danielle the state she was in. Sandra didn't think her daughter was conscious of the changing faces asking her the same questions, otherwise she would have told the posh bloke to leave Danielle alone.

Yanking sheets off the bed, Sandra piled them into the wash basket. As she straightened up there was a twinge of pain that she had to take a moment to breathe through. She had painkillers but didn't like to take them. Now was not the time to be out of it; there'd be time enough for all that.

She clenched her jaw and hauled the basket up onto her hip for the trip downstairs. It was probably a bit late to be putting on another load, but the weather was bound to break soon and she wanted to get the house as sorted as she could for Danielle.

Of course, she should have done more for Danielle years ago. She'd been angry, and selfish. She hadn't been so old herself when Danielle announced that she was pregnant by that silly boy she was seeing, and Sandra had been done with kids. She wanted to do something for herself and have some fun. She had a good job and was just getting to do some of the stuff she'd felt she'd missed out on – nights out, spending money on herself, weekends away, the odd flirtation that went further than a wink over the counter of the newsagents while being nagged for sweets. But now she realised that, once you have kids, they're your responsibility, however old they are, however much trouble they get themselves into.

Adam Peters hadn't so much been trouble as a complete waste of space. Full of all that when he was down the pub talking about how he'd got his woman knocked up, how he had boys, proper boys who liked rough and tumble, football, could take a fall without crying. He barely knew the kids and he barely did a day's work.

When he finally buggered off, Danielle was up to her eyes in debt and so depressed that she spent most of her days in bed. That was what Sandra had heard. To her shame, she'd not seen it for herself. There'd been a falling out. Sandra had told Danielle that she was making a mistake when she got caught up with Adam and again when she said she was pregnant. When she told her she was pregnant again, with Callum, Sandra told her not to have it, to get rid of it. There'd been a lot of things said that couldn't be taken back and Sandra had kept her distance for a good while. Maybe if she hadn't... But what was the point of maybes?

So, when Adam had first left, Callum and Shaun had briefly been taken into care. Sandra had found out and helped sort Danielle out, agreed that she'd be around to help from then on. It'd been too late for Shaun – and Callum as it turned out. Some kids were damaged, broken, from the start and then there wasn't a lot could be done to change that. You had to protect their innocence, keep them safe when they were little, to give them a chance.

Sandra half dragged, half carried the dirty bed-linen down the stairs. She heard the police asking about Shaun again. They knew he was out of prison. They thought Danielle must know where he was. She didn't. Sandra had made sure of that. Shaun was bad, through and through. He took after his granddad, and the day that bastard had gone had been the best of Sandra's life.

It had taken too many years, but she'd finally stood up to him. She'd thought it was a romantic adventure moving out to Cambridge as a newly-wed. It didn't matter that she didn't know anyone because – Christ Almighty, she'd been a fool, must be where Danielle got it from – because they had each other. Yeah, she really had been that naïve.

He went out to work and she stayed at home. She had Dean and, apparently, she let herself go and let the house go, was too preoccupied with the baby, so he didn't like coming home. So she took more care of herself, got her figure back. So then he was jealous and didn't want her going out and flaunting herself at other men. The odd slap and black eye certainly put her off going out too much.

She got pregnant again because, apparently, Dean needed a brother or sister. So along came Danielle and it started all over again.

She told her mother she wanted to come home and she told her that she'd made her bed; she was a married woman with kids, and had to make the best of it. It's what she did for years. She didn't want her kids coming from a broken home and Brian wasn't mean all the time, at least that was what she told herself. And Dean had turned out okay. Got himself apprenticed as a plasterer and emigrated to New Zealand. Married now. A little boy. He sent pictures. They had a lovely life over there. He talked about her visiting. It wasn't ever going to happen, even before.

It'd been a determination that Dean wouldn't see his dad raising his hand to a woman that made her stand up to Brian in the end. She told him that if he hit her again then she'd kill him in his sleep. She'd been perfectly calm when she'd said it. He'd looked into her eyes trying to see if she meant it. Whatever he saw there, he didn't do it again. He didn't know how she'd grown up, but he must have seen something of it there. Would she have left him eventually? Perhaps. Sometimes you had to be hard, do the hard thing.

Sandra thought of the letter she'd sent to Shaun in prison. She'd asked him not to come home. There was nothing back in Cambridge for him; the police would be keeping too close an eye out for him to return to his old habits and his old business, and yet it was inevitable that he would return to them. Sandra had made it clear that she wasn't as daft as his mother and knew what was going on. She wasn't going to let him come back, waltz back into their lives and pick up where he'd left off.

It hadn't stopped him trying. He'd turned up outside her flat a week ago asking for money, asking to stay. He did, at least, realise that Lee wasn't going to be letting him back in the house. Sandra didn't want him anywhere near.

He'd been sitting on the front step when she came back from the shops. 'All right, Nan?'

'They let you out, then?'

'Good behaviour.' He'd grinned. It might have softened her more if he hadn't looked the spit of Brian sucking up on another morning after. 'Any chance of a sandwich? Stay a few days, maybe?'

He'd looked genuinely shocked when she said no. 'Not a good idea, Shaun. I thought you got that.'

'I didn't think you meant it, Nan.'

'I did.'

'So, what am I meant to do then? I've got no money, have I? Where am I supposed to go?' He'd stood up and was looming over her. He was scrawny and hard, muscles on bone.

Sandra had stood on the step to reduce the height difference. 'I'll give you money if you leave.'

'You're that desperate to get rid of me? That's cold, Nan, that is.'

'Do you want the money?'

'Not going to say no, am I?'

'Just so we're clear, Shaun. If you come back asking for more, if you give your mother and Lee any trouble, I'll tell the police that you threatened me and stole the money.'

Had there been a flicker of doubt, even hurt, in his face? Maybe. He'd recovered and straightened out his shoulders, flexed his hands. She'd wondered if he would punch her and tensed ready. In the end, he'd kicked at a can lying in the grass and just said, 'How much?'

It'd cost her her savings. She didn't care what he did as long as he stayed away and gave the rest of the family a chance. She'd suggested that he go to Manchester, to his dad's, but she was pretty sure she'd caught a glimpse of him in the cemetery on one of her walks there. She liked it there, for the quiet. She knew, though, that there were those who didn't go there for the birdsong and green – people like Shaun.

Should she have told the police he'd been back in Cambridge? Save them the trouble of trying to find out if he'd had anything to do with Callum? They hadn't asked her, so she didn't have to think about that right now.

Sandra slammed the door of the washing machine and switched it on. The door mechanism clicked and, after a pause for thought, the growl started up. Out of the kitchen window, Sandra could see Alfie sitting on the dusty excuse for a lawn playing with his Action Man. Above him, a previous load of washing hung limply on the line. Not even a breeze today; the washing would be baked dry. Amongst Lee's work T-shirts and underpants, alongside Alfie's faded pyjamas and little shorts, hung a couple of T-shirts and a pair of jeans belonging to Callum, like abandoned skins. Still in-between sized, not quite a child and not quite a man.

Sandra realised that she was crying. Her eyes stung and tears overflowed and ran down her cheek. She clenched her teeth. No tears. Hard.

31

JENNY

Jenny was walking back home past Rose's. She wasn't going to knock. She had no desire to interrupt Rose's time with her new grandchild. She was walking on the other side of the road to avoid being seen. She'd considered walking the other way, but this was quicker. She regretted the decision when she saw Tommy's car pull up. It was like they couldn't avoid each other.

Then she'd seen Emma, travelling at some pace, along the pavement towards him. That was too much. That was one family reunion she really didn't want to be part of. Not that she was ever keen on being the third wheel in chats with Tommy – or should she say *Thomas* – and Emma. Luckily, they were on the other side of the road with a double barrier of parked cars between her and them – and neither Tommy nor Emma was taking in the sights. She ducked behind a high-sided van to avoid being seen. And they didn't see her, thank God.

It was pretty clear from the look on Emma's face that something was up. It was clearly going to be some kind of domestic. She felt bad about lurking and eavesdropping, but what was she supposed to do? It wasn't her fault that their conversation was so public and so loud.

From the get-go, Emma was yelling. 'Where is it?'

Tommy was looking around to see if anyone was listening – it was so annoying when he did that. And pointless given that he didn't see her behind the van.

'Emma, keep your voice down.' He was using his calming voice, pitched low and slow and designed to bring you down to the same level. Also bloody annoying.

Jenny couldn't see Emma's face now, but her body language was full of tension and rage. 'I will not keep my voice down. Where is it?'

What was the *it* about?

'She's perfectly safe.'

It. She. It seemed odd. What were they talking about?

'Why didn't you keep it with you? Why here?'

'Emma, don't make a scene. It's perfectly reasonable–'

'Perfectly reasonable to lie? To let me come back to an empty house? To leave it *here*? Without asking me, without telling me?'

It seemed like maybe they were talking about the baby.

'Emma – shhh!'

'I will not shhhh. Get the baby out of there away from that…'

It was shocking to hear Emma speak about Rose like that. She'd never liked Emma, obviously, but never thought her capable of such nastiness. And about Rose. And – whatever her feelings about Rose as a person – about her husband's mother.

Tommy was up close to Emma now, his hand on her arm trying to calm her. It was too intimate. Jenny kept her head low and her eyes fixed straight ahead, walked on as quickly as she could. No way she wanted to be part of whatever was going on there, or to have them know that she'd been a witness. She just hoped that Rose hadn't heard what Emma had been saying, that Tommy managed to calm her down before she came to the door. Emma was not one of her favourite people – for obvious and myriad reasons – but she had never seen her like that. It wasn't her business, but something wasn't right there.

On the walk back she met Jack. He was sitting on a wall looking at his phone.

'You all right, love?'

He shrugged.

'Coming home?'

He shrugged again but got to his feet, pocketed his phone and started to walk alongside her – not too close – him in the road and her on the narrow pavement.

'You know that boy Dad was talking about?' Jack kicked at a can lying in the gutter.

She cast a look over at him. 'Which one? The one that was killed?'

His eyes stayed on his feet and the gnarled road surface. 'No. The other one. Will. Will Collinson.'

'I think so. Year above you?' She tried to remember what Tommy had said, further back to whether Jack had mentioned him before. The names piled up over the years: playgroups, nursery, primary, secondary, football teams, best friends, enemies, siblings and kids of friends. 'He lives on St Barnabas Road?'

'Yeah.'

'I do his neighbour's garden, I think.' Enormous front hedge. Bloody nightmare. When had she seen the neighbours? Out when she was sweeping the cuttings. 'He seems like a nice boy. Dresses smart. Always very polite. Wouldn't hurt you to be a bit–'

'Yeah, right.'

'What?' They'd been walking more or less side by side, but now she sensed him pulling back, slowing to let her walk ahead.

'Doesn't matter,' he muttered.

It was so easy to say something wrong. He'd been going to tell her something and she'd criticised him. Why had she done that? She needed to think before she opened her mouth. She told

Tommy off about it and she was no better herself. She'd try to get him back. 'What about this Will? I, obviously, don't actually know anything about him.'

'Exactly.'

'Sorry. So, tell me.'

'Doesn't matter. Nice haircut and lives on St Barnabas Road. You think I should be just like him. Right?'

'Stop saying that.' Teenagers. Bloody teenagers. Look tough but sensitive as greenhouse orchids. She'd apologised. She was all ears but now his pride had been hurt. She was the enemy again. 'What did you want to say about him?'

'Nothing. No point.' He refused to say any more and she had nothing left to persuade him; they walked the rest of the way home in silence.

He'd gone to his room when they'd got back, come down to eat the pasta she cooked for him.

They hadn't properly talked about what had been said at school. She grated some extra cheese for his pasta and ventured a comment.

'You know your dad was in lots of fights in his time. Mostly it was about some girl or other. Even me sometimes. Although I was also known to fight my own battles. I once slapped a girl because she tried to get your dad to buy her a drink in return for a snog.'

'Too much information, Mum.'

'Okay, possibly. The point is that we weren't saints, your dad wasn't a saint.'

Jack took more cheese with his fingers and stuffed it into his mouth. It probably wasn't the moment to tell him to eat with a knife and fork. She stayed quiet.

Finally, he said, 'You know the girl from earlier?'

'The pretty one we saw outside your gran's?'

He made a face. Whether at the fact she'd said the girl was

pretty or because he didn't buy her pretence of not quite remembering, she couldn't know. Both probably.

'It's not like you think. We're just friends.'

'Okay. Boys and girls can be friends.'

'Thanks for clearing that up.'

Her child was a sarky arse, but that conversation could wait. She stayed silent. She really should get some kind of medal for the restraint she'd been showing just recently. Her reward was that Jack spoke again.

'The stuff at school. It was because Callum was messing her about and I told him to lay off.'

'Good for you.' It was good; it was good that he was standing up for a friend, but at the same time... The boy was clearly trouble and now he was dead. Just let him talk.

Nothing. She'd have to try a prompt. Something neutral. 'So that was it, was it?'

Jack was pushing a last piece of pasta round his plate. 'Sort of.' He stabbed the twirl with his fork. 'She's going out with Will Collinson now and everyone thinks he's Mr Perfect – even you – teachers love him, even though he's a total...'

'You know him better than me. Never judge a lad by his haircut. Consider me told.'

Jack put the fork down. 'Everyone knows – apart from the people who need to know, like teachers and parents and the police – that he's well into drugs – not using, selling. Thinks he's going to be the next Richard Branson, starting with drugs. Goes on about how he's going to business school and going to get a Porsche and stuff, and be a millionaire. He's in with all these lowlifes, but no one can see it.'

'If that's true, Jack, don't you think you should just tell your dad?'

She knew she'd said the wrong thing – or the right thing at the wrong time – as soon as the words were out of her mouth.

But this was what she was afraid of – violence, drugs – and she didn't feel equipped to deal with it on her own.

Jack pushed his chair back from the table. 'No. And you're not to tell him anything. I can handle it on my own.'

'What do you mean "handle it"?'

'I'm going to show people what he's really like. He thinks he's like some secret agent, but all us kids know what's going on. I just have to show the people who need to know, and don't.'

'So *you're* going to tell your dad?'

'Leave it, will you, Mum?'

'I'm worried. You can't blame me. You say this lad, Will, is trouble. That boy in the park. Callum. You know him. You were in a fight with him.'

'You too, eh? You think I had something to do with that? Like Dad does?'

'He doesn't. I don't. Your dad loves you, Jack.'

'Right.'

'He does.'

'Just not as much as his new family.'

'Jack–'

'Don't defend him. We both know it's true.'

He'd interrupted her, but Jenny hadn't known what she was going to say. It was what she thought too. She needed to say something, though, not for Tommy but for Jack. She tried to start again. 'Look–'

Jack was on his feet and headed for the door. 'Thanks for tea. I'm going out.'

The answer to her question about where was drowned out by the slam of the front door. Maybe he'd heard her instruction to be back by ten and maybe he hadn't. Time would tell. Parenting was a shit job.

32

SANDRA

Sandra ripped off a piece of kitchen roll and wiped her eyes, went to the sink and splashed her face with cold water. Alfie was commando crawling across the ground with his Action Man held out beside him, chattering away to himself. He was what mattered in all of this. Dean had come through and got out. It was up to her to see that little Alfie got the same chance.

Shaun had helped take that chance from Callum, if it had ever been there. Callum was going to do the same to Alfie. He wasn't going to let him stay innocent. Sandra was mad at herself that she hadn't seen it coming.

Danielle didn't pay as much attention as she should. Callum knew that and took advantage. That morning, just the day before, he'd thought his mum was taking Alfie to nursery, like she usually did. But Sandra took him. Danielle was on her period and saying she felt grim, so Sandra told her to stay put and she'd come back and make her a cup of tea.

The nursery was only round the corner. Alfie liked to show that he was growing up, could be trusted to not hold hands and was walking a few steps ahead – not so far that Sandra couldn't catch hold of him if she needed to. A lad cycled past, got off his bike by Alfie and came right up to him. It happened so quick. This lad put his hand in Alfie's pocket and then he was on his bike and gone.

Sandra had caught up to Alfie. 'Do you know that lad?'

Alfie had shaken his head.

'What was he doing? Did he put something in your pocket?'

Alfie had looked at the pavement and shrugged. He knew something but wasn't saying.

'Come on, let me have a look.' Sandra had crouched down next to her grandson and put her hand in his little pocket. She'd found a small plastic bag and, inside, a twenty-pound note. Alfie was given the odd 50p, a pound coin, but not paper money. 'Where's this come from, Alfie? Did that lad put it there?'

Alfie wouldn't look at her. 'You're not in trouble, sweetheart, but I do need you to tell me why you have this money.'

'He said I wasn't to. It's a secret.'

'We don't have secrets. I'm sure he wouldn't mind you telling your nan. You know you shouldn't keep secrets from me.' Sandra had already had the conversation with her grandson about how important it was not to keep secrets from the grown-ups who looked after you. She'd seen enough of the dangers in the world for kids to know that she'd needed to prepare and protect him. It hurt to stay crunched up on her knees on the pavement, but she waited, waited for Alfie to speak.

'It's for Callum. I mustn't lose it. It's sweets for Callum's friend. I'm not to eat them and I'm to give him the money.'

Callum had his little brother selling drugs for him. Sandra had pocketed the money. 'Okay. I'll give it to Callum, shall I? So you don't lose it.'

Alfie had nodded and gone happily into nursery. As she'd watched him go, she'd tried to think what she could do. There was no point telling Danielle. Could she talk to Callum? She could keep a closer watch on Alfie; she could do that at least. She hadn't wanted to go straight back to the house, so she'd taken a walk, down through the back streets, into the cemetery and round its overgrown paths. The dead under their crosses were offering no help. Neither was the Virgin Mary, standing in stony silence, half hidden in a thicket of trees and shrubs. Who'd be a mother, eh?

Now, Sandra heard the front door open. It would be Lee. Automatically, she reached across to pick up the kettle. He'd want a cup of tea.

A few minutes later, Sandra opened the door to the sitting room and found it already too full of people. Danielle was curled in the corner of the sofa, head bent, knees tucked up under her chin, arms wrapped across her body, as though protecting herself from physical blows. The policeman – the posh one again – was sitting on a dining-room chair, legs crossed, arms crossed, back straight and a look of moral superiority all over his face. If a bunch of fat-cheeked angels appeared at his shoulder singing hallelujah, she wouldn't have been surprised. Who did he think he was?

Something had clearly gone wrong in the few minutes since Lee had come in. He was on his feet and had a face like thunder. He was shouting, 'What the fuck are you accusing us of? How dare you sit in my house and accuse us of having anything to do with drugs?'

Danielle was rolled tight against the noise and the hurt and the shame. Sandra wanted to throw her body in front of her daughter's, cover her with a blanket, cover her ears, protect her little girl from these too-big men and their cruel words and their badness.

Janice, the family liaison girl, looked scared. She was standing against a wall like she hoped it would absorb her. The policeman's face was paralysed somewhere between *like I care* and *oh shit.*

Lee carried on. 'How were we supposed to stop him doing whatever he was doing? You're the police. What did you do? I suppose we could've guessed after his bloody brother, but we couldn't do anything with either one of them. That's your job. Where the fuck were you before this happened? When something could've been done? And they're all still out there now, doing their dodgy little deals, getting off their heads on who-knows-what. And what are you doing? You're sitting in my fucking front room doing fuck-all.'

Lee seemed to have emptied himself and he slumped down into the chair behind him. Sandra was glad to see that the policeman took a moment to reanimate himself and find words.

'I can see that you and your wife are very upset.' He closed up his notebook and popped a very fancy-looking pen into his top pocket. 'We'll leave you in peace now.'

As the policeman stood up, Sandra saw him roll his neck and jut out his chin. Amazing he had a chin, with a voice and manner like his. He added, 'We'll be in touch.'

Sandra looked at Lee. It was okay, he wasn't listening. He'd gone back to staring tragically at Danielle. Sandra crossed in front of the policeman to hand Lee his tea and then turned back. 'Shall I show you out?'

As she led the few steps to the front door, she couldn't help adding, 'I'm Sandra, by the way.' He hadn't even asked who she was, let alone what she knew.

After the incident at the nursery, Sandra hadn't had a chance to catch Callum until he'd skulked into the kitchen nearer teatime than breakfast. She'd put the plastic bag containing the money down on the kitchen counter in front of him. He hadn't looked at her as he covered it with his hand and picked it up. Neither of them had said anything as he'd left the kitchen and she heard him go out shortly afterwards.

She'd waited until later that evening to speak to him. Alfie was asleep and Danielle had gone up to bed. She got up when she heard his bike drop on the path outside and confronted him in the hallway. She pulled him into the front room and told him what she'd seen, what had happened outside the nursery. 'You cannot use your brother like that.'

Callum had stood sullenly silent, staring her down.

She'd raised her voice to try to get through to him, make him listen and take what she was saying seriously. 'Do you hear me? You cannot use your little brother as a drug mule. That's what they call it; that's the name for what you're doing.'

That had been when Lee had come into the room behind them. They hadn't heard him come in the front door. It was immediately obvious that he'd heard at least what she'd just said.

'What the fuck? You little fucker–'

Sandra had stood between them while Lee shouted and Callum looked bored. Then Callum had darted past. He'd gone out the front door, leaving it open as he ran down the front path.

Lee had gone after him.

33

EMMA

I made a mistake earlier, said things I shouldn't. I arrived at his mother's house as he drove up. I lost control. *Bitch. Witch. Evil.* It made him angry. I saw that. I couldn't stop myself. I have to stop myself. Maybe it made me do it, made me say those things. Tricking me so they'll think I'm the mad one, I'm the dangerous one. I'll have to be more careful.

We didn't talk in the car. Back in the house, I apologised. 'I'm sorry, darling. I was worried when you and the baby weren't at home.'

'Worried, Emma? Those things you said.'

'I know. I'm sorry. I think I'm just tired.'

'You must be. I know that.'

It was the right thing to say. It fits with what he thinks.

'We could've left Isabella with Mum. You could get some sleep? What did the doctor say?'

'Nothing to worry about. I'll be fine. I'm fine. I'll nap when she naps later. Then I'll feel much better.' I pull my lips into a smile.

'Did you talk to the doctor about how you're feeling?'

'How I'm feeling?' Smile again. 'I'm feeling fine; don't worry.'

'If you're sure…'

'I am.'

'I just need to sort out this case. Murder. A child. It's big.'

'I know. I'm sorry. I'm fine. Really.' He's about to come over to me. He'll put his arms round me. 'I'll just pop up and get a quick shower. After the doctor's. You know.'

He hesitates.

'I'm fine. Really.'

He seemed to believe me; it's what he wanted to hear. I shouldn't have said all those things. I need to keep quiet while I'm still trying to sort things out. I hurt Thomas. I never meant to hurt Thomas. I want to protect him. But it wasn't supposed to be like that. The baby was supposed to stay with Thomas and then he would see and then I could explain to him because he would have seen for himself and then we'd be able to deal with it together. But he gave it to them. How could he do that?

But maybe it isn't Thomas's fault. Maybe they're drawn to each other and it's not Thomas's fault. Poor Thomas. Both of his children. It'll be hard for him when he knows. I shouldn't be angry with him.

I feel better after my shower, cleaner. I am fine. I don't know why I lost control. I mustn't do that again.

When I come downstairs, Thomas is on the sofa with the baby lying on his chest. It's not what he should do. They shouldn't be like that. I have to breathe. I can't breathe. My chest feels too tight, like it's gripped, gripped by a band of iron that is tightening, tightening round my ribs, stopping my lungs, stopping me breathing.

No. Calm. I have to stay calm. I can't say anything. I can't watch. I'll go back upstairs, put washing away, until I can take it off him, find a reason to separate them.

Upstairs in our bedroom. It's cooler. Quiet.

Thomas used to put his own clothes away. We were equals. Now I'm here, in the house, and he's out there at work, I'm doing it all. At least it means that I can keep order, keep everything clean and in order. He used to just stuff things in his drawers, but now I can fold things, place them in neat piles so they stay smooth. It's easier if you take everything out, refold on the bed and replace neat stacks, one by one.

It falls to the floor as I take out the final heap of T-shirts, falls to the floor with the heaviness of a stone. I pick it up. Cool in my palm, now lighter than I expected. I can't believe what I have in my hand. It's not the same. I'm sure I've not seen this one before.

Downstairs. Walking slowly. Step by step. Breathing. One hand gripping the stair-rail, squeeze and release, squeeze and release.

He's still lying where I left him. Now with his eyes closed. Both of them quiet together. Mustn't raise my voice. Must ask him without letting him see. 'Thomas, what's this? Why do you have this?'

He opens his eyes and shifts to sit up, lifts the baby onto his shoulder. 'What?'

He's still holding the baby. The cot is there; he could put it down in the cot. 'You can't have this. Why? Why do you have a knife?'

He's looking confused and then, then something else. What? I can't tell what he's thinking.

I'm holding the knife in my hand, heavy on my outstretched hand, showing it to him. 'Thomas?'

He's sitting up straight now, on the edge of the sofa. He hasn't asked me how I found it. He knows where it was. In the drawers in our bedroom. In his drawer. He put it there, hid it there.

'Emma, love, come and sit down for a minute.'

Inside of my lip between my teeth. Squeeze. Stay in control. Sit down. I sit in the chair.

'I'll tell you what happened, all right? It's nothing, but I'll tell you.'

Sit still. Feet want to twitch and flick. Stop them. Still. Listen.

'The knife has nothing to do with work.' He pauses. 'It's Jack's.'

Jack's. That boy. The boy had a knife.

Still. Listen.

'Jenny found it–'

Her as well. All of them. Don't react.

'She gave it to me.'

He's looking at me, waiting for me to react. I'll just listen.

'Boys… It's quite common…'

I'm shaking my head.

'I'm not saying it's not serious. I've talked to Jack about it and I'll talk to him again. I'll get rid of it. I just… I just put it there until I had a chance–'

'Jack had a knife. You say it like it's nothing. He's been in our house. A knife.' I'm on my feet. The walls are too close. The room is too small. 'Knives are dangerous. You can't protect him, you know. He could hurt someone, kill someone, with a knife. Do you know how easy it is to kill someone with a knife? Cut an artery, even nick an artery, and you bleed out, bleed to death. A knife can do that. Neck, groin, heart. That boy has been in our house, with a knife. Was he there at your mother's today? What if he'd had a knife then?'

'Emma, I have his knife, you have it in your hand. Are you worried about Isabella?' He strokes the baby's back. 'Jack would never have a knife out near the baby.'

He's standing, looking like he will come towards me, still cradling the baby against him. I move away, further away. 'How do you know? He could've.' I'm not worried about the baby; I'm worried about Thomas. 'Anyone can have a knife and you wouldn't know. All sorts of people carry knives. Did you search him? He could've had a knife. He could be carrying one now, a new one. He could've been carrying one for months. When he was here. All the times he's been here and been with you.'

He's watching me pace, following me with his eyes. 'Calm down, Emma. It's all right. There's nothing to worry about.'

'Of course there is. It's everywhere. Blood. Evil. That boy out there.' I'm pointing, waving my arms. Stop it. Arms at my sides. Calmer voice. 'You saw him. The blood. You saw it. You must have seen it. You must realise. Don't you realise?'

'Realise what? You don't think I'm aware of the dangers of knife crime? That I don't take it seriously when kids carry knives?' Frowning, raising his voice – not much, but it's there.

'You see, I knew. I knew it was down to me. No one sees!' Now he's looking confused. Stop speaking. Listen. Look at him. Be calm.

But no. Oh, God, no. I hadn't seen it before. Now I do. Now I'm looking at him, I can see it. 'Thomas!' Blood. There's blood.

He's looking around, like he thinks it's something outside of him. 'What? What's the matter?'

'Thomas, you're bleeding. Put the baby down.'

'What do you mean I'm bleeding?' He sees where I'm looking and follows, twists his hand to look. 'Oh, this?'

A small bead of blood swells from the ripped cuticle by his thumb. He's brandishing it, throwing the fumes into the air, it's near the baby, right near it, the cut, it'll get in through the cut. In or out. It's not clear anymore. Blood. He's bleeding. 'Give me the baby, Thomas.'

'It's nothing. Don't worry. I've been chewing my cuticles again. You'd think I'd have learnt by now.'

'Give the baby to me. You're bleeding.'

He's laughing. 'Just a tiny bit of blood.'

He's laughing at me.

'Can't believe this worries you. You've been away from work for too long. Have a look.' He's waving his hand towards me. 'Go on. Smell it. You love it, you know you do. Nice bit of blood.'

How had she ever found this, anything like this, amusing? 'Don't, Thomas. It's not funny. Don't do that.'

He's showing his thumb to the baby, putting it right in front of her face. 'You're not frightened by a little bit of Daddy's blood are you, Bella Boo?'

'No!' I said that too loud. Quieter. He doesn't understand. Mustn't alarm him. 'Don't do that, darling. Please give the baby to me. Let me get you a plaster.'

He hesitates. What is he going to do?

He stands up. 'Okay, you win, you take her and I'll run it under a tap.'

I'll put the baby in the cot. It's asleep, or pretending to be asleep. It knows. It's part of all this; the root of all of this.

34

JENNY

Jenny opened the door to find Tommy on the doorstep.

'Can I come in?'

He looked done in. Usually she'd make some smart comment, there'd be a bit of banter – humoured or ill-humoured depending on how things were going – but he didn't look in the mood. She just let him in and he followed her through to the living room.

She could imagine why he might he looking a bit grey around the gills. She'd seen what happened outside Rose's earlier.

She looked at her ex, her son's father, slumped on the sofa they'd bought together a decade earlier, arguing in DFS about something, she couldn't remember what now. They'd been paying for the thing for four years after. The sofa and the man had seen better days.

He'd only just started in the police when they split, but there'd been times when she knew that what he'd seen at work was getting to him. And this latest thing was close to home in too many ways, too close for comfort. And then there was the new baby and whatever was going on with Emma. It would be easier if she could just be angry with him, like Jack. Though that wasn't easy either. He just looked so bloody tired, though. 'Tea?'

He nodded.

She came back from the kitchen and handed him a mug – Cambridge United – she'd had it for years, in fact it might've been his originally, a Christmas present.

He hadn't moved and was staring into space. 'Thanks. For the tea. For letting me in.'

'That's okay. I think it's a bit like the rules of vampires. Have a child with someone and they have the right to come into your house.'

He looked like he wanted to smile but it was too much effort.

'Something up?'

'I needed to get out for a bit.'

Jenny didn't say anything. This wasn't like Tommy. It wasn't his way to be disloyal. He seemed to realise the same thing himself.

'Strike that. I didn't mean it. Small babies. You remember.'

'Grim.'

'Hard. Tiring. Emma's doing brilliantly–'

'Yeah.'

'It was always going to be hard. She's not got a mum around – I told you she died when she was born.'

He had. One of the many tales of the wonders of Emma she'd been forced to endure. 'She's got Rose, like I had.'

'Emma's not close to Rose like you were.' He hesitated and then spoke again. Change of subject. 'I wanted to see how things were with Jack. With everything that's going on. And the stuff earlier. And, you know.'

'The knife.'

'Yeah.'

'We've not talked about it any more. I think he was going to tell me something earlier about the Will Collinson kid you mentioned and then I said something wrong and he clammed up on me.' Should she tell him what Jack had told her? She'd said he should speak to his dad and he'd been clear that he didn't want to. She should respect that. She didn't want him to stop telling her things, to think he couldn't trust her. There'd been too many secrets already.

Tommy was blowing on his tea. 'If saying something wrong was an Olympic sport I'd have a good shot at a gold.' He paused before adding, 'I shouldn't tell you this, but we think Will Collinson might be involved in the death of Callum Peters.'

Jenny nodded. 'Okay.' She tried to stay focused on what Tommy was saying rather than going off into her own thoughts and speculations about what this might mean, trying to join up what Jack had said and what she was hearing now.

'You won't say anything to anyone, will you?'

'What, call the *Evening News* and offer an exclusive? Nip down the pub and tell my bevy of friends?' Tell Jack was what she was thinking – because this meant that Tommy didn't think Jack was involved, didn't it?

'I'm serious, Jen.'

'I won't say anything to anyone. You clearly just need to say it to someone.' The fact that the someone couldn't be Emma had to remain unspoken. Should she really be feeling a sense of smug satisfaction? Shut up, Jenny, and listen.

'We haven't got any real evidence yet. I really shouldn't be talking about this but with it happening right outside my front door and the involvement of Jack and with Emma and–'

So he did still think Jack might be involved. 'It's okay. You talk and I'll listen, and then that will be that.'

'We don't have the weapon and we're waiting for the post-mortem results to get something more solid. Still *sharp object*. Obviously knife seems most likely.'

Jenny remembered the feel of Jack's knife in her hand and stayed silent.

'There was only one wound. Not deep. Unlucky, or lucky,

depending on your point of view. Cut to the aorta caused the boy to bleed out, probably quickly. No other injuries.'

'So whoever did it might not have meant to kill him?'

'Or meant to do it and was very efficient, knew what they were doing, where to stick the knife to do the most damage.'

Horrible thought. Jenny released a heavy breath and took a sip of her tea.

'The investigation seems to be pointing towards an involvement with drugs. We know Callum Peters was selling drugs. Kids like him – in and out of the care system, trouble at school – it happens more than you want to know. His older brother's in prison, or at least was. It seems like he's out now.'

'But Will Collinson's not like that, though, is he? He lives on St Barnabas Road.' Whatever Jack said, could the boy really be as bad as he implied?

Finally, something that Tommy seemed to find amusing. 'Nice middle-class parents? And so he has to be clean living and law abiding?'

'Okay, that was a stupid comment.' Jenny remembered her conversation with Jack. You'd think she'd have learnt. Would Jack be amused that he and his dad were in agreement?

'His name and face have come up in places that suggest that he's got his fingers in pies that he shouldn't have. Kids like him are just better at not getting those fingers dirty – or not getting caught. Often because people, like you, assume butter wouldn't melt.'

Just what Jack had said.

'We might've missed him if it wasn't for the fact that he's going out with Callum Peters' ex-girlfriend.'

'Is she involved as well?'

'Nothing to suggest so. Pretty bad taste in men, though.'

'Thankfully not a criminal offence.'

Tommy raised his eyebrows but didn't pursue the topic. 'We're pretty sure that Collinson is connected with some nasty types bringing drugs up from London and selling around schools. But we can't prove it. So, in the meantime, we have to look at all possibilities. We think the older brother might be back in the city. We're looking at the stepfather. There's no CCTV on that bit of the park but we're still looking at stuff from cameras around the area. Door-to-door hasn't turned up anything – apart from a general distrust of the Peters boys and a scant amount of sympathy. No one liked the kid, Jen.'

'Shouldn't stop them being sorry he died, though.'

'Exactly.' He went quiet for a moment. 'Look, Jen, I know I've been a bit crap recently but I'm always here for Jack; I'm still his dad.'

'I know that. Jack knows that. Whatever I might say sometimes, you're a good dad.' She grinned. 'Though I have to remind you that this conversation is off the record and cannot be used in evidence. I'll deny everything if I have to.'

'Understood.' Thomas put down his mug and slapped his knees. 'Better be getting back. Jack upstairs?'

'No. He's out.' Jenny waited, waited for the questions and criticisms that were going to sour their peace accord.

Tommy seemed to be going through responses in his head before he said, 'Okay. Would you mind texting me when he gets in? Just so–'

'I can do that.' She nodded, as much to acknowledge what he hadn't said as what he had. She was worried about Jack being out, about his constant disappearances and refusal to share where he was going and who he was seeing, but she wasn't about to tell Tommy that.

35

EMMA

Thomas has gone out. *Work* he said. Another evening when he should be at home. Out. Work. Should I believe him? Is he lying? I would never have thought that he would lie to me. Now I'm not sure. It's changing things.

The washing machine is on. Everything they touched, might have touched, everything that's been close to the contagion, everything must be washed. Hot water. Detergent. Bleach. Frothing up. It's churning, like food in the gut torn apart by acids, fighting it, pushing at the glass porthole to be released. Let the chemicals and the heat do their job. Will it be enough?

I shouldn't have brought his blood into the house. The knife. A different knife. Blood on the knife. I wrapped the shoes in plastic and put them out. I soaked my clothes and then washed them, the hottest wash. Would it be enough? Is it killed by heat? Not everything is. Can it protect itself, lie dormant and then bloom again? And the knife. I had to keep it. I might need it.

And the other knife. Jack's knife. Knives are dangerous. Jack, he's a problem. I didn't realise before how serious a problem. I was distracted. I saw it so clearly in one boy. Jack was too close. But now the evidence is right in front of me. Why can't Thomas see? Jack is part of the evil. Maybe he sees it but can't admit all of it. He doesn't know what he's seeing, refuses to know. Thomas shouldn't be angry with me; I'm trying to protect him.

Jack and that woman and his mother, they are trying to distract Thomas and keep him away from us. I need to make Thomas understand, about Jack and the baby, and the others out there. He should listen to me, shouldn't lie to me, go behind my back. He'd said we'd be together, do it all together. I hadn't been sure I could. I hadn't had a mother. How could I know how to do it? My mother is dead; I killed my mother. Could someone who killed her mother, be a mother? Is this how I will be punished?

But Thomas said it would be all right; together we'd be all right. But I'm on my own, always on my own, like now, and it's so much worse than I imagined.

I poisoned my mother's blood and my mother is dead. Or was my mother the poison? And now the baby. My baby. It hates me. It's part of something bigger that hates me and is evil and will hurt me and will hurt Thomas.

It isn't fair. It's too hard. I'm on my own. I was always alone. I can't be alone again. It wasn't supposed to be like this. Thomas promised it wouldn't be like this. It wasn't his fault. He wouldn't lie. I love Thomas. When it's just me and Thomas, it will be good again. He wouldn't lie, wouldn't leave me, not unless someone or something made him. I must stop that; remove the risk.

36

JENNY

Jack was in just before ten. Jenny had already gone up to bed, not to sleep, to wait. He shouldn't know that she was waiting. She lay in the dark with the light off and waited till she heard him come in.

Front door unlocked, banged shut. Into the kitchen. The lid of the biscuit tin. The fridge opening and closing. Up the stairs. Into his room. Back out and into the bathroom. Click of the light. The fan coming on. Loo flush. Water running. Creaks back across the floorboards to his room. A heavy creak, more like a crack, as he chucked himself onto his bed.

He was going to break that bed; she kept telling him. He was too big now to go throwing himself down on furniture like that. With walls between them, she'd lain quietly in the dark waiting for him to fall asleep, just like she used to do when he slept in the cot in the corner of their room.

At least she'd managed some sleep, once he was in, once he was settled. She got up early – with the sun – to go and water the Harrisons' lawn. She'd forgotten to do it the previous evening. Thankfully, the pots were on an irrigation system, so they were fine.

The forecast said the weather was due to break. Thunderstorms coming in. She couldn't take the risk and the grass wouldn't mind a double soaking if it came. Given the impending break in the weather, she went from the Harrisons' to mow a lawn, pull some weeds, refresh some hanging baskets and feed some tomatoes at a couple of other clients'.

She'd left a message for Jack and said she'd see him at lunchtime. Now it was lunchtime, she was back home and there was no sign of Jack. She knew he was up. There were signs of breakfast having been eaten in the kitchen, but the house had that hollow feeling that said no one was in.

She made some tea and took it to sit out on the front step. It was her favourite spot; it got the sun for most of the day, she couldn't see the chaos in the back garden and all the jobs she should be doing but wasn't, and she could have a neb at what was going on in the neighbourhood. Who knew how the guy opposite could afford that new car? It wasn't through his job, that was for sure. And an inheritance from a rich relative seemed unlikely.

She was telling herself off for being nosy and judgemental when she noticed that someone – a girl – who'd been walking down the road towards her, had stopped before next door's gate and was turning on the spot, looking back the way she'd come, out across the road. She was watching and so caught the girl's eye as she walked on again and stopped at the end of Jenny's path. She smiled. It was the pretty girl they'd seen outside Rose's. She was wearing the same baggy sweatshirt. What had Jack said her name was? Adele.

The girl didn't return Jenny's smile. She said, 'Is this where Jack lives?'

'It is.' This was a new development. A girl turning up to look for Jack. A pretty girl. Even if Jack had said they were just friends – and hadn't Tommy said this girl had bad taste in men? Well, tastes could change. Could this girl – Adele, pretty name – be the explanation for his recent absences?

'Is Jack here?'

'No. I'm sorry, he's out at the moment. Do you want to leave him a message?' *Preferably one that tells me the nature of your relationship with my son and whether I have anything to worry about.* Jenny tried not to reveal the degree to which she was examining this girl to see if she might be good daughter-in-law material. The distraction meant that it was a shock when she realised that the girl was standing out on the pavement crying, proper sobbing.

Jenny stood up. She didn't go down the path in case she spooked the girl. 'Hey, what's the matter?' No response beyond more tears. 'Do you want to come in?' No response, but no flight either. 'Come on, come in and I'll get you a hanky.'

So, now the girl was sitting in Jenny's living room clutching a glass of water and a fistful of soggy tissues. She'd still offered no explanation for the visit or the tears. 'Do you want to tell me why you're upset? In case I can help?'

Adele dabbed at her snotty nose. 'I wanted to see Jack. I wanted to tell him, to make sure that he was all right. Because it's my fault.' Another outburst of sobs.

'Why wouldn't Jack be all right? What's your fault?'

'It's all my fault!'

Jenny's sympathy was waning as her concern for Jack was piqued. 'Could you just take a breath, try to stop crying and tell me?'

'I'm sorry.'

'I'm sure you've got nothing to be sorry for.'

'I'll never forgive myself if I've, like, got Jack in trouble. He's nice. He's always been lovely to me. He stood up for me when Callum was being horrible.' That set off more tears.

Jenny could feel her heart beating in her chest and her sympathy was all but shot to pieces. 'Can you tell me what you think you've done? Why you think Jack might be in trouble?'

'I'm soooo sorry.'

'Just tell me what's happened, yeah?'

Something about Jenny's changed tone gave Adele a shake and she stopped crying. 'I used to go out with Callum, right? You know about Callum, yeah?'

Jenny nodded.

'But I wasn't going out with him. We, like, broke up.'

'Are you and Jack going out?'

A sniff and a shake of the head. 'No, me and Jack are, like, just mates. Jack's so nice but–'

Jenny couldn't help herself. 'But you like the bad boys.'

'You sound like my mum.'

'I sound like *my* mum. Sorry, I interrupted. Carry on.'

'I'm going out with Will now.'

Thus proving Jenny's point.

'So, like, we were out last night at the leisure park and I noticed Jack and he seemed to be, like, watching us. And then I saw him later and he was watching us again. And then Will saw him and he, like, kicked off, going on about what you looking at and f–'

She looked at Jenny to see if she was going to tell her off for the near swear word, like Jenny cared about that. Jenny nodded and Adele carried on.

'Well, you know, and so Will was, like, going to go after Jack–' Adele must have seen Jenny shift in her seat because she added, 'But I didn't let him, right, I stopped him and Jack went off and it was all right.'

Jenny excused herself. 'Stay right there. Drink your water. I just need to pop to the loo.' She went out into the hallway and texted Tommy.

> Can you come round? Now. Girl called Adele here talking about Will C and Jack. Worried.

Coming back in, she sat down again and kept her voice level.

179

'So what's happened now? Has something happened since last night to bring you here?'

Adele bit her lip. 'Will came round my place this morning after Mum went to work. He was, like, going on about Callum being a dick.' An eye flick at Jenny to check her reaction.

Jenny thought she'd probably quite like Adele's mum.

'And then he said that Callum, like, got what he deserved and then he started going on about Jack and how he was, like, hanging round after us and how he must fancy me – he doesn't, we're mates and I told Will that. And then he, like, started saying that he was going to sort Jack out and tell him to f– leave us alone. So I said that he should, like, leave Jack alone and that Jack knew someone in the police.'

Jenny felt cold.

'He does, doesn't he? I saw him with someone that's police on Catharine Street.'

Jenny nodded. She decided not to add *that's his dad.* 'What happened then?'

'Will was, like, raging, going on about Jack talking to the f-ing pigs, going on about Jack being a grass and, like, grassing him up and how he'd, like, shut him up and teach him to go telling tales to the pigs and how he didn't know what he was dealing with. And he sounded really, really mad and was, like, walking up and down and punching things and I thought he was going to break something of Mum's and I asked him to, like, stop and calm down, you know? And then he went in my mum's kitchen and I heard him open the kitchen drawer and when he came back in he had one of Mum's knives, like one of the good ones she uses to cut up meat, and then he left. And Mum'll kill me if he doesn't bring that knife back. It's, like, expensive and she uses it all the time. She'll kill me.'

Jenny felt sick. *Shit, shit, shit, shit.* She had to get up and walk, look out the window to see if Tommy was coming, if – please God – Jack might be walking up the path.

Adele had started sniffing and crying again, 'It's my fault, isn't it?'

Jenny wanted to say, *Yes, it's your fault and if anything happens to my boy...* She couldn't think straight. What should she do? Should she call Jack's mobile? He wouldn't answer; he never did. Should she text a warning? What could she say? *Kid after you with a kitchen knife?*

Shit. Shit. Shit. She really was going to be sick. She sat down on a chair, stood up again. She saw a car draw up outside. *Thank God.*

Jenny met Tommy halfway down the path and, in a hurried half whisper, provided as succinct a summary as she could of what Adele had told her. Tommy nodded a lot but said nothing until they entered the living room. Adele looked up from her soggy ball of tissue, her eyes full of alarm. Jenny marvelled at how calm Tommy sounded when he spoke, when she was pretty certain that he was doing his nut as much as she was.

'Hi, Adele. I understand you know my son, Jack.'

'You're his dad?'

'I am. But I also work for the police, as I think you know.'

Adele looked at him in what appeared to be stunned awe.

'I've asked my colleagues to look out for Jack and for Will Collinson, your boyfriend, yes?'

She nodded. 'I'm so sorry. It's all my fault.'

While Jenny was silently agreeing that it was all her fault, Tommy was telling her that it wasn't.

Adele said, 'Has Jack been, like, telling on Will to you?'

Tommy shook his head. 'No, Adele, he hasn't.'

'I didn't think he would. He's nice. When he, like, got in that fight with Callum and took the knife off him, he never told anyone. But Callum was so mad, you know?'

'Did anything happen after that?'

'Not really. Callum and Will – they were still friends then – they tried, like, winding Jack up a few times, but he ignored them, and, anyway, they always seemed to have their own stuff going on, and then it got, like, complicated when I, you know, broke up with Callum. Will thinks I still want to be with Callum. Like I went out with him just to get back at Callum. It's all so, like, fucked up.' Adele looked up at Tommy with enormous, scared eyes.

Jenny could feel her face twisting with annoyance and impatience. Romeo and bloody Juliet while some nut job was out looking for Jack with a kitchen knife.

Tommy's voice held steady. 'Adele, do you know anything about either Callum or Will and drugs?'

Suddenly Adele was on her feet and pacing the tiny floorspace. She wrapped her arms across her body and started hitting herself. 'Fuck, fuck, fuck. My mum is going to kill me. She's going to go, like, mental and then she's going to kill me.'

'Adele, please just tell me what you know about the drugs and then we'll worry about your mum, okay?'

'I knew Callum took a bit of stuff – and he knew people. But I never did, honest, never. Tell my mum that. I didn't. And Will didn't. But Callum said Will was, like, selling the stuff and making money off his mates. He said Will was involved with a bad lot, like he was some gangster or something. But Will's not like that, I'm sure he's not. My mum is going to kill me.' Adele looked between Tommy and Jenny, huge eyes trying to convey the horror of the situation she found herself in. Then she carried on. 'But then Will started being, like, really odd and now he's gone off on one about Jack. And my mum is going to kill me.'

'Adele, do you know where Will might have gone?'

The girl shook her head.

'How long has he been gone?'

'I dunno. About an hour, maybe?'

An hour. This psycho kid had been out looking for Jack for an hour and they had no idea where either of them were.

37

EMMA

Pretending to sleep. Again. Always pretending. It's what he wants to see. It makes him happy – well, calm. And now he's gone. Again. I heard the front door, the car. And it's crying. Again and again.

Back at the window. Clear blue hot sky. Already hot. Sweat down my back, between my breasts, useless breasts. Heat through the glass of the window, seeping in, passing through glass. I hadn't thought of that.

They took the body from the bushes. Where will it be now? Will it be sealed away, safe? They are all fools; they don't know what they're dealing with. Although, I think maybe when the blood is out the evil goes with it and the body is left pure. When I looked at the boy's face, you could already see the changes, he was looking younger, less angry, more innocent.

I will study it and defeat it. Objective science. But right now I have to save my family, keep Thomas safe.

I'm keeping watch again.

The park. Out there. That woman is there. She's one of the gardeners and I've seen her in the Co-op, working there, behind the counter. I've seen her here before. She was here yesterday, looking, staring. I saw her with a little boy. Then I saw her again. Now I'm seeing her again. She's standing at the fence and staring at where it was. What does that woman know? Why does she come now? Is she like me? Can she see it? To share would be a relief. But it could be a trick. I need to stay quiet. They might try to stop me if they know.

Keeping watch over the baby. Look at it lying there. Its red glow is stronger, a deeper scarlet, thick, congealing. And the noise, fizzing, like from a giant wasp nest, menacing, preparing to swarm, attack. It's been fed, again, has sucked down the milk until it frothed out of its mouth. Now it's briefly drugged to silence. Silence in which I can think.

Thomas can't see, won't see. I'll have to act alone, again, alone.

38

SANDRA

Sandra had the stuff she needed to do day-on-day so down pat that she barely needed to think about it. Her hands made tea, spread butter on bread, loaded the washing machine, wiped down kitchen surfaces mysteriously covered in crumbs and scum not five minutes after she'd last done it.

Her feet made the journey to and from her flat, to and from the shop, up and down stairs. Her mind was left free to wander. She'd have liked more of a distraction, something to keep her in the present moment, out of the future, away from the past.

Alfie was pulling on her arm as they walked up towards the crossing. She kept hold. 'You can press the button when we get there, I promise. Just wait.' He always did the same thing. She always said the same thing.

Today her mind was on Keith, her little brother.

Keith was nine. Like all the kids on the estate, Sandra and Keith were free to come and go, take themselves out for the day, round to friends' houses, up on to the rec, just so long as they didn't leave the estate, didn't do anything stupid, didn't annoy anyone and were home for tea. There weren't the restrictions there were now.

Sandra was twelve. She and Keith didn't have the same friends. It was a dry day, not sunny but warm enough for just a T-shirt and shorts, the sky sealed with smoke-white cloud. She'd already been at the rec, not playing, chatting about nothing with her friend, Susan. Susan was sitting halfway down the slide, eating a tube of Smarties, tipping it up to pour the sweets into her open mouth, and Sandra was perched at the top of the steps with a perfect view out beyond the wooden roundabout and rocking horse, out across the chalk-marked tarmac, over the scuffed, brown grass to the blocks of flats beyond and the road that ran in front of them.

Had she seen Keith coming? Could she have shouted to him to stop kicking his football so close to the road? Could she have told him to look, stop and look, like on the Green Cross Code advert? Could she have shouted a warning? Could she have stopped what happened? She could never be sure; she'd always wonder.

Keith was with some mates. It was always considered safe if you weren't on your own. They were on their way to the rec to play football, kicking the ball between them as they went. The ball got away from them, Keith chased after it and didn't stop as it bounced off the kerb and on into the road. He didn't look. The driver was going fast, too fast for the road, didn't see him, but must have felt the impact as Keith was flung up onto the bonnet and then back down onto the road. The car didn't stop, didn't hesitate, kept going and disappeared round the corner.

There was silence, a moment where everything seemed to be on pause, and then people started to run, Sandra with them. She'd yelled at her friend to get out of the way and shot down the slide, almost falling over as it threw her off the end.

Keith's friends had formed a huddled wall in front of him and a woman was knelt down in the road. Sandra pushed through. She saw her brother's bare legs lying at strange angles in the muck of the gutter. Their mum would be so mad if he'd ruined his new T-shirt.

Another grown-up led Sandra away. Should she have resisted and insisted on seeing Keith, sitting with him as he lay on the road? There were sirens, flashing lights, more people and then no people – she was sat up in her bedroom listening to her mum crying.

No one asked her what happened. No one asked her what she'd seen. When the police came to talk to her parents, she went and stood inside the door to the living room. Her mum told her to go back to her room. When she tried to speak, the policeman led her out into the corridor and closed the door. As he was leaving, when her mum and dad were still in the other room, Sandra went to the door and whispered to him. 'I saw. I saw the car. It was green, silvery green. It was a Capri. I saw it.'

The policeman patted her on the head and went away. She never saw him again.

There was a funeral, more crying and then no one talked about what happened, no one talked about Keith, no one asked Sandra what she'd seen. The grown-ups were sad and angry, they talked behind doors and over her head.

Sandra waited. She didn't just know what car had hit Keith and driven away, she knew who was driving. She knew because her dad had pointed out the silvery-green car when it arrived on the estate. She'd thought the colour looked pretty, not like other cars she'd seen.

Her dad told her it was a Capri. He told her that he'd've had the silver blue, not the green, if he could afford one. He told her that Chick Standish had more money than taste. Chick Standish drank in the same pub as her dad and gave her dad work on his building sites, but they weren't friends.

It was Mr Standish's car, but it hadn't been Mr Standish driving; it'd been Mark. Sandra had seen the car and seen who was driving before the accident. That was why she'd been watching so closely. The car that her dad so admired was being driven by Mark Standish, Mark who was in her class. He could barely see over the wheel and looked tiny up in the front seat. She recognised his short, short hair and the red jumper he always wore – even at school where it wasn't allowed.

Eventually Sandra couldn't wait anymore. She asked her mum. 'Will he go to prison?'

'Will who go to prison?'

'Mark Standish.'

'Why would Mark Standish go to prison?' Her mum had been annoyed and already impatient with Sandra's questions.

'Because he killed Keith.'

'What are you talking about? Your brother was killed by a hit-and-run driver. Some bastard who didn't even stop. No one saw who it was.'

'That's not right. It was Mark Standish. I saw. He was driving his dad's car, the one that dad kept talking about.'

'Sandra! What would make you say a thing like that? Just because you don't like someone in your class, you can't go making stories up about them, horrible stories, like that.'

'But I'm not–'

Her mum had sent her to her room. When her dad came home, he was sent to talk to her. He told her that she mustn't make up stories, that no one had seen who hit Keith, that no one had been able to identify the car or the driver.

Sandra didn't see the silver-green car again. It had disappeared from the parking space it always sat in and was replaced by something else, a red car she didn't know the name of. Back in school, Mark Standish wouldn't meet her eye. When she passed him in the dining hall and looked at him, he turned his head and then started shoving one of his mates to kick off a half-hearted fight that got them told off and sent outside. Once she saw him turn and walk the other way down a corridor when he saw her coming. She knew. He knew she knew.

She told her friend Susan what she'd seen and she told her parents. They must've told the school because Sandra got another telling off for making up stories. 'It's a very serious thing to accuse someone of, Sandra.'

Like she didn't know that.

A year later, Sandra heard Mark Standish boasting that he could drive, that his dad had shown him how and he'd taken his dad's car out while his dad was out. He went quiet when he saw Sandra watching him. That weekend, Sandra took the small knife her mum used to peel potatoes from the kitchen drawer and used it to scratch up the side of Chick Standish's new red car. No CCTV back then, so no one found out. The scratches weren't repaired and sometimes Sandra would walk round that way just to have a look at them, to run her fingers along the scars in the shiny paintwork.

Mark Standish was always in trouble. When he left school, he went to work for his dad on the building sites. He ended up stabbing some black lad outside the bowling alley. He didn't get away with it that time. He went to prison. But if they'd listened to Sandra, then Mark Standish would've paid for killing Keith and the black lad would still be alive. No one believed her. The police either didn't believe her or did nothing. You couldn't rely on other people. She'd learnt that lesson young and had regular reminders over the years.

Sandra still wondered what Keith would've looked like as a grown man. Her mum had kept photos of him on the windowsill – a studio one of him as a toddler and a picture of him and Sandra on the pier in Clacton, both of them grinning over sticks of candyfloss, sitting under a wooden shelter as it chucked it down with rain. New pictures were added over the years. Sandra in her school uniform, in her wedding dress, holding Dean as a newborn. She got older in the pictures. Keith never did.

Sandra and Alfie reached the crossing and Alfie pressed the button. He hopped up and down beside her as they waited for the green man and the beeps. Sandra made him wait and check the road before crossing, like she always did.

As soon as the beeps started, he tried to step off the pavement and she pulled him back. 'Check first, poppet.'

'But there's the green man and the light is red. It tells the cars and they have to stop.'

'It does, but sometimes they don't stop, even though they should.'

'Why? That's against the law.'

'Sometimes because they don't see the light, or because they're going too fast, or even because they just don't want to stop and think that no one will see. Hitting us will hurt us more than them, so we're extra careful.'

Alfie nodded and gave the driver who, in fact, had stopped to let them cross what he thought was a warning look. Sandra hoped Alfie remembered the lessons she was trying to teach him, hoped she was doing enough to keep him safe.

39

EMMA

I can't go in there. It's screaming and the fizzing is louder and the red light is throbbing bright bright bright bright. I'm in the hallway, crouching by the stairs, keeping low, but it's stretching closer. I could go. It wants me to go. But I can't. It's my responsibility.

Pulsating sound-waves bouncing off walls, a chaos of jagged lines, smashing against and into each other, taking over every space in the room, in the house, inside my brain. I can't think, taking my breath, I have to think. I have to stop it.

I have to get up and go into the red and get it. The noise is squeezing my head, it's going to squeeze out my brain, displace it, take the space for itself, the scream will win, like a fire, it will burn into my brain and then it will be in my blood and it will rage through my body, burning it up, destroying, killing me and I will be nothing, dead inside, hollowed out. The screaming. I have to get away from the screaming.

I need Thomas. Thomas could help me. Together maybe. Thomas could stop the screaming. I've seen him do it. If I could get Thomas here. Thomas would stop it. Make it stop. Make me stop. Make it stop.

I'll have to call him.

'Thomas, you have to come home now, I need you to come home. I can't do it. I will do it.'

'Come home.' …

'Now, Thomas, please.'

Not answering. Not listening.

They have him. So, it must be me, on my own.

I need quiet to think; it won't let me think. And without the light and the fizzing, my mind would be free to think. I must put it out, that's the only way. I must go in there and put it out. No other way. Put it out. Make it stop. Stop. Out. Blood will have blood. I know that from somewhere. I remember that. It's important. Blood will have blood. That's right. That's what I must do.

40

JENNY

Tommy had gone and taken Adele with him. He'd told Jenny not to worry and that they'd find Jack. He told her to stay put and call him if Jack came home.

She crawled backwards out of the cupboard under the stairs clutching a pair of Spider-Man wellington boots. Sitting back onto the hall floor, she let the boots rest in her lap. Jack must have worn these when he was about nine. Wasn't it simpler then? Or did every new phase feel like the hardest?

It was too hot to be clearing out cupboards. She had to do something. Wearing only shorts and a vest shirt, she was still too hot. When Jack was little, they'd get the paddling pool out on days like this and sit in it together, Jack naked and she in her underwear. Yogurt pot boats and bum-bump tsunami.

Jenny heard her mobile phone ringing. Where was it? Kitchen? No, front room. She scrambled to her feet and over the obstacle course of shoes, bags, boxes of who knew what and plastic tubes from the old hoover to reach the front room. She reached for the phone just as it went to voicemail. Bugger. She saw Tommy's name and number disappear from her screen. She punched the recall button. Engaged. She was about to punch it again when the phone started ringing.

'Is he home?'

'No. You haven't found him?'

'No. We're looking. I'm sorry. You must hate me.'

'Why would I hate you, Tommy?'

'Because it's my fault. If I'd been around more, he might not have got involved with these boys. If I'd handled things better, he might not have done a disappearing act. If I wasn't his dad and wasn't police, he'd not be in danger now.'

'Lots of ifs.' Jenny had a list of her own.

'I let you down, you and Jack.'

'You didn't let us down. You're here now, aren't you?'

'A lot of use that I am. I'm no use to anyone. I left you and Jack. Emma's losing it and I don't know if it was a mistake us having a baby and I don't know what to do. And I'm not doing my job.'

'I don't know about the rest of it, Tommy, but I'd say we kind of left each other. We'd have killed each other if we hadn't.'

Jenny detected the slightest of smiles in Tommy's response. 'Yeah, I suppose so.'

'So, what do we do now?'

'You stay put and let me know if you hear from him. I'll call if they find either Jack or Collinson.'

Jenny kicked the shoes and the other crap on the hall floor back into the cupboard. The plastic hoover tubes fought back. She slammed the door on them and left coils of them hanging out like massive entrails. She'd already called Rose, disguising her question about whether Jack was there inside an enquiry as to whether Rose wanted her to send someone round to look at the broken fence, like she used to hide vegetables in Jack's pasta. When he was little, those worries about whether he was eating his five a day, would grow up into one of those people who only ate white food, seemed so huge. Would he ever be able to say 'helicopter'? Would he learn to tie his shoelaces? Would he clean his teeth without being told? It had all seemed so important and, in fact, none of it mattered.

She had to do something, something more useful than cleaning cupboards. She'd call Jack's friends, or the parents of the kids that Jack was friends with at some point, anyway. It was all she had.

She opened up the contacts on her phone. There were a few names of mothers she remembered from primary school. Their kids had gone to different secondary schools and Jenny had been relieved to let the friendships with the families wither away. She wasn't good with mummies – their suspicions about her intentions towards their husbands, her being a single mother, had not helped. The other single mothers, on the other hand, had been desperate for her to join them on nights out clubbing and spa weekends, neither of which were really her thing.

Once Jack had gone to secondary school, she'd been happy to wave goodbye to all that school-gate bollocks. But now she wondered if she should have made more of an effort. Jack made his own social arrangements these days. There had been some boys who had come round. The more polite would mutter what might have been a hello before darting upstairs to Jack's room, but that was the extent of her contact with them. Sometimes she provided food. Mainly, she left them to it.

She must remember some of them. There was a lovely Asian lad called something beginning with R and an Adam. Something beginning with R had gone to the same primary as Jack. She hadn't known his mum, but Olivia's mum had known everyone, PTA and all that. She was a stripy. Mums were either stripies, after their Boden catalogue Breton-striped T-shirts, or pikeys.

She could ring Olivia's mum and ask if she knew Adam's mum; she had her number on her phone under O for Olivia. She used the home phone, just in case Jack or Tommy called on the mobile.

The conversation with Olivia's mum wasn't the easiest – Cheryl, Sherilee, easy mistake to make. However, although Sherilee didn't know 'R', she did think she knew Adam's mum, because his sister went to Brownies with Olivia's sister Grace.

Jenny couldn't believe that she'd stayed calm during the ridiculously inane conversation she'd had to endure to get Adam's mum's phone number. She had definitely been rude in the end, but hopefully she'd never need to speak to the woman again. The only thing that mattered was finding Jack.

So, Jenny called the number and spoke to Adam's mum, something beginning with T, Tami or Tania, maybe. Adam was friends with Jack, but he wasn't with him now. Adam was at home on his Xbox and had been all day. They had another mutual friend, Aidan (Jenny tried to remember if she had any memory of this name), but he was on holiday with his family.

How come Adam's mum knew so much? She'd been keen to have a chat about Jack, and Jack and Adam, and the new term and school uniform, and even suggested that they met for coffee one day. Jenny had been rude to her as well. That was how crap she was at this mothering thing. All these mums out there who knew each other, knew their children's friends, were all part of this lovely support network and all knew where their children were. And all of them would now know that she was a crap mother who didn't know where her son was and had to phone other people to find out contact details for her son's friends.

Where was Jack? Why didn't she know? Jack needed more care and attention, more discipline – Tommy was right – and now he was in who-knew-what trouble and there was nothing she could do.

Jenny tried Jack's phone. It was switched off. She tried not to imagine where it might be, why it might be switched off, why Jack wasn't answering.

Jenny had been pleased that Jack didn't seem to have any kind of serious girlfriend, given what had happened with her and

Tommy. Now, she wished he had. He might have brought a girl home and then she'd have talked to her, because girls talk more than boys, and she might have met her parents, and now Jack might be safely tucked away snogging, or whatever, and not out on the street or in a park where boys died. At least Tommy had his knife, but the other boy had a knife so would it be better if Jack had one, or worse?

Tommy rang again. He hadn't found Jack. He was still looking. He'd hoped she'd found out something. But she hadn't. Tommy had sounded scared. He was never scared. Apart from that moment when he'd first held Jack after he was born. He'd looked terrified then.

But not for long. He'd got the nurse to show him the right way to hold a baby and then he'd been forever telling her off – support his neck – one hand under his head and another under his bum – don't suffocate him – he'll slip off if you hold him like that. Jack was a wriggly baby. And bloody hell he'd screamed. Except when his dad carried him around, then he'd be quiet. A daddy's boy. Tommy was always so steady, so calm. Jack must have felt safe, known he was in safe hands. But now he'd slipped out of their hands; their boy was in danger.

If anything happened to Jack there would be nothing, there would be no reason for her to be. She wouldn't be able to be. She couldn't be a childless mother. She only had Jack. There was her and Jack. She couldn't exist without Jack. Nothing could happen to him.

Who would want to hurt Jack? Everyone liked him. He'd always been such a gentle child. At playgroup when some kid pinched his toy car or whacked him over the head with a wooden brick, he'd always looked at her with confusion – why had the child done this to him? What was he supposed to do? And how had she let it happen? She should never have let that happen.

But they were all just children. And they were still children now. But that boy in the park, he'd been a child too and maybe he had a mum who thought she was looking after him and now he was dead. He'd disappeared and he didn't come home, would never come home.

Stuff happening to kids was in the news all the time. All that testosterone out there, raging through young bodies, out there in streets where community didn't exist anymore, where there were closed doors, closed minds, closed eyes. Boys got caught up with fighting and knives, with no one to see them or stop them.

She'd always thought that was other sorts of boys, though, not her boy. Jack was a good boy, a kind boy. They didn't believe in violence as a solution to problems. He didn't even play the really bad shooting games on the computer, not the war ones. He understood that killing and violence was wrong.

But he had a knife. And the school said he was in a fight. With that boy who was dead. Could Jack really have changed that much, and her not have noticed?

Jenny decided that she didn't care what he'd done, she just wanted him home safe. And then she'd lock him in his room and never let him out again. She'd even send him to live with Tommy and that woman if it would keep him safe. Safe. Jack had to be safe. God, Jesus, Buddha, Shiva, the Goddess, the Elements of Earth, Water, Fire and Air, Jenny would believe and worship them all if they would just keep her boy safe and bring him home. She would be good. She would never have sex again. She would join the PTA and make cakes. She would dedicate herself to being a good mother, a better mother, just so long as she could have him back, safe.

Jenny had been pacing around the house. She'd rinsed a couple of mugs in the kitchen, straightened out the sofa where Tommy had sat earlier, stared at the empty bed in Jack's room. The whole house was airless and suffocating and empty. She decided to go outside. She had her phone clutched in her hand, alert to any tiny vibration. The phone was hot. Her hand was wet with sweat. She looked at the screen again. Nothing. Pulling the front door open, it snagged against a small wellington boot. The pressure behind her eyes told her she was going to cry.

But she wouldn't. She wouldn't cry. She'd water the garden, Jack's old job, and she'd be outside to see when Jack came sauntering down the road and up the garden path. She'd shout at him and make him help with the watering and she'd call Tommy and their boy would be safe.

41

EMMA

Suffer the children. Suffer the children. He wants them. He does. I don't. I can't have it here. Sometimes I think I can control it. Then I don't know. When it screams and cries and rages at me. When the air is full of the red raging and I can't think. Then I don't know. It's stronger than me. Look what it did. What should I do? What should I do? I need to do something.

Call Thomas again.

'Please. The screaming is too much for me and the fizzing, it's like wasps, and the red, the glow. Red. You haven't seen it, but it's there.' … 'You don't understand but you must trust me. You must come home.' … 'It is happening. It has been happening since the beginning. I couldn't make you see.' … 'I need to make it stop.' …

It's hot. It's hot outdoors and it's hot indoors. I can't breathe. Maybe that's making it worse, making the evil grow faster. It's blooming in the heat, opening, unfolding, multiplying, spreading. The red of its skin, that's it rising to the surface, pushing at the skin, pushing to get out and spread further. I've tried keeping it in but I can't. Who can I save? Who should I not? Once the evil has hold, there's nothing worth saving. Is there? But can I? Will Thomas understand?

42

JENNY

Jenny realised that she'd been watering one patch of grass for so long that a pool of water had formed and was now seeping into the front of her shoes. She couldn't stand around at home watering the garden while Jack was out there being hunted down by some psycho. She dropped the hose. She turned off the tap and reached into the house for her keys. She slammed the front door.

Walking up towards the park, Jenny scanned front gardens and doorways for signs of Jack or his bike. She saw a couple of lads about Jack's age on the pavement just ahead and caught up with them. 'Hey, do you know Jack O'Keefe?' Jack would be appalled if he could hear her.

One of the lads ignored her and carried on looking at his phone, but the other deigned to look at her. 'Why? What's he done?'

'Nothing, I just need to find him.'

The boy shook his head and looked away.

Jenny walked through the park. There were a few groups sitting out on the grass, some young kids playing kick-about with a football, a couple of women with prams sitting on a bench. She used to do that, take Jack out in his pram when he wouldn't settle, or when she decided that they both needed some fresh air, sit and stare at the trees, too exhausted to focus on anything else.

The gated playground was deserted, except for a lone policeman standing over by the area still marked with crime-scene tape. Beyond that was Tommy's fancy new house. Was the park view quite such an attractive feature now? It wasn't that she was jealous – who was she kidding? Of course she was jealous. Would all this be happening if she and Tommy had stayed together? It's what you were supposed to do – stay together for your children so that they could have two parents and a stable childhood. That Will kid had two parents, though, lived in a nicer house even than Tommy's new house. What about the lad that was killed? What did any of it matter as long as Jack was safe and she could hear him slam his bedroom door and see his sullen face again?

Mill Road was still a major tributary leading into the city, despite being barely wide enough for two lanes of traffic. The usual lunatic cyclists did battle with delivery vans and buses and stop-start cars. The traffic was as bad as ever and the air full of exhaust fumes, not that it seemed to bother the people sitting outside the various trendy cafés that had popped up between the charity shops and hairdressers recently. They seemed to be happily kidding themselves that they were enjoying the sunshine out on some continental boulevard.

Jenny noted that another curry restaurant had been turned into a café. How much coffee could people drink? Who had the time to be sitting around in these places? While they were paying out for shots of overpriced caffeine, down the alleys behind, kids were knocking down fences, passing around pills like sweets and threatening each other with knives.

They'd cleared the drunks and druggies from in front of the church by removing the benches. They must be taking their haul of methadone from the pharmacy and lager from the Co-op to enjoy elsewhere.

The bus stop opposite the Sally Army place used to be a favourite. Jenny wasn't going that far, not over the railway bridge. Mill Road bridge signalled the end of the last buffer district between the city and Romsey – it started at the lamp-post they called Reality Checkpoint in the middle of Parker's Piece, which marked the 'humorous' boundary between Town and Gown. The graffiti on the bridge was painted by local artists and reflected the rather optimistic view they had of local culture. 'Diverse' was just a fancy way of saying anyone not quite like the ruling classes who still roosted up around the colleges. Jack and his friends rarely went into the city centre.

There weren't many youngsters in evidence on Mill Road, so they must be hanging out somewhere else.

Jenny turned off and headed up towards Coleridge Park. It was bigger than the park near hers – and not the site of a recent murder – so maybe the teenagers had gone over there. They couldn't all be indoors on their technology, certainly Jack and Will Collinson were out somewhere.

It was the school holidays and the sun was still shining, so the park was busy. Mums and the young children were mostly camped out around the splash pad, neon swimsuits and multicoloured towels, skin turning a dangerous shade of pink, squeals and splashes.

Although there were a few little kids running around, the playground area was dominated by a group of teenagers, boys and girls, who were spilled out across the play equipment. A row of three girls sat smoking on the swings, idly pushing themselves back and forth. A couple were unselfconsciously snogging on a bench. A mixed group were flung across the different parts of the climbing frame like discarded laundry. Jenny was jealous of their languid boredom.

As Jenny approached the teenagers, a couple hid cigarettes

and a couple more didn't bother. One lad stared at Jenny, daring her to say something, so she spoke to him. 'Can I ask you a question?'

The boy looked at his mates, before attempting a drawl to say, 'It's a free world.'

A girl sitting at the top of the slide said, 'Not everywhere it isn't. What about Guantanamo?'

Jenny ignored her. 'Do any of you know Jack O'Keefe?'

A boy had walked up behind Jenny and said, 'You his mummy, are you? Has Jack been a naughty boy?'

Someone shouted, 'Naughty Jack!' and a few laughed. The Guantanamo girl said, 'Shut up, you idiots.' She addressed herself to Jenny, 'Is he in trouble?'

One of the idiots said, 'Will little Jack be getting a smacked bottom? Is he *grounded*?'

The girl told him to shut up and asked Jenny, 'Why do you want Jack?'

That sounded like she knew him. Jenny said, 'I'm his mum. He's wanted at home.'

Guantanamo studied Jenny, as if deciding if she was a grown-up she was willing to speak to. Finally, she said, 'We've not seen Jack today.'

'Thanks,' Jenny said. 'How about another lad you might know, Will Collinson? Do you know where he is?'

'We don't have anything to do with him.' It was clear that this was the end of the conversation as far as Guantanamo was concerned.

One of the boys attempted to blow smoke in Jenny's face and said, 'You looking to buy some stuff then, are you?'

Guantanamo gave loudmouth a shove. 'Shut up, you twat.'

Jenny made one final attempt. 'You've none of you seen Jack O'Keefe or Will Collinson today then?'

There were a few nos and a few shakes of heads. Jenny turned to leave.

Guantanamo girl said, 'What should we do if we do see them?'

'If you see Jack, ask him to come home, please. Tell him it's important but he's not in trouble.'

Jenny considered walking on over to the leisure park – Adele had said Jack had been there the night before – or she could head over the bridge into town. Youngsters hung out on Parker's Piece when the weather was good – at least that was in sight of the police station – or down on Midsummer Common. Jack could be anywhere. What chance did she have of finding him wandering the streets on her own when the police hadn't found him? And he could be home by now, raiding the fridge, laid out on the sofa with his filthy trainers still on. God, she hoped so.

Jenny was walking home when her phone rang. Not Jack but Tommy.

'What? Have you found him?'

'Not yet. But I know where he is.'

'Tell me. I'm on my way.' Jenny stopped walking and checked where she was, assessing how quickly she could get to different parts of the city, to wherever Jack was.

'It's not that simple.' Thomas broke off to speak to someone who was with him. His voice muffled.

'Is that Jack? Is he with you? Is he all right?'

'Jack called me. It turns out that he's been carrying out some kind of vigilante surveillance on Will Collinson.'

'What the hell?'

'I know, I know. I've told him and I'll tell him again. Right now he's watching some kind of meet-up and I need to get over there.'

'So what are you doing talking to me?'

'I'm going, Jen, I'm going. We're heading out now.'

Jenny heard scuffling and a door slam. 'Tell me where.'

'No. I can't do that.' He hesitated. 'Look, I need you to do something for me. Emma.'

'No. I'm sorry but I don't care about Emma. And she doesn't like me.'

'I know. But I can't be in two places at once. Something's up. She's been leaving messages, weird messages. I'd not picked them up because I was focused on Jack. And now she's not answering the phone.'

Jenny could hear that Thomas was in a moving car now, travelling at speed. Despite a voice in Jenny's head shouting *fuck Emma and fuck her bloody baby. Just go bring home my baby,* she said, 'Okay. Spit it out. What do you want me to do?'

'Can you go over to the house and see if everything is okay? Her phone is probably just out of charge but… something's not right. Please, Jen. I know I shouldn't ask. I've got to go now.'

'Okay.' The phone in her hand went dead. Thomas had gone, gone to find Jack. She didn't care about anything but Jack, but now she had to check on Emma. She switched directions, her phone in her hand so that she could pick it up as soon as Tommy called back.

Be okay, Jack, be okay, you idiot.

43

SANDRA

Sandra had always been fond of Mill Road Cemetery. It lay just off the main road but it was always quiet. You needed to know it was there, enclosed behind the grey-brick Victorian terraces just beyond the city centre, a secret space where you could walk and think with only the forgiving company of the long-dead. Were they forgiving? Certainly, they kept their judgements to themselves and that would suffice.

There were no new graves; no room. The stones here were all old, crumbling, fighting a losing battle with lichen and ivy – and the vandals, of course. Little buggers. Who did that? There were signs of their work everywhere: a headless angel, a broken cross, faded spray-paint scrawls. At least there wouldn't be many living relatives around to see their handiwork. There was the big cemetery out on the road to the airport now, although so many opted for cremation over burial these days. That was what she wanted. She didn't fancy rotting in the ground. People always said that they wanted a place, a stone, to visit. How many did, though, really?

There'd have to be a funeral for Callum, of course, once the police released his body. Like the one they'd had for Keith. All wrong. Not a gathering of old people for one of their own, not like how it should be. Parents grieving for their children. The young, shocked that life could be over so quickly. Children in black. Children should never wear black. Parents should never have to bury their children. How was Danielle going to cope with that?

A problem for another day. One day at a time, that was all she could cope with right now. One foot in front of the other. Keep going for Alfie. (She'd tell Danielle not to make him go to his brother's funeral.) She'd have to talk to Danielle soon. She needed to get a grip.

The hot weather of the past weeks had dried out the grass between the graves leaving it yellow-brown and dusty. It needed the rain that she'd heard forecast on the radio that morning. Nothing so far; just a heavy cloud cover that kept the day stuffy and colourless.

Sandra took her usual route, taking the main pathway to the centre of the cemetery before turning off onto the winding path that followed the walls around the edge. She headed for her favourite spot by the statue of the Virgin Mary.

Sandra wasn't religious; she didn't believe that anyone or anything was going to save her, or forgive her, and the life you had was all there was. Still, something about the statue appealed to her, the calm of it.

She'd been so busy, kept herself busy, looking after Alfie, sorting out the house, making constant cups of tea for the people coming in and out of the house, she'd not had time to think. It wasn't that she wanted to think now, but she needed to breathe, needed just a few minutes on her own. She'd said she was going to the shops.

She'd needed to pick up her prescription from the chemist. She'd dropped into the newsagents to pick up a comic for Alfie. She'd looked at the local paper. Nothing on the front page now. Just an article on the inside, a couple of paragraphs, a photo of the crime scene with the white tent and tape, no names. *Boy, 15, found dead in park.* Most of it had been about calls on the police to crack down on county lines operations in the city. Everyone knew that Callum's death was connected to drugs. They weren't wrong, of course.

Sandra stopped to pull away a spiked snake of bramble that had grabbed a-hold of her sleeve. As she did, she saw a movement on the path up ahead. She wasn't the only person to walk here; she often saw other walkers, people eating lunch on the benches beneath the yew trees, drinkers hopping over the back wall into the beer garden of The Cambridge Blue.

These looked like youngsters though, their heads shrouded in the hoodies they all loved. Now she remembered seeing a couple of teenagers lurking near the gate and a bike sprawled out at the head of the path she'd taken. She'd heard stories of people mugged in the cemetery but chosen to ignore them. You couldn't let things that happened to other people stop you getting on with your life. No point being reckless, though.

She looked behind her and listened beyond the birdsong for anything that sounded off. There were voices up ahead. If they were talking then they weren't lying in wait for her. She considered going back the way she'd come. No. She was just being silly. She carried on the way she'd been going, but she did walk a little faster, did reach into her pocket and take hold of her phone.

As she approached her statue, she saw that there was a knot of youngsters in the clearing where it stood. She hesitated. As she did, a flash of light in the corner of her eye made her blink. She and the group under the trees turned to see where it had come from. A boy, a teenager, maybe Callum's age, had stepped forward from the bushes with a mobile phone held out in front of him. He must've taken a picture with it and, in the shadows, the flash had been activated. For a moment, it was like the taking of the picture had frozen its subjects just as they were in that minute. Then there was a lurch of movement and a series of yells, swearing, threats.

Sandra stepped back so that she couldn't be seen but could still see what was happening. The boy with the camera disappeared back into the bushes and was followed by one of the group from the clearing, chasing. The rest shouted their encouragement. Sandra could hear the running feet out of sight, hear the snap and crash through the undergrowth, then the two boys emerged onto the path she'd just walked down and faced each other. Then she saw it. The chaser was holding a knife out in front of him, a kitchen knife, huge and threatening in the way it was pointed at the other boy.

'Fucking Jack. Fucking *grass*. Give it over.' The words were coarse, but the voice was well-spoken, clear and confident.

The boy with the phone shook his head and took a step back, pushing the phone into the pocket of his jeans.

'You can't get away, you know, Jack. Chuck over the phone and I'll give you a chance.' The boy gestured sharply with the knife and looked set to launch forward.

'Oi!' The sound was out of Sandra's mouth before she realised. As soon as it was, she knew that it was stupid. That boy with the phone might be able to get away, but she didn't have it in her to outrun a teenager. She almost laughed at the situation she'd put herself in. Well, maybe there was a God after all.

Then, as both boys turned their eyes towards her, the harsh alarm call of a magpie. The boy with the knife looked startled and then laughed. He lunged forwards, the knife in front of him. The other boys dodged to the side, just managing to avoid the blade. He was twisting away to start running when he was grabbed by his shirt and the knife flashed. Unbelievably, it sliced only air again as the boys fell onto the dusty path and scrabbled together. Sandra tried to keep track of where the knife was, terrified when she couldn't see it for even a second.

Then she became aware of movement among the watching

crowd of teenagers. A pounding of heavy feet and shouted orders from both ahead and behind made heads jerk and limbs scramble into action. Figures in black and yellow from all sides. Police. A dozen or more. Suddenly all around. Three of them in uniform with bulky body armour lunged towards the boys, who were still rolling and wrestling on the ground, and pulled them apart. One continued to struggle while the other hung limp in his rescuer's arms. The knife had now been dropped into the dirt. Sandra scanned for blood but couldn't see anything. She felt a hand on her shoulder and dragged her eyes away.

'Can you come with me, please. This way.'

She let herself be led away from the confrontation. She tried to look back but was taken around a corner. 'There were others,' she said. The group under the trees, how many had there been? She was trying to remember. Huddled together. Conspirators.

'It's okay. We got them.'

'The boy took a picture of them.'

'Did he? Well, that was very foolish of him. Are you together, you and the lad?'

'No, I was just out for a walk. On my own.'

'Okay, perhaps you can tell me everything you saw just now.'

Sandra nodded. 'I think–' Her heart was pounding in her chest and she had a horrible feeling that she might faint. Her head felt odd and her vision slurred. She focused on her hand, noticed the slight tremor, focused on the knuckle at the base of her first finger, a single point in focus. She was not the fainting type. She concentrated on breathing. 'I think I might need to sit down.'

'Do you feel unwell? Can you walk?'

Sandra nodded again. 'Just give me a minute.'

Sitting on one of the benches at the centre of the cemetery, Sandra told the policeman what she'd seen. He wrote down what she said and took her contact details. She wondered if he'd know who she was, but he didn't seem to. He thanked her and offered to have someone drive her home. She refused. She just wanted to be away. It was everywhere, these boys with their dirty dealings, with their knives. Like weeds. Everywhere.

'Was it drugs?' she asked.

'I can't say, madam.'

It was drugs. How many more of them were there? Where was safe? She caught sight of Alfie's comic in her bag. Spider-Man. Heroes and villains. At least you knew who would win. At least it was clear in that world which was which.

44

JENNY

Jenny walked up the short path to Tommy's front door. It was open, which was strange. She could see into the hall with its polished hardwood floor. She stood on the doorstep and shouted into the hall, 'Emma? Are you there?'

She wasn't sure how to announce herself – *it's Jenny, the mother of your husband's son, hello?*

There were no signs of life inside. She pushed the door open further and leaned in, looked down the corridor to the stairs, tried to detect any signs of movement in the rooms beyond. The house was silent. No radio. No baby crying. No signs of life at all. Jenny scanned the street and looked up at the windows. Nothing. She was going to have to go in. She'd told Tommy she'd check on Emma and she wasn't going to be able to do that standing on the doorstep on her own. 'Emma? Hello? It's Jenny...'

Jenny had only been inside Tommy's house once before, when she'd come to collect Jack for some reason. Dentist, maybe? Tommy usually collected Jack and brought him home. She assumed that Emma preferred it that way. Emma was never rude when the two of them met, but it wasn't comfortable – think ex-girlfriend but a million times worse.

It wasn't fair to hate Emma. It wasn't her fault that there was a before and that she was the before. Tommy was pre-loved but back on the shelf when Emma found him. She didn't take him away; he was already gone. It wasn't a furtive affair; it was a proper grown-up relationship between two free people who'd chosen to be together. And Tommy had married Em. Proper wedding. Not like the register office thing that they'd once been considering to try to placate Tommy's dad. Jenny had never thought that Tommy was into that stuff – frocks, speeches, church even. Emma had suggested that Jack could be a page boy. That was never going to happen. But it was a nice gesture. *Nice.* That was still the best interpretation Jenny was willing to put on it.

Jenny stood in the hall. Nice floor. She was inside now. She couldn't bring herself to shut the front door though.

She still couldn't hear any signs of life. Except now she was inside, she could hear something. Tommy still had that damn clock. Tick TOCK. Tick TOCK. She'd made him take it with him when he left.

Jenny was wearing trainers and they squeaked as she made towards the stairs. They were carpeted in a beautiful pale golden oatmeal stripe. Should she take her shoes off? She looked behind her for a clue. There was a pair of neat leather sandals by the door, set at right angles to the mat and skirting board. She should take her shoes off. Instead, she checked the soles to make sure that there was nothing there likely to leave a mark on the carpet. She wanted to be able to leave as quickly as possible, leaving zero trace, when she discovered that Emma was asleep or in the bath, or whatever else she was doing so silently.

She peered through to the back of the house. It looked empty. She listened but couldn't hear anything over the noise of the clock. She walked as softly as possible down the hall, which was mad because she didn't want to be caught looking like she was trying to creep in. She looked into the sophisticated sitting room and the open-plan area at the back, both decorated in Scandinavian shades of blue and white. Everything was spotless and as tidy as a show home. It could be a show home. Not that Jenny would want to live like that, and it would never stay like that with Jack around.

No, she wouldn't think about Jack. Tommy would look after Jack and she would look after Emma and Isabella until he was back.

Isabella. There was no sign that there was ever a baby in the house: no bottles, no pram, no toys, none of those muslin squares that you had everywhere to wipe up spit and milk and protect your clothes; no wet wipes either – though you shouldn't really use those, too many chemicals.

Back in the hall, Jenny looked up the stairs. She was going to have to go up. She stepped onto the first step. She'd try shouting again, in case Emma was asleep. 'Hello? Emma? It's Jenny. Tommy asked me to come.' Oh, no, she wasn't going to like that. Oh, fuck it. Louder. 'Are you there?'

Emma couldn't be up there or she would have answered. Maybe she'd just gone out; gone for a walk to cool off. She'd probably just been mad at Tommy and wanted to give him a fright. Jenny remembered how frustrating it had been being left at home with a crying baby. No crying baby here, though.

Perhaps she should just leave. Pull the door shut behind her and assume that Emma had gone out and left it open by mistake. On the other hand, she couldn't just walk away. Not without checking, or knowing that the baby was all right, Tommy's baby, the little girl she'd never had, would never have. No, she couldn't let herself be distracted by errant thoughts. Not now.

Too much silence. Too much creeping about. 'Emma? If you're there, I'm coming up.' Jenny ran up the stairs before she could change her mind.

On the landing, there was what looked like the door to a bathroom and beyond it an open door to, what? Another bedroom. The nursery now, she supposed. There was a closed door which must be to the master bedroom. Jenny wasn't going in there unless she really had to.

She walked down the hall and it was only when she was standing in the door to the nursery, that Jenny saw Emma. She was sitting in a nursing chair staring out of the window, not moving, barely blinking. She wasn't asleep, yet she didn't seem quite awake.

'Emma? Are you all right?'

No response. No response at all. Emma continued to stare. What was she looking at? Jenny stepped past Emma and looked out of the window. It overlooked the kids' playground. It overlooked where that boy had been killed. Why would Emma want to sit looking at that?

Jenny bent down to try to catch Emma's eye, but she looked straight through her. She turned and looked into the cot. It was empty.

'Emma, where's the baby? Where's Isabella?'

No response. In films, they slapped people when they were like this, but she couldn't slap Emma. (Although there had been so many times when she'd wanted to.) But where was the baby? Could she be with a friend? Tommy hadn't mentioned any friends. Neighbours? A babysitter? From what Tommy had said, this wasn't how Emma had been earlier. Had something happened?

Jenny touched Emma's arm. 'Can you just tell me where the baby is, Emma? Please.'

No response. None at all. Not even an acknowledgement that she'd been touched. Then she saw it.

Emma's hands were bunched up in her lap but now Jenny saw that she was holding something. A knife. A penknife, like the one Jack had had. Was it the same one? Had Tommy left it somewhere and she'd found it? What was she doing with it now?

Jenny took a step back. Her eyes went between the knife in

Emma's hands and the empty cot. She was out of her depth. She couldn't call Tommy, not while he was finding Jack, making sure he was safe. She had her phone in her hand and checked the screen again. No messages. He was bringing Jack home. She couldn't interrupt him. But she had to do something.

Rose. She'd call Rose. She'd know what to do. She'd always known what to do when Jenny lost it when Jack was little.

Jenny made the call. She hadn't needed to say much to Rose, just that she was at Tommy's house and needed help with Emma. 'There's something wrong, Rose, and I don't know what to do. And Tommy, he can't come right now.'

Rose didn't ask any questions, just said that she was on her way.

Jenny had asked, 'Will you be okay? Walking over, I mean.'

Rose had tutted. 'I'm not too old to walk yet, young lady. I'm on my way.'

Jenny hadn't realised how little she'd been breathing. She tried to take a deep breath and found that only half of her lungs were functioning and it hurt to try to breathe any more deeply. Her chest was tight. Her diaphragm had stopped moving. She needed to take deep breaths, yoga breaths. She sat down on the floor opposite Emma, who still sat unmoving in the chair, and crossed her legs over each other. The floor was a lot cleaner than at her house, and fancier, no expense spared.

Jenny waited for Rose and breathed. Every time her thoughts strayed to Jack or the missing baby or the knife or what Tommy was doing, she dragged them back. Rose was coming and she would know what to do.

Rose was always in charge, even when Tommy's dad was alive, even if it didn't look like it from the outside. Tommy's dad, Old Tom, was just a big bully. He'd never have coped if Rose had gone first.

When Jenny had told her mum that she was pregnant, she'd lost her rag completely and told her she had to get rid of it. She told Jenny that she was ruining her life, but really it was her own life she was worried about; she was ashamed, worried about what people would think if she had a daughter up the duff at sixteen. Although it was a point of principle for Jenny that she'd had Jack when she was seventeen, because that sounded better than sixteen.

Rose was different. It wasn't what she'd hoped for her son, but she got on with it. For once, she stood between Tommy and his dad and made it clear that the baby was happening and they would be happy about it. Old Tom had grunted and gone along with it. He'd come to see Jack when he was born. He'd said, 'A boy. Good.' Then he'd gone back to reading his paper. Rose got on with doing all the stuff you hoped your mum would do – cooking meals, washing blood-stained knickers, cleaning the flat, taking Jack for walks so Jenny and Tommy could sleep. She was amazing.

Jenny had thought that Rose would do all those things for Emma. She'd asked once about Emma's mum and been told 'she wasn't around'. But Rose said that Emma didn't want her, didn't want her near the baby even. It'd clearly broken her heart. They'd talked about it, trying to find a reason that wasn't too hurtful or mean, and agreed that, with Emma being older and having a career, she'd probably wanted to be in charge more. Although, secretly, Jenny had concluded that Emma was a selfish bitch.

Jenny hadn't felt in charge of anything when Jack was born. Having babies seemed like a totally out of control thing, something you just had to go with, like giving in to the ocean. She'd never have made it without Rose.

Rose was older now, but Jenny was confident that she would still know what to do. Jenny would just keep breathing and watch Emma – and the knife – and wait for the phone and stay calm until Rose arrived and Tommy called.

45

EMMA

Clean and white. Sun-bleached, sterile white. And still. And quiet. So lovely and quiet. Turned the sound down. Mute. Rest now. Between the sheets. Let it bleed out. Put it away. Out. And then there is nothing, lovely, lovely nothing. Shhhhh. Inside the bubble. Shhhh.

46

JENNY

Jenny had moved and was sitting on the floor of the hall upstairs, in the relative cool. She hadn't been able to bear looking at Emma – and that knife – any longer. Although it was late, the heat of the day was clinging in the air. No breeze. No air at all. But here at least, away from the windows, the light was dim. She waited in the silence.

She'd left the front door open and heard Rose's soft steps on the floorboards as she came in.

'Jenny, love? Where are you?'

Jenny answered in a half whisper. 'Up here. Hold on a minute.' At the top of the stairs, she said, 'Thanks Rose. For coming.' She was so relieved not to be alone with–

'Phew.' Rose waved a hand in front of her face in an attempt to fan herself. 'I'm not as young as I used to be and it's too bloody hot out there. Now, what's up?'

'Can you come up?'

Rose looked at the stairs. 'Just about.' Then she began a slow ascent.

Jenny willed her to hurry up.

'Getting there, love. Where's Emma? It's very quiet.'

Jenny knew that what Rose really meant was *where's the baby?* She started talking as Rose's foot hit the top step. 'There's something wrong with Emma, she won't look at me and she's not said a word, she's just staring, not at anything, just staring. And Tommy said she left some odd messages and I know she's been a bit, you know, off. She's not saying anything at all now. She's just staring. And the baby isn't here. And she's got a knife in her hands.'

Only one bit of the information seemed to have stuck. 'What do you mean, the baby isn't here?'

'I've looked. Not in the cot in the nursery and not anywhere else that I can see. It's too quiet, Rose. You don't think...?'

Jenny had heard stories about mothers not coping. There'd been a woman a few doors down when Jack was little. They hadn't been friends. Jenny hadn't had time for friends. They'd seen the police cars out there one morning – assumed it was a domestic or some early morning raid – and then seen it in the paper. She'd hung herself from the bannisters. Husband had been on night shift. Came home to find her hanging there and the baby crying. Jenny saw the house go up for rent. Heard the husband had moved away, back to his mother's. Now Emma was here, like this, but not hanging from anything at least. But where was the baby? She'd heard other stories but didn't want to think about those now.

Rose followed Jenny down the hall to the nursery, peering through doorways, obviously hoping to see the baby, or signs of the baby or to hear something. Jenny had already looked. Every room in the house was spotless. The bathroom looked like one of those cleaning adverts.

Jenny tried her best to keep the house reasonably clean and tidy but nothing like this – and Emma had a small baby to look after. It wasn't until months after Jack was born that she and Tommy could walk across a room without stepping over or round the rash of baby mess. She could imagine that Tommy's habits might have improved, but this level of tidiness wasn't his work. It wasn't normal. How was Emma looking after the baby and keeping the house like this?

Rose must have been thinking the same thing. 'It doesn't seem right, does it? It's too–'

'Clean.'

'It doesn't feel right.' Rose was shaking her head. 'Tommy should've said something.'

'Perhaps he didn't realise. He is a man. And Emma has always been a bit of a neat freak.'

'Not like this, though. How has she managed to keep it like this and look after the baby? And where is she? Isabella? Could she be with Tommy?'

'No.' It wouldn't make Rose feel any better if she explained how she could be so sure.

'I should've known something was wrong. When they were round the house…'

Jenny remembered what she'd witnessed from behind the van opposite Rose's. How much had Rose heard? She was so loyal. Even now she didn't want to share the things that Emma had said.

'Of course, Emma doesn't have a mum around. No mum. No sisters. She never seemed to have many girlfriends.' Rose shook her head. 'I should've made more of an effort, been more understanding. So busy having my nose put out of joint. I'll never forgive myself if–'

'It's not your fault, Rose.'

'It is. I always thought – hoped – that you and Tommy–'

'It was never going to happen.'

'She's so not like us. She's so clever and… different. But I should've tried harder, should've seen that she wasn't coping.' They were outside the nursery. 'Is she in here?'

Jenny nodded and followed Rose into the room. Emma was still sat in the low chair by the window. The sky was darkening outside. A storm, they'd said on the weather. Jenny had put the light on and Emma was pale, bone white in the bright light.

'Emma, love, it's Rose. Are you all right?'

There was no response, not even a flicker. Even now, Jenny half expected Emma to shout at them, tell them to get out.

Rose was bending down to speak gently to Emma, like she was a child. 'Sweetheart, can you just tell me where Isabella is?' Still nothing. Rose looked down at Emma's hands – the knife was still there.

Should she pull Rose away? Jenny was unsure. Emma hadn't moved. But she could do anything in this state. But, surely, not that.

Rose waved a hand in front of Emma's face. No reaction.

Jenny stayed watching from the doorway. Rose spoke to her, while not looking away from Emma. 'Has she been like this since you arrived?'

'Yes.'

'But she rang Tommy? Why didn't he come home? Where is he?'

'Jack's in trouble. He had to go.'

Rose seemed to take a moment to absorb this latest blow before speaking again to Emma, 'Okay, love, now why don't we get this thing out of the way.' Gently she pulled Emma's fingers apart. She didn't resist and Rose took the knife. The blade was out. She pushed the blade down so it disappeared into the hilt. She crossed the room to put the knife on the chest of drawers, out of reach, and then went back. 'Emma, love, can you tell me where the baby is? Please Emma, I'd just like to check that she's okay. I won't take her anywhere, I promise.'

She stroked Emma's leg. There was no response to her words or touch. The only signs of life in Emma were a slight rise and fall in her chest and a slow blinking of her eyes.

Rose turned and spoke to Jenny. 'Right. We need a doctor for Emma. And we need to look for Isabella.'

Jenny didn't move. A doctor? What kind of doctor? An appointment or an ambulance? What about the knife? And where were they supposed to look for the baby? Where would she have left Jack? With Rose. That was where she'd always gone when it got too much. But what if she hadn't had Rose?

'Jenny, you're going to have to help me out. I'm going to stay here with Emma and you're going to call the doctor. I saw a documentary about women who got a really bad sort of post-natal depression – not like the baby blues – psychosis they called it and it was much worse, but people got better, as long as they didn't do anything really stupid.'

They both looked over to where Rose had laid the knife.

'If you can't get through to the doctor, call 999. I think we need the mental health people. Then we'll look for the baby. If we can't find her, we'll call the police. Okay?'

Jenny nodded.

'Right, off you go. You've got a mobile phone, haven't you, love? Tommy keeps important numbers in the drawer in the kitchen.'

Jenny could feel Rose willing her on her way. She did as she was told. She went downstairs and opened all the drawers in the kitchen until she found the one with the list of numbers. Then she called the doctor – an out-of-hours message. So then she called 999. She'd never done that before and was surprised that the operator sounded just like they did on the telly. She answered that she needed an ambulance and tried to explain how Emma was behaving, only remembering a couple of sentences in that she'd had a baby. She didn't mention that the baby was missing. It seemed, maybe, disloyal, or maybe, just too frightening to put into words to a stranger. Rose had said they'd look for her. They'd find her. Wouldn't they? She'd be all right. She had to be. Tommy wouldn't be able to bear it if…

As she disconnected the call to the ambulance service, her

phone rang. She thought it would be them again, that she'd forgotten to tell them something.

Instead, it was Jack. 'Before you freak out, Mum, I'm fine.'

'Where are you? What happened? What–?'

'Later. Dad's here. He wants to talk to you.'

Jenny knew she should tell Tommy what was happening but, completely selfishly, she wanted to know about Jack. 'He says he's all right. Is he?'

'He is. He's a bloody idiot but he's all right.'

'What happened?'

'Long story short. He gave us the opportunity to pick up Will Collinson and some of his associates with enough evidence to hold them – definitely on drugs charges and quite possibly for the murder of Callum Peterson. It's a bit of a reach at the moment, but my boss is confident that it'll pan out.'

'Was Jack in danger?'

'He could've been. I'll let him tell you the whole story. He's at the station. You'll need to go down there before they can take his statement.'

'Right.' She needed to tell him about the baby and how she'd found Emma, what she'd found her holding. 'Look, Tommy, you need to come home.'

'You're at the house. What's going on?'

'I don't think Emma's well, Tommy. We've called the doctor.' She couldn't bring herself to say *ambulance*.

'Why? What's happened?'

'She's not hurt. It looks like, maybe, she's had some kind of breakdown. Come home.'

'Leave Jack?'

'If you have to. We can't find Isabella.'

That was enough for him to know. He ended the call.

Jenny ran back up the stairs to Rose, no longer worried about creeping around.

Rose's eyes were wide as Jenny rushed into the quiet nursery.

'He's okay. Jack's okay. I'm sorry. I know I shouldn't smile, but Jack's okay. That was him.'

Rose smiled. 'That's great, love. Did you get the doctor?'

'I called an ambulance. I told them what she was like and they're sending some special team. And I told Tommy to come home.'

'Did he understand that it was important?'

'Yes. I told him we couldn't find Isabella. He put the phone down.'

Rose was leaning against the windowsill. Now she knew that help was coming, that Tommy was coming, she seemed to have deflated; she looked very old. Of course, she was old. Jenny felt terrible for having loaded everything on her when she should've taken responsibility herself. 'Rose, I think you should sit down.'

'I need to look for Isabella.'

'I'll look for Isabella. You stay and watch over Emma. If she is in here somewhere, she won't want her to be left with me.'

Jenny went to find a chair for Rose. It felt so wrong going into Tommy and Emma's bedroom. She made herself push open the door and looked again for any signs that Isabella might be there, sleeping on the floor maybe. Nothing. Every surface clear and shining, the bed-cover pulled tight and smooth.

She found a chair and carried it back to the nursery.

Rose still protested. 'She's my granddaughter. I can't sit here doing nothing. Who knows…'

'You're not doing nothing. We can't leave her here alone.' Jenny nodded towards Emma. She couldn't stop her eyes straying to the drawers where the knife had been placed, couldn't stop her mind going to places she didn't want it to go. 'She's probably left the baby with a friend or a neighbour.'

'If anything's happened to the poor mite–'

'She'll be fine. You stay here and wait for the ambulance people – or Tommy, whoever gets here first. I'll start with the neighbours.'

Rose slumped into the chair. 'And if–'

'We'll find her.'

Jenny went slowly down the stairs. The fear was rising in her belly like sick, acid at the back of her throat. Not really expecting to find anything, she checked the downstairs rooms and the garden again. There was no sign of the baby. No trace that a baby had ever lived in the house. No pram even.

Maybe that meant that Isabella was in it somewhere out of the house. If the baby was in the house, wouldn't she have cried by now? So, now to check with the neighbours.

She couldn't check with Tommy whether they knew their neighbours, so she'd knock anyway. Tommy might have a better idea as to where Emma might take Isabella, but she couldn't wait around until he got back. She'd go look.

She left the front door open, so that the ambulance people could get in, and went out into the stuffy late afternoon. A rumble of thunder made her look up at the sky. Not raining yet.

47

EMMA

They can't reach me. Moths against the glass, wings like powdered silk. I'm inside, safe in the clean, clear air. Shhh. Don't listen. Don't hear. Shhh. No more. No more. I'm swimming away. Floating away.

48

JENNY

Jenny walked slowly down the long garden behind the house, not just looking for the pram but for anything. It was a relief to be out of the house.

She'd spoken only a few words to Jack. He'd obviously been told to ring her and say that he was all right. She'd never have accepted anything but the sound of his voice. Now she wanted to know what had been going on and wanted eyes on her son, wanted to see for herself that he was as all right as he said he was. But for now she had to do this. For Tommy.

She started down the street knocking on doors. Some houses there was no one in. At one there was no answer, but she could see that lights were on, so she kept knocking till they answered.

Most people were obviously dealing with dinner or relaxing in front of the television. A couple were ready with a speech about not giving to charity or buying things at the door, the door shutting even as it opened a crack to deliver the dismissal. They weren't pleased to have someone, a stranger, coming to their door and disturbing them, inserting themselves into their lives. It wasn't the Cambridge way; people didn't drop in on each other in Cambridge.

When Jenny explained why she was calling, reactions ranged from embarrassment to concern to disinterest. A couple of closer neighbours said that they'd maybe seen Emma on the street once or twice with a pram, though not that day. A couple more said that they'd never seen the people in the last house by the park at all. No one knew Emma and certainly no one had any idea where the baby might be. Carrying on knocking on doors further down the street was going to be a waste of time.

As Jenny was walking back to the house, she felt what she was sure was a drop of rain. That was all – a single drop, like she'd imagined it. She heard a car coming too fast up the street behind her. She didn't need to look, knew it would be Tommy.

It seemed he was out of the car even before it stopped. He was walking towards her and talking at the same time.

'Where's Emma? What's happened?'

'She's upstairs with Rose.'

He looked confused.

'I called her and I asked her to come over. I wasn't sure–'

He interrupted. 'Where's Isabella?'

'We don't know.'

'What do you mean? You don't know? She isn't with Emma?'

'No, and she isn't in the house.'

'So where–'

'We looked for her. She's not here; not in the house and not in the garden. I've talked to the neighbours. They don't know anything. Does Emma have anyone she might have left her with?'

'There's no one.'

'Someone from NCT classes, a friend?'

'No. We dropped out. Well, I never went really. Work. And then Emma said she didn't want to.'

'What about friends?'

'She's got a couple of old college friends she's in touch with, but they live miles away.'

'Doesn't Emma have friends at work?'

'At the lab? Yes, of course. But it's mainly men. Emma always got on better with men.'

Something of her thoughts must have shown on her face because he added, 'Not like that. Just as friends.'

'Okay, Tommy. Just if you can think of anyone, you need to ring them. If we don't find the baby soon, you'll need to call the police.'

Tommy gave her a look. 'I am the bloody police.'

'I know, but you know what I mean. We might need some help to look for her.'

Tommy was scanning around as though he might see Isabella. He must be feeling what she'd been feeling earlier looking for Jack. Except Isabella was a tiny baby. They were utterly helpless at that age. That soft spot on their heads... 'Tommy, I've not seen anything that makes it look like anything bad has happened, but...'

'But what, Jenny?'

'Emma had a knife.'

'What?'

'She was kind of sitting there and she was holding a knife. Rose took it off her and it's upstairs.'

'What sort of knife?'

'It looked a bit like Jack's knife, but I couldn't remember exactly what that looked like.'

'It's not Jack's.' Tommy hesitated. 'I had it in the house and then I put it in the boot of the car. I keep it locked and I have the only key.' He waved the car key. 'Did you see any–'

He couldn't say it but she knew what he was asking. 'I didn't see anything bad, Tommy. Just the knife and Emma. She wouldn't tell us where the baby was, she wouldn't say anything. She wouldn't even look at us.' Jenny hesitated but then had to ask. 'Did you not see any signs?'

'Signs? No. Yes. I don't know. Maybe. Now this... But I never thought anything like this... Where's the knife now, Jenny?'

'Rose took it off her and put it on the chest of drawers, upstairs, in the nursery. Should I have done something with it?'

'No. I'll deal with it.'

Jenny could see the struggle going on in his head. How could he decide where to go, decide between his wife and his missing child? Jenny wanted to touch him, to pull him into her arms and tell him that everything would be all right. But she couldn't know that. And couldn't do that, even if she did. 'Go up and check on Emma and your mum. An ambulance is on its way.'

'An ambulance?' A look of fear in his eyes.

'For Emma. We thought it the best thing.'

'You think it's that bad?'

What could she say? She nodded. 'Sorry. Hopefully they'll get here soon. I'll carry on looking for Isabella. Emma probably just took her out in the pram and left her somewhere. Do you remember when I left Jack outside the post office?'

'Yes, but you didn't even get all the way home before you realised.'

'I ran all the way back and Jack was right where I'd left him. No one had even noticed but I felt such a terrible mother.' She paused. 'I don't think Emma's been well for a bit, Tommy.'

He nodded. He looked up towards the house but didn't move. 'Where will you go?'

'I'll take a look round the park. She might've taken her for a walk and then got distracted, or not felt so good. If I don't–'

'Yeah, okay. You look there. I'll see if I can get anything from Emma.'

Jenny nodded, though she doubted very much if Tommy was going to have any more luck getting Emma to speak than she or Rose had. Maybe though. Hopefully. She watched him disappear inside the house before turning away.

The sky overhead was a dark black-grey and the rumblings of thunder were coming closer. The park was almost empty. Jenny scanned the main pathways but saw no sign of a pram. Would

Rose have seen it when she walked across earlier? Probably not. She wouldn't have been looking. She'd have been focused on getting to the house to find out what was wrong.

Jenny started walking round the main path, making herself stay calm, walk steadily and look properly, peering behind the benches and out towards the fence. There was a woman sitting on one of the benches, older, not as old as Rose; she looked worn down – like she was carrying the weight of the world, Rose would say – and you could see that she'd been crying. Jenny's eyes were still scanning for the pram, her mind still on the baby, but she couldn't ignore the woman. 'Do you need anything? You all right?'

The woman looked startled and then, seeing Jenny, nodded. 'Yeah, I'm fine. You know, life.'

'I do,' Jenny said. 'You haven't seen a pram, have you?'

The woman shook her head. 'Sorry, no.'

Having completed the circuit of the main green, Jenny pushed open the gate into the playground. She had to push the weighted gate hard to make it move and it clanged shut behind her. She used to bring Jack here when he was little. He never wanted to leave. Used to hold onto the bars of the climbing frame till she prised his fingers away.

There was something sad-looking about an empty playground. A couple of fat drops of rain fell onto the ground at her feet. Then she saw it, just poking out of some bushes at the edge of the playground. The back of a pram. Jenny had never seen Isabella's pram, but this looked like the kind of thing that Tommy and Emma would buy – black and red, huge wheels and a tiny space for the baby, hooks and baskets and cup holders.

Her heart hammered in her chest as she pulled the pram free of the undergrowth. She looked inside. Empty. It couldn't be a coincidence. This had to be the pram, so where was Isabella?

The pram hadn't been outside long. There was a clean white blanket, pushed aside as though it still held the imprint of a tiny baby, of Tommy's daughter, little Isabella. But where was she? Not in the pram. So where?

Then she heard it. A cry like a cat, high and insistent, coming from within the bushes, under – she now realised – the wall of Tommy's house. Of course, she couldn't know that it was Isabella. She did, though. There were still pieces of police tape attached to the bushes. This was where... Jenny couldn't think about that now; she held back branches and pushed through towards the sound of crying.

And there she was, lying on the ground in amongst the dirt and dead leaves. Tiny, angry, scared, hungry, screaming. Jenny bent to pick her up. So light. You forgot so quickly how very small babies were. Nowadays, Jenny looked at Jack – looked up at him – and couldn't imagine how she'd carried him inside her body.

Knowing she now had someone's attention, the baby screamed louder. She gulped for breath between new wails of misery and fury.

'Oh, I know, I know.'

Carrying the baby against her shoulder, Jenny pushed back through to the path. Coming out into the open, she felt raindrops on her face and held a hand over the baby's head. 'Can't have you getting wet on top of everything else, can we? Come on, let's go find your daddy.'

As Jenny pushed the pram through the gate with one hand, while still holding Isabella against her shoulder with the other, Tommy was coming out of the house. He stopped.

'Is she...?'

'She's fine. Hungry, I think, and pretty grumpy, but I think she's come through her adventure pretty well.'

Tommy took Isabella from Jenny and kissed the top of her head, just like he used to kiss Jack. 'Where did you find her?'

Jenny pushed the pram ahead of him towards the house. 'Don't worry about that for now.'

Emma had left her baby lying outside on the ground, hidden from view, right where that poor boy had died. How could she do that? What had she been thinking? How could Jenny tell Tommy that? How could she put that picture in his head? So she said, 'How's Emma? No sign of the ambulance yet?'

He was about to speak when they became aware that the street ahead was lit up by blue flashing lights.

Now they waited for the paramedics to arrive, for whatever was going to happen next to begin.

Without taking his eyes off the lights as they came closer and then switched off, Tommy said, 'You'll need to go to the police station. They'll want to interview Jack about what he knows and what he saw.'

'Is he in trouble?'

'Only with me. But they'll ask him about everything. They'll keep me away from the case now. You need to go. I don't like to think of him down there on his own. Can you call a taxi?' He pulled out his wallet from his back pocket and handed Jenny a twenty-pound note.

Jenny had long ago got over any concerns about taking money from Tommy. She became conscious that she was just wearing a vest top – fine for gardening but not too great for a police station. 'Can I borrow a shirt or something?'

'Upstairs in the wardrobe. Take whatever you need.' He put his hand to his face and squeezed his fingers into his eyes. 'She's so tiny, Jenny. What if…?'

'But it didn't happen. Now you need to look after Emma.'

'You'll–'

'I'll be fine. I'll look after Jack. You look after Emma and your daughter. Message me, yes?'

He nodded.

49

SANDRA

Sandra was reading Alfie his Spider-Man comic for the umpteenth time as he sat on the sofa next to her. He'd heard it so many times that he was mouthing the words and vibrating with anticipation long before Spider-Man swung in to rescue the innocent and take down the villain. Lee had gone into work and Danielle was still in bed.

The night before, Sandra had tried talking to Danielle.

First, she'd cooked sausages and mash for their tea. Lee had watched something on the television while Alfie played with his toy cars on and around him. Danielle had been upstairs in bed and Sandra had gone up to see her. 'Tea's nearly ready, love.'

Danielle had barely turned her pillow-creased face in acknowledgement.

'Come on, love, why don't you get up and come down to eat. It's sausages and mash. You like that.'

'I'm not hungry.'

'You've got to eat. We could all sit up at the table together.' Sandra was forever telling Danielle that Alfie should be eating his meals at the table, properly with a knife and fork, rather than having plates on his lap on the sofa and using his fingers.

236

As usual, the table had been lost under unopened mail, carrier bags, toys and, embedded in the mess, dirty plates and crushed beer cans. Sandra had cleared it and wiped down the sticky surface, laid out the knives and forks like she'd been doing since she was a child.

It was her job. Keith was younger – and a boy. *Lay the table,* her mum would say and she'd go to the drawer in the kitchen and fetch the cutlery, carry it through to the other room and lay out a place for each of them, knives on the right and forks on the left, her mum and dad at the heads of the table, she and Keith on the longer sides, opposite, where they could kick each other under the table. It'd seemed lopsided after he'd gone, looking over at the empty chair, the wall and the sideboard with the fruit bowl and the crystal vase.

She'd made the kids, Danielle and her brother, eat at the table when they were little. She'd given up trying to get either of them to actually lay the table; it'd been easier to do it herself.

In the dim light of the sun through drawn curtains, Danielle had pulled the covers back up so they half covered her face.

Sandra had stood over her and tried again. 'Just get up for a bit. Have something to eat and then, if you want, you can come back up. You should spend some time with Alfie.'

'I can't.'

Sandra was using her best jolly mum voice. Really, she wanted to shake her daughter. She may have lost Callum, but she'd lost him long ago, him and Shaun. There was still little Alfie. He needed her. She could still be a mother to him. Bad things happened but you couldn't lie around feeling sorry for yourself. Not when you had children. She tried again. 'You'll feel better if you get up and splash a bit of water on your face. Put a brush through your hair and come down and eat with your husband and son.'

'I said I can't.'

Sandra had sat on the bed and tried to pull the covers away

from her daughter's face. 'Danielle, love, I know this is hard, but you can't stay like this. You have to look after Alfie.'

'He's all right with you.'

'I'm not his mum. He needs his mum.'

'He doesn't need me. I can't do it.' Danielle had rolled over to face the wall.

Sandra had rested a hand on the heap of duvet. What could she say? Should she tell her daughter that none of what had happened was her fault, that she was a good mother? Should she tell her that it *was* her fault and that she needed to do better? Should she tell her that she had to look after her son because she was going to be all he had? How much truth should she tell? How much truth could either of them bear?

She'd said none of it. She'd patted the lump in the bed that was her daughter, stood up and gone back downstairs. She'd handed Lee a plate of food to eat in front of the television and made Alfie come to the table and eat with her, saying nothing, though, when he speared his pieces of sausage with his fork and refused to touch the knife she'd put out for him.

She'd spent the night again, sleeping in the bed next to Alfie's, Callum's old bed. At some point in the night, Alfie had come and crawled in next to her, curling his hot little body into the curve of her own. She hadn't slept after that, not that she'd slept much before. She'd listened to his snuffly breaths, to the rain now falling outside, growing stiff from lying so still and cramped, but unwilling to move and risk disturbing his sleep.

Of course, she and Alfie had been first awake and first up. Now, from her seat on the sofa, Sandra saw the car arrive, saw them get out and walk up the path. Two of them, an older man she hadn't seen before and Janice, the family liaison girl. Sandra waited for them to ring the doorbell before hauling herself up to let them in.

Janice introduced the man. 'Sandra, this is Detective Sergeant Miller. Can we come in?'

Were they back to talk to her this time? That would mean she wouldn't have to disturb Danielle and Lee. She led them through to the front room. Alfie barely looked up. He'd got used to people coming and going and even police uniforms didn't impress him anymore. *Scooby-Doo* was his world for now.

Sandra didn't have the energy to engage in pleasantries, so she just waited for them to get on with it.

Janice spoke again. 'We've come to update you on some developments in the case, Sandra. Could we talk to you all together? Are Dani and Lee here?' The girl had a really annoying sing-song voice. She looked round as though Danielle and Lee were tiny creatures who could be hiding somewhere in the cramped room. Where did she think they were going to be at this time of day? Down the back of the sofa? Tenerife?

'They're in bed. Can it wait? Or will I do?'

'We wanted to talk to you all before you heard through any other means. I'm sorry we've disturbed you so early.'

She didn't look sorry.

'Would you mind? You know? Disturbing Dani and Lee for us?'

The old guy tried to smile in what he must think was a friendly and encouraging way. It didn't suit him. He looked like he'd had a few too many late nights from the drooping skin under his eyes. He didn't have much hair and she noticed that he had very long ears. She'd put a bet on them being hairy if you got up close. What could they think was so important to drag themselves out at this time? They'd been coming and going for days. She'd had to get more teabags and she'd been out for milk twice.

Sandra left Janice and the old guy sitting with Alfie, watching cartoon teenagers chase criminals disguised as monsters, and went to shake Danielle and Lee out of their bed. They weren't happy and it took a while. Danielle was still dosed to her eyeballs. Lee was awake straightaway but not keen on getting up. She held out his dressing gown to him. 'Come on; it'll be all right. They just want to tell us something.'

Sandra was in the kitchen making tea – more tea – when she heard them clumping down the stairs. Janice had offered to help – tea-making was clearly a vital part of family liaison training – but Sandra preferred to be doing something and preferred her own company. Her hands made tea on automatic pilot and she could let her mind disconnect. It was how she'd done most things over the last couple of days. Just going through the motions. The incident in the cemetery had shaken her but the fug had soon descended again.

Janice was sitting pertly on the edge of the armchair and Deputy Dawg had stood up to leave the sofa free for Danielle and Lee. Lee looked in Sandra's direction, but she indicated that he should sit. She'd rather stand than keep sitting down and getting up again. She handed out tea and they all waited.

Janice said, like she was presenting a prize at a dog show, 'I'm pleased to tell you that we've arrested someone on suspicion of murdering Callum.'

Deputy Dawg coughed and Janice continued, 'Obviously it's early days and we're still building the case – no formal charges have been made, but we're confident – we thought that you'd like to know.'

Danielle still looked bleary, the blanket of tranquillisers muffling any effect this news might have. Lee was wide awake, though. 'Who've you arrested?'

Janice looked to Deputy Dawg and then said, 'Yesterday, as part of a raid on a drugs operation, we arrested a number of suspects including William Collinson and we have accumulated convincing evidence that he was responsible for the death of your son.'

Was that what Sandra had witnessed in the cemetery? She tried to remember the boy on the path with the knife. Smart-looking, nice haircut – short, not long like so many of them insisted on wearing it. Was that Will Collinson? Why did they think that he killed Callum?

Lee put his arm round Danielle; she'd started to cry. 'You're sure it's him. You've got evidence?'

Sandra interrupted. 'I'm sure they've still got things to work out, Lee – is that right?'

Janice nodded and explained some of what would be happening next. She sounded so bloody perky, full of such confidence. They thought they'd done their bit. Just a job and they'd got it done. Would they all be down the pub tonight congratulating themselves? And what about the boy they'd arrested? Where would he be? There had to be a difference between how they treated someone arrested for drugs compared with murder, actually killing someone.

Sandra struggled to concentrate on what was being said. The arrest was a shock. A child, not a very nice child by the sounds of it, but still a child, like Callum. Sandra wondered what Will Collinson was like, what his parents were like, how he'd come to get himself into so much trouble.

Sandra watched Danielle and Lee; looked over at the useless police officers. If only this could really be the end of it. Danielle was going to have to come off the tranquillisers soon and start trying to cope without them. She couldn't put it off for too long. Alfie was going to need his mum.

Sandra was tired and her back was killing her, a sharp ache grinding deeper and deeper into her muscles and chewing at her belly. She'd like to go back to sitting in the armchair with her mug of tea while Alfie sat at her feet watching *Scooby-Doo*. Just for a bit.

50

JENNY

Jenny poked the last of a pile of washing into the machine. Tommy's shirt that she'd borrowed the night before. Was it only a few hours before that she'd been standing with him outside his house with the baby missing, Emma in that weird state, Jack at the police station – bloody idiot child getting himself involved in who knew what. One crime-busting hero in the family was more than enough.

She'd been getting in the taxi when the paramedics came down with Emma, leading her like she was sleepwalking. It'd started raining by then, loudly, heavily. Tommy and Rose had been standing inside, watching from the front doorway, as the paramedics tried to shield Emma's head and avoid the quickly forming puddles on the pavement as they took her out to the ambulance. Tommy had looked stricken. Rose had been cradling the baby and talking to her. What would they do now?

Jenny pictured the knife lying where they'd put it. What if there was blood on it? What would it mean if there was? What would Tommy do? He could clean it, get rid of it. He'd know how. He wouldn't though. She knew he wouldn't.

As the taxi had driven off ahead of the ambulance, Jenny's

thoughts had been on Jack. She needn't have worried; he was fine. The police – thank God – had told him what an idiot he was but still thanked him for doing the right thing. It might be the right thing from their point of view, but it wasn't the right thing from her point of view, from his mother's point of view. The right thing was never taking any risks, staying out of anything that might be dangerous, being at home, with her, for, well, forever.

Jenny had sat with him while he gave a statement. He'd been following Will Collinson – she'd say again, bloody idiot – and had phoned in to the police when he saw the meet-up coming together in the cemetery. He'd taken a photo of them.

When he recounted how the Collinson lad had chased him and pulled a knife on him, the fight, Jenny hadn't been sure whether she needed to be sick or slap him round the head. She couldn't let herself think about what might have happened if the police hadn't turned up.

She banged the door of the washing machine shut and stabbed the button to make it start. After the rain of the night before, the skies were clear again, so she'd be able to hang it out – and get Tommy's shirt ready to give back to him. It didn't seem right for it to be in the house, be in her washing basket. She liked the feel of it, though. Wearing it had made her feel like he was there with her, a bit, like they were together, Jack's mum and dad, like they used to be. Silly of her. She'd taken it off as soon as they got home, dropped it in the washing basket and then taken it out and put it on top of the closed lid.

She'd thought the storm might clear the air, bring the heatwave to an end, but it was already hot again. At least the downpour would save some lawns – and her some watering. She pushed open the kitchen window and went to open the ones at the front, get a bit of through-air going.

She saw Tommy as he drove up and pushed himself out of the car. He looked bloody awful. When had he gone so grey? He stood looking at the house but hadn't seen her. He looked as though he might cry. But that could never happen.

When she opened the door, the first thing he said was, 'Where's Jack?'

She said nothing about the absence of social niceties. 'Still in bed. Sleeping off yesterday's adventures.'

He nodded.

'Do you want to come in?' She assumed that the answer was *yes* and let him follow her through to the kitchen.

As she turned to offer him tea, he slid down the wall until he was sitting on the kitchen floor.

He rested his head on his knees. 'It's all my fault, Jen. All of it. I didn't see. How could I not see?'

'Neither of us knew what Jack was up to.'

'Yeah, but I should've seen it. He should've been able to come to me about it. Instead, he thought I wouldn't believe him. Christ Almighty, Jen, he thought I thought he could've killed someone.'

'You didn't think that. Not really.'

'Didn't I? I don't know anything anymore. He had a knife. He'd been in trouble at school, fighting with the boy... But, still, what kind of father does that make me? How could I suspect Jack?' He raked a hand through his hair leaving it in messy tufts.

'Even good boys can get themselves into trouble with the right help. You must see that all the time. At work.'

Tommy tipped his head back against the wall. 'You trusted him, though, didn't you?'

There was no right way to answer that question, so she decided not to try. 'It was okay, though, wasn't it? It didn't have anything to do with Jack.'

'No. Except he did know about the drug dealing, about the lad they arrested yesterday, and he didn't tell me because he didn't think I'd believe him. And because of that he put himself in danger. He could've ended up like the lad in the park.' He banged his head against the wall.

'But he didn't, though, did he? He's fine.'

'He is now.'

'That's okay, then, isn't it?' Jenny looked down at Tommy slumped on the floor and wished there was something she could do to make him feel better, stop him beating himself up. 'Look, I'm bloody furious with him and I might have to make his life a little miserable for a while, but Jack really is fine. I think, in a way, he wanted to make you proud of him.'

'And that nearly got him killed. He should just *know* that I'm proud of him.'

'So you can tell him. If he ever deigns to get out of bed.'

Tommy rested his head down onto his knees again. 'It's all such a mess. I've been getting up, going to work, and all the time the people who needed protecting, looking out for, were my own family. I'm a detective and I couldn't see what was going on right under my nose.'

'Jack's fine.'

'And what about Emma? And Isabella?' He was chewing his nails again.

'Did Emma say why she left the baby out there?'

Tommy laughed, a sound totally without mirth. 'Emma hasn't told anybody anything. She hasn't spoken. Not a word.'

Jenny wasn't sure what to say, so she said nothing.

'She's in the hospital. They've sedated her, told me to leave them to get her settled. Whatever that means. Postpartum psychosis is what they're calling it.'

'I'm so sorry. I've read about it. It's awful, but people do get better. It's the hormones. They seriously fuck with your head.' She couldn't look down at him any longer. She sat down on the floor opposite him. The floor was filthy and the grown-up world of kitchen gadgets and food and crockery cupboards loomed above. It felt safer down there, and cooler. She leant back against the cupboards, fixing her back to their solidness to stop herself reaching out, crawling over to take him in her arms and holding him like she used to when a night shift had left him broken; when his dad died; when they finally acknowledged that they just couldn't stay together any longer.

'How did I not see it happening, Jen? Psychosis. Emma. She's the least mad person I've ever known. I just thought she was tired. I'm such an idiot.'

So, he'd be okay if someone told him *she* was mad? The spark of new annoyance with him made her feel better, safer.

Tommy shook his head. 'That's not all, though.' He hesitated, like he wasn't sure he could say any more.

Jenny waited.

'Everyone assumed that it was kids – or kids and drugs. We looked at the boy's family – the father, the brother and the stepfather.'

Jenny nodded. Could families really be that bad that they'd kill one of their own? There'd been some bad arguments in her house, she and Tommy had thrown some stuff in their time, and she'd had some very unpleasant fantasies about Emma. But murder?

Tommy continued his monologue. 'Everyone had an alibi. We looked at his friends and I actually thought Jack–'

'We've been over that; you don't need to worry about that anymore. I thought you said they'd arrested Will Collinson?'

'We did. They did. He and Callum were friends. But they fell out. And there was that girl involved.'

'Adele.'

'Yes. But Adele and Callum broke up before she got together with Will and he didn't seem the type to fight over a girl.'

'Maybe. You punched David Baker over me once.'

'But I loved you and he was out of order.'

He had loved her. Back then. They'd loved each other. And David Baker had been well out of order. He'd cornered her in the corridor on the way to the loo at The Portland Arms and tried to stick his tongue down her throat.

Tommy was still talking, as much to himself as to her. 'I don't think it's to do with fights over a girl. Business is more likely. Money. Callum was selling drugs and so was Will.'

'That would make sense.'

'Yes, but Will wasn't taking drugs and his business was doing well. Callum was small fry compared to the thing Collinson had going. So, what would be the motive for murder?'

'An accident?'

'But there was no reason for Will to be in the park with Callum. They hadn't been hanging out together since school finished. I just don't think it's him. I suppose it could be someone we haven't found yet, or...'

'Or what, Tommy? What are you not saying?'

'You saw the knife.' Tommy lifted his head and looked across at her.

'The one Emma had?'

He nodded.

'You can't think...'

'It's not like Emma's about to explain anything. She's not speaking. Is she still even in there? There was a dead body outside our door and she's got a knife with blood on it – and she's clearly not in her right mind. And I have no idea when it started, why it started, what the hell happened.'

Jenny didn't know what to say.

'It's not just what I think anymore. I took it into the station last night, had to tell them where you found it, what's happened to Emma. They think it was the knife that killed the lad in the park.'

'That's insane. Why would they think that?'

'There was blood on it. It's his.'

'You can't know that.'

'Unfortunately, I can.' Thomas hesitated before continuing. 'I shouldn't know, but a mate–'

'What does that mean? They can't think Emma–'

'They can. And she's not in a state to tell them anything different.'

'But isn't Will Collinson still under arrest?'

'Yes. But the evidence for his involvement in the murder is circumstantial. They hadn't found any physical evidence. And now they've got this knife. I've sent Mum home to hers with the baby. Forensics have been in the house. They found shoes, Emma's shoes, with blood on them.'

Jenny tried to keep the horror out of her voice. 'Blood? Not–'

'They don't know yet. The lab'll be working on it. But, yeah, I think that's what they'll find. It was his blood on the knife. The boy's blood. Emma's fingerprints.'

'There'll be some explanation, Tommy. There has to be. It happened right outside your door, didn't it?'

'Yes. Exactly. And I know Emma went out that night. For a walk, she said. But–'

'Emma couldn't do anything like that.' Jenny couldn't help remembering how she'd found Emma, sitting in the nursery, her face, the knife.

'I would've said that. But you saw how she was and now – looking back – too bloody late – I can see that she's been acting odd over the past few days. Something was wrong.'

Jenny remembered the scene outside Rose's house and, again, the look on Emma's face. She'd hated the woman for so long, but this couldn't be true. To kill someone? To stab a random teenager in the park? She couldn't have done that. Could she?

She'd read stories about women with postpartum psychosis, the delusions, the things they'd thought were real, the things some of them had done. No. Hardly any of the women were actually violent. What reason would Emma have, even if her mind was disturbed, to stab a child? Because that was what he was, a child, Jack's age. How would Tommy come back from something like that?

Tommy looked like he might cry again. 'It's my fault. I don't know what to do. What will I do if–'

Jenny couldn't help herself. She reached across and laid a hand on his leg. She hadn't touched him for years; again, she couldn't help remembering the time when touching was as natural between them as breathing.

Tommy didn't acknowledge her hand and she pulled it back, the space between them feeling too great to keep stretching across. She felt the tears pricking behind her eyes.

No. She couldn't do this. Sending psychic thanks to her yoga teacher, Jenny rose to her feet and channelled Rose at her most pull-your-socks-up-and-get-on-with-it. 'There's no point thinking about ifs. The first thing to do is get up off my mucky kitchen floor.'

Tommy turned a puzzled look on her.

'Yep, up you get.'

He struggled up and she was a little disappointed that he hadn't witnessed how much more easily she'd returned to standing. They were the same age, after all.

'You don't know what happened and I'm guessing that they're not going to be letting you anywhere near the case.'

He nodded.

'So all you can do is look after your daughter and your wife.' It still hurt to say those words. *Daughter. Wife.*

She seemed to be having the right effect on him. He ran his fingers across his hair to flatten it and straightened his shoulders. 'You're right–'

She hadn't heard those words very often.

'–I need to get a grip.'

'What will you do first?'

'Go up to the hospital and see Emma.' He glanced up at the ceiling. 'I wanted to see Jack, though.'

'Jack can wait.' Tommy was about to protest but she interrupted him. 'I'll explain what's happened to Emma – just how she's ill, for now. He'll understand. I'll make sure he knows that you came to see him, that you wanted to see him.'

'Will you tell him that I'm sorry?'

'I will but you can talk to him properly another time. You need to talk to each other.'

'I know. I'm sor–'

'Not now, Tommy. Jack is safe – thank God – and he's not leaving my sight for a while, so he'll be here when you can talk.'

'You're a good mum, Jen.'

'And you're a good dad. We're none of us perfect, though. We'll just keep muddling along. I think Jack has actually turned out rather well, so we must both of us have done something right.'

Finally, Tommy smiled. 'The lads at the station were saying how great he was.'

'Well, there you go. If Cambridgeshire Constabulary think he's okay, who are we to argue?'

Tommy brushed at the back of his trousers. 'That floor is pretty disgusting actually.'

'Cheeky bastard.'

Jenny saw him to the front door. 'Let me know when you know anything, yeah?'

Tommy nodded. 'And tell Jack–'

'I'm not telling him that you love him. That's your job.' Of course that was exactly what she would tell him, exactly what she'd always told him. *I love you. Your dad loves you.*

Jenny watched Tommy walk down the path and get back into his car. She still loved him. Always had. Always would. Because he was the father of her son. Because he was Tommy O'Keefe: best-looking boy in her year, funny, clever, cocky, infuriating, good kisser, the first boy she'd slept with, the first man she'd loved. The only man she'd ever been in love with.

51

SANDRA

After the police had left, it'd been on the radio about the arrests. They weren't giving out any names yet. There'd been journalists ringing the house for a comment all day. She'd got fed up in the end and turned the phone off. They'd get fed up and find something else to talk about soon enough.

Lee was full of it. Now he felt safe, felt the weight of suspicion lifted from him. Now he could rage. 'Little bastards. Fucking druggies–'

Sandra had widened her eyes and indicated Alfie.

'He's not listening. You could tell him he was going to Disneyland when he's watching that, and he wouldn't hear you.' He pointed at the television where some teenagers in multicoloured costumes were taking on a giant, city-crushing robot.

'Are we going to Disneyland?' Alfie looked up at them from his place on the floor, far too close to the screen.

'No, love. Can you sit back in the chair. You'll hurt your eyes sitting right up near the television.'

Lee had carried on his rant about drug pushers and users and how the police should do more and how at least the bastard who killed Callum would be locked up, how they should throw away the key.

Sandra stopped listening and got on with making tea. She'd made a casserole for Lee and Danielle and was doing some fish fingers for Alfie. She wasn't hungry. She was never hungry anymore.

She persuaded Alfie to eat at the table, put a knife and fork in his hand and showed him how to cut up his fish fingers and use the knife to push the baked beans onto his fork.

She'd left Lee and Danielle to help themselves to the casserole. She needed to be out of the house. Her legs had taken her to the park. She walked around the path and pushed through the heavy gate into the children's playground. It was quiet. Teatime, bathtime, bedtime for the little ones. And too early for the older ones. Apart from some breakages in the shrubs and some extra trampling of the grass, all signs that anything had happened were gone now; no police tape, no warnings. Like nothing had happened. Except it had.

It was pleasantly warm, more comfortable than it had been over the past couple of weeks. End of August. It would be September soon and the weather would start to change and it'd be freezing and Christmas before they knew it. Christmas and then New Year and Easter and onwards. Time went so quickly. It seemed just yesterday that Callum had been born, Shaun, Danielle... where had all that time gone?

She wasn't that old – not even sixty. She'd thought she'd have so much longer. Her mum had been in her late seventies when she died, and she'd been a miserable woman who didn't even like life. Maybe that'd been losing Keith. Was that how it would be for Danielle? She had Alfie, though. Sandra's mum had only had Sandra left, and she'd never been enough. Just a girl.

Sandra liked life. All the stuff that had happened, she'd never been one to give up on living.

Everything had happened so quickly. She'd been expecting to

hear that her biopsy and scans were positive for cancer. That's what had killed her mum and the speed with which they'd rushed it all through had told her that they thought something was seriously wrong. She hadn't been expecting the word 'terminal' though. She'd imagined a fight, chemo, sickness, pain, operations, but not death.

In ten years, maybe, five even, but not so quickly. She'd thought she'd have time. They'd said they could maybe buy her a little more – with treatments that would have meant being alive but not living. She'd opted for quality over quantity. Maybe that'd been wrong. Too late now. No point crying over spilt milk. Though, to be honest, she felt like she could blub right now.

The pain was bad, sometimes worse than others, and she was getting a lot more tired. Maybe it would help if she could sleep. They'd given her pills and they would give her more, as and when she needed them. What she couldn't bear was the ticking clock in her head, counting down the remaining days, hours, minutes that she had left. Bugger it. Why now when she'd realised all the things she'd done wrong and all the time she'd wasted and how much there was to make up for? If only she'd done something sooner.

Sometimes she looked at little Alfie and she wanted to wrap him in her arms and run away with him to somewhere safe, but she couldn't because there was no running from what was coming for her and she couldn't stay to keep him safe. She'd done what she could for him. Didn't make it right, though.

There was a man with a pram sitting on the bench. Men did that these days, pushed prams, looked after their babies. As she walked closer, she recognised something about him, his shape, the solidity of it. She hadn't seen him like this, though. He was looking down at the baby but looked up as she approached. Catching her eye, he nodded, looked a little uncomfortable. He must have seen her frown.

'You probably don't recognise me.'

Suddenly she did. 'I do. The policeman. You were the first one who came, who told us about Callum. Irish-sounding name. O'Keefe. Sorry, I can't remember your proper title.'

'It doesn't matter. I'm off duty.' He indicated the pram and the small baby inside, weeks rather than months old. 'How you doing? Sorry, silly question.'

'We're okay.' How was anyone supposed to know what to say? 'They came and told us that someone had been arrested.'

He shuffled his feet and looked down at the baby before answering. 'Yes, that's right.'

'They didn't tell us much else.'

'They'll tell you more when they can.'

'It won't be you?'

'No.'

He looked like he was going to say more and Sandra waited, but he seemed to change his mind. 'Do *you* think he did it? The lad they've arrested?'

'It's not up to me to say. I can't talk to you about the case.' He leant into the pram to tuck in the thin blanket covering his baby. 'I'm on leave right now.'

The pink flowers on the blanket said *girl*. How many years since Danielle had looked like that? 'The lad was dealing drugs?' she said.

'Yes. He was definitely doing that.'

'But not a murderer?'

He hesitated.

'What's her name?' Sandra nodded towards the pram.

'Isabella.' He smiled. He looked handsome when he smiled.

'Pretty name.'

'Yes, it is, isn't it?'

'She's quiet.'

'She is now, but she isn't always like this. I think she likes the fresh air.'

Sandra tilted her face up to the setting sun and closed her

eyes. 'It's cooler after last night's rain.' She watched as he placed a hand on his daughter's belly, so gentle he was barely touching her.

When the policeman spoke again, it made Sandra jump. She'd been lost, way down deep in a tunnel of thoughts.

'I think my wife tried to kill our baby last night.'

Sandra twisted round to look at him. She turned too quickly and winced.

He saw her and looked concerned. 'I'm sorry, I shouldn't have said that. Are you all right? Do you want to sit down?' He moved along the bench to leave more room for her.

Sandra smiled and nodded. She sat down. 'Where's your wife now?'

'She's in hospital. I'm sorry. I really shouldn't have said anything.'

'It's all right; sometimes you just need to tell someone. What happened?'

'They're saying that it's postpartum psychosis. It must have been building for a while and I didn't see it. Who knows what she could've done.'

'Having children is hard. It's hard when they're babies and when they're teenagers and when they're grown up and when they have their own kids. No one really talks about just how hard it is. You want everything for them, you want to be the best mum – or dad – you can be, but at the same time, it's hard.'

'But you've been a good mum,' he said. 'Look how you've been there for Danielle, and I've seen how you look after little Alfie.'

'I wasn't always there for Danielle, or her kids.'

'I'm sure you did your best.'

'No, I didn't. Maybe if I had, Shaun and Callum wouldn't have turned out how they did.'

'You can't know that.'

'No, but I wanted to make sure things went differently for little Alfie. He has a chance.'

'Every chance. He has people in his life who clearly love him. And he's got you.'

'I wasn't going to let Shaun or Callum corrupt him. I paid Shaun to stay away, you know?'

'Did you? He's broken his bail conditions, so he'll probably end up back in prison.'

'Good.' Sandra flicked a look at the policeman's face to see what judgement was there. His face seemed passive. He was watching his daughter, that's what you did when they were babies – you watched them breathe and you thought that was as scary as it was going to get.

He didn't turn his head, but he spoke. 'How was Callum going to corrupt Alfie?'

'He had him passing on his drugs. He wouldn't have stopped there. He'd have dragged him into the whole mess with him.' She paused and he waited for her to carry on. 'We were arguing about it – me and Callum. Lee heard us and there was a row, a big row. Callum stormed off and Lee went after him.'

'Did he find him?'

'No. I knew that's what you'd think. Lee might look a bit rough around the edges, but he wouldn't hurt anyone. I found him. I found Callum.'

'You did?' He sounded curious but not shocked.

'I just wanted to talk to him. Make him see that he needed to leave Alfie out of it. When I found him, he walked away from me into the bushes. He was laughing. I knew he'd taken something and I should've let him be.'

Sandra remembered how Callum's eyes had looked, how he'd been fidgeting on the spot, the laughter. *About time the little runt made himself useful. No one's gonna stop a little kid, are they? Too fucking perfect.* She'd just wanted to make him understand that it couldn't go on.

She'd forgotten that anyone else was there until the

policeman spoke again. 'You didn't, though. You didn't let him be?'

'No. I followed him.'

It'd been like when she played hide and seek with Alfie. Pushing through the bushes to find him hunched against the wall, vibrating with the thrill of it all, loving being hidden, loving being found. Callum, though, he hadn't expected her to follow him and was angry. *What you want? Just fuck off and leave me alone. Go back to your precious Alfieeee.*

'It made him angry. He wasn't himself; wasn't in control. I should've realised.'

It had taken her a moment, in the dark, to realise, to see it in his hand.

'He had a knife. I don't think he meant to use it. I think, now I think, that he was just showing off. That's what they do, isn't it? These boys. They carry knives because they think it makes them big and then, and then people get hurt.'

The baby was grizzling and the policeman jiggled the pram.

'I told him to give it to me; the knife.'

He'd laughed and waved it at her, waved it in her face. You couldn't let kids behave like that, let them think they had the upper hand, especially boys. Boys who threatened women grew up into men who did worse.

'I grabbed his wrist to try to make him drop it. I don't know how it happened.'

She couldn't say it.

'What happened, Sandra?'

His voice sounded so calm, kind even. She didn't deserve anyone being kind to her.

'He looked so surprised, not in pain, just surprised. I wasn't sure what had happened at first. I should've helped him, called for help. Instead, I walked away. I left my own grandson to bleed to death on his own. When I came out of the bushes, I saw a woman with a pram coming through the gate across the other side of the playground. I dropped the knife and walked away. I don't know what I thought was going to happen. He'd be found? That woman would find him and call for help?'

'And when that didn't happen? When he didn't come home?'

'I suppose I knew. What good would it do to tell anyone? I had to look after Alfie, look after Danielle, protect Lee. I could be more use with them. It wasn't like I could bring Callum back. I couldn't save him any more than I could Shaun.' Or Keith.

'Why are you telling me this now?' The baby's grizzles were turning to cries and her father lifted her out of the pram to rest against his shoulder. He'd have to move soon to soothe her or feed her or something. That was the thing with children, they always needed something. You think when they grow up that'll change. It doesn't.

'They've arrested the wrong person. I didn't think you'd arrest someone else.'

'What did you think would happen?'

'I thought you'd let it go. That you wouldn't find anyone and then...' She shrugged. 'I thought we'd lost enough; Danielle had lost enough. I thought it wouldn't matter. People knowing who did it wasn't going to bring Callum back.' She paused. 'I did love him, you know.'

She looked at the man beside her and he nodded.

'That Will Collinson boy,' she said. 'Whatever he did, he's not a murderer.' She looked at the baby lying tiny against her father's shoulder. 'What'll happen now? Will you tell them?'

'It would be better if you did it.'

'I'm not sure I can.'

'Do you want me to?' he said.

'Yes.' Sandra looked out to the spot in the bushes where her grandson had died and lay in the dark all night. He'd been afraid of the dark when he was little. 'Can you give me an hour to talk to Danielle?'

'I can do that.'

The baby's cries were full throated and angry now. Sandra turned and reached out to run the back of her finger down her soft cheek. 'I think you need to take this little one home for her tea.'

'I think you're right.' The man slid the baby back into the pram and stood. 'I'm sorry for your troubles, Sandra. I'll give you an hour before I call in what you've told me.'

Sandra nodded and watched the man walk away. It was time. She needed to tell Danielle everything. More pain. She wished she could save her daughter from the pain.

52

JENNY

J enny was standing in the doorway while Rose went through the drawers in the nursery looking for something for Isabella to wear. She was more comfortable in the house than when she'd first come in, but it still felt strange being there, being in Tommy's house that was his with someone else. It was a lovely house, far nicer than her council house with paper-thin walls and a tendency to mould. She would definitely want more colour on the walls, though – more colour everywhere.

The cleaning obsession had been part of the psychosis, but Jenny had always found Emma a little sterile. She'd put it down to her being a scientist and a bit posh, and a cold-hearted bitch, that too, of course. Even after everything that had happened, seeing Emma so clearly unwell, it was hard to remember not to dislike her, a lot.

Jenny had accepted that she was never going to be okay with Tommy being with someone else. Just because they couldn't live together, didn't mean that she could bear him being with anyone else. Tommy and Jenny forever – they'd scratched it into the bark of one of the trees on Parker's Piece. And thus it would live forever, like *Fame.*

Tommy had been round every day over the past week, talking to Jack – well, exchanging monosyllables while they played computer games together – and staying to drink tea and talk to her.

He'd asked her to come over and check on Rose while he was at the hospital. Rose insisted that she was perfectly capable of looking after her grandchild however long Tommy needed to be away, but he worried. It was all he did now. Worry. The lines on his forehead seemed to be becoming permanent gouges. So many times she'd had to stop herself reaching out to smooth them, reaching out to pull his fingers from his mouth and stop him biting his nails raw, reaching out to pull him back to her.

The baby was lying on the changing table, naked but for a clean nappy.

'I've asked Tommy to go shopping. All the poor mite has to wear is these white babygros and vests. Nothing but white. I don't know–' Rose caught herself and stopped talking. Then she pulled something from the back of the drawer with a hah of triumph that made Isabella take her eyes off her toes for a moment and look over at her grandmother. 'I gave her this.' Rose was holding up a cotton dress covered with tiny pink flowers. 'Look, it's got matching knickers. Isn't it adorable?'

It looked like something the royal family would dress their children in some time in the 1940s. Not Jenny's taste at all. She smiled though. 'Very pretty.' Was this the kind of thing that normal, non-mad Emma would like for her child? Or was this an outfit that was always destined to be shoved at the back of a drawer and forgotten about?

Jenny had had some of those. Firstly, everyone seemed to buy newborn stuff, that babies grew out of in, literally, a couple of weeks – after which no one bought anything, and you ended up scrabbling around the charity shops of Mill Road to find stuff that was stain-free and didn't look like it'd been washed to death. And secondly, who thought it was a good idea to buy first-time parents baby clothes that did up with anything but poppers up the front?

Rose was now deftly manoeuvring Isabella into the dress, taking the opportunity to kiss her and tell her how beautiful she was.

Rose tickled the baby on her belly. 'I always hoped I'd have a little girl. Not instead of Tommy, of course. But I'd have liked another. I always wondered if Tom would have got on better with a girl.'

'Tommy and his dad did clash at times.'

'Oh, they did. But Tom did love Tommy. I wouldn't want you to think—'

'No. I know. And Tommy loved his dad. They just clashed horns. Like Jack and Tommy do.'

'They're all right now, though, aren't they? After…?'

'They've largely called a truce. Mainly by not talking about it. What happened.'

Rose lifted Isabella from the table and rested her against her shoulder. 'Tommy feels terrible. About it all. He blames himself.'

'I know. But it's not his fault.'

'I've told him that.' She hesitated and then added, 'I don't like to ask him about it – didn't someone come forward and admit to murdering that boy?'

'Yes. It was all to do with family in the end.' Tommy had come round to tell her what had happened, how the grandmother of the murdered boy had admitted to killing him.

Jenny tried to imagine Rose doing something like that, to Jack. It was impossible to imagine. But things happened to people, to families, and it did things to them. When she remembered how frightened she'd been when Jack was missing, when she thought he was in danger. What would she have been capable of? Hopefully she'd never have to find out.

Patting the baby's flowery bum, Rose said, 'So, they think Emma found the knife, found the body. I can't imagine–'

'It's what they think, but she's still not said anything about it. The police are hoping she'll be able to tell them more when she's better.' That's what Tommy had told her, though neither he nor anyone else knew how long it would be until Emma was 'better', or what 'better' would look like. No one knew what had been going on in Emma's head, but they'd seen what it had made her do – and how she'd ended up.

Rose carried the baby over to the window and lifted her to see out at the cloud-splattered blue sky and the parched park below. After the rainstorms, the dry weather had returned and Jenny was back lugging watering cans and waving hosepipes around thirsty gardens. The grass in the park was yellow-brown. It was hard to believe that it could recover, that it could ever be green again. It would be, though. The big kids would be back in school and the little ones would get their playground back to themselves, at least until nightfall.

'Do you think that's maybe what sent her funny?' Rose spoke as much to the clouds as to Jenny. 'You know? Seeing the boy? Like that?'

'I don't think that's how psychosis works.'

'When I think about how she left little Isa, where she left her...'

'She wasn't in her right mind, Rose.'

Tommy was up at the hospital now. They were arranging for Emma to go to a specialist unit. They'd take the baby in and rebuild their relationship. It didn't seem fair on Tommy that he'd be separated from his daughter – Tommy or Rose, who was clearly loving the opportunity to step into the breach and get to know her granddaughter.

Rose's thoughts must have been following Jenny's. 'Tommy said it could take months. Emma and the baby could be away at that place for months.'

'He'll be able to visit.'

'Yes.'

Rose was silent. Jenny knew what she was thinking. Tommy would be able to visit, but she wouldn't. She'd be separated from her grandchild again. She wanted to say but you'll still have Jack, have us, but she knew that wasn't it, wasn't enough.

Rose was still looking out of the window. 'You know, love, being a mother means always being on the edge of heartbreak. We'd fight packs of hungry wolves for them, sacrifice anything, but, in the end, it's them, our kids, who hurt us most – and maybe we do the same to them. Family. Trapped together like ferrets in a bag.'

THE END

AUTHOR'S NOTE

This story features a character affected by postpartum psychosis. This is a very real condition, but this is fiction, I do not profess to be an expert and I am not suggesting that my depiction of the condition represents the experience of all. Postpartum psychosis is a severe mental illness experienced by over 1,400 women each year in the UK. It begins suddenly following childbirth and symptoms include hallucinations and delusions, often with mania, depression or confusion. It is very frightening for women and their families – but most women make a full recovery with the support of healthcare professionals. If you or someone you know is affected by postpartum psychosis there is help available from GPs, midwives or health visitors. You can learn more at www.app-network.org

ACKNOWLEDGEMENTS

For making this story into a book, I'm grateful to Betsy Reavley and her team at Bloodhound, especially my editor Clare Law whose attention and insight helped make the book better. Tracey Seagrove was correcting my tenses back when the novel first began and grew me a whole new eagle-eyed reader, in the form of Poppy Seagrove, who corrected them again at the end. The shortlisting in the Good Housekeeping Crime Novel Competition helped me believe in this story and some words of wisdom from Lisa Milton at the Primadonna Festival gave me the kick to do one final re-write. My National Centre for Writing Springboard gang provided me with support, comradeship and positive energy when I was ready to give in – all the times I was ready to give in. The writers from my Cambridge Community Arts classes have inspired me with their creative energy and commitment to writing – I hope you'll get to read their stories one day. I'm grateful for the company and sisterhood of all the strong women in my life. I wish the original of those women, my nan, Dot, was here to see a book with my name on the cover – and to know her grandson, for whom, doubtless, she would have fought dragons. Thanks to Ben and Soo for not being horrified when they discovered that I'd made their house into a murder scene. And, finally, all my love and gratitude to Adrian for his love and patience and belief in me (and for bringing me tea every morning), and to Alexander for making me a mother and always making me proud.

A NOTE FROM THE PUBLISHER

Thank you for reading this book. If you enjoyed it please do consider leaving a review on Amazon to help others find it too.

We hate typos. All of our books have been rigorously edited and proofread, but sometimes mistakes do slip through. If you have spotted a typo, please do let us know and we can get it amended within hours.

info@bloodhoundbooks.com

Printed in Great Britain
by Amazon

33476197R00155